D0396974

How to Disappear Completely

ALI STANDISH

HARPER

An Imprint of HarperCollinsPublishers

Library of Congress Control Number: 2019946024
ISBN 978-0-06-289328-4

Typography by Laura Mock
20 21 22 23 24   PC/LSCH   10 9 8 7 6 5 4 3 2 1

First Edition

For Aki,
who fills even the stormy days with sunshine

Glory be to God
for dappled things.
—GERARD MANLEY HOPKINS
"Pied Beauty"

Would Sarah and Jack have clasped
hands and stepped into the tunnel if you or
I could have warned them of the darkness
that awaited them on the other side?
I suppose I like to think they would,
or there would be no story to tell.
—R. M. WILDSMITH,
The World at the End of the Tunnel

1

The spot appears on the morning of Gram's funeral.

It arrives unannounced and uninvited, like a fly buzzing around a picnic.

Not that my life is a picnic today.

Or maybe the spot has been there for a while, and I just haven't noticed. Maybe the only reason I notice the little white circle now is because I've been staring at my lap ever since I sat down in the front pew.

If I were wearing black tights, like Mom told me to, I probably wouldn't have noticed the spot just between my big toe and my second. But when I searched my room earlier this morning, every pair I owned seemed to be ripped, or covered in Boomer hair.

We didn't have time to run to the store to buy a new pair. I know because Mom said that three times before saying I would just have to go to the church "as is."

"As is" is an insult when it comes from Mom.

"It's still warm out," I reminded her. There's a whole week left before school starts, after all. "I don't need tights."

Just then, Lily came gliding down the stairs, flawless as usual, from her shiny long hair to her own sleek black tights.

Lily is my older sister, in case you didn't know, which you didn't, because I've only just started the story.

There are two other things you need to know about Lily:

1. She is perfect.
2. She is going to Yale to study English next year, even though technically she has not applied yet, but she will definitely get in (see #1 above).

She stood shoulder to shoulder with Mom. You can tell that Lily is Mom's daughter, not because they have the same complexion or eyes or hair, but because they are both the same kind of very polished pretty. Lily had spent the hour before locked in the bathroom we share, curling her hair and perfecting her makeup.

I can't remember the last time I looked at my

reflection in a mirror except to get something out of my teeth.

Dad came rushing down a moment later, and I was relieved when Mom pounced on his crooked tie, forgetting all about my tightlessness. Then we were off.

And now here I am, sitting in the church, staring at the white spot on my left foot while the minister talks about God and heaven and angels.

Now that I've seen the spot, I can't stop staring at it. I blink at the paleness of it against my skin, like a tiny bright moon.

I think of this one time Gram took me to the meadow by the river to sit with her while she painted. Well, we did that all the time, but *this* time, I started pulling the paints from the old leather satchel she carried them around in and reading all their names. They were called things like "icebox plum" and "whitening willows."

"What color would I be?" I asked.

Gram looked at me thoughtfully. Then she said, "You, Emma, are the color of afternoon light settling on the trees in the Spinney."

"You can't fit that on the back of a tube of paint!" I protested. Gram was always saying stuff like that, like she was a poet instead of a painter. But secretly, I'd been proud.

Spinney is an old-fashioned word for a little forest,

by the way. And *the* Spinney is the place where I wish more than anything I could be right now.

I think the spot must be some kind of stain. I lick my finger and lean down, rubbing at it. It doesn't fade like marker or paint would. Another, more alarming thought floats into my brain. What if I've managed to bleach my skin somehow? It seems like something I would do. If I have, Mom. Will. Kill me.

As if to prove me wrong, she reaches an arm around my shoulders and gives me a reassuring squeeze. She probably thinks I'm looking down because I'm crying. I cross my right foot over my left so she can't see the spot.

It seems like almost everyone in Lanternwood has shown up today for Gram's funeral. A glance back reveals Ruth and Gloria and the rest of the garden club sitting directly behind our pew, all of them wearing big black hats. Old Joe and Older Joe (who used to be Young Joe and Old Joe) have taken the morning off from the farm and sit side by side, their few strands of hair slicked back and their heads bowed respectfully.

Even villagers who didn't know Gram very well showed up to say goodbye to her. There are lots of people I know by face but not by name, like the Apple Lady. She never spoke to Gram as far as I could tell, but this morning she's in the back pew, next to a family with two little kids I don't recognize. Their mom is sniffling into a tissue.

I know I should probably be crying, too. I should be thinking about Gram, not some weird spot. And you should know that I *do* think about her, all the time since she died. It's just hard for me to think about her here.

The old stone-and-brick church is just down High Street from her house, but I never saw her come inside. Sometimes, we would take Boomer and walk through the graveyard, searching the mossy gravestones for funny names or making up stories for how the people under them died. (In the old section, of course—not the new one, where people still put flowers by the stones.)

Anyway, you would be surprised by how many people died in the killer skunk attacks of 1919, including poor Billy Snagglehook, May God Rest His Soul.

But mostly, we spent our time in the Spinney or down by the river, where Gram told me fairy tales while she painted.

In fairy tales, things are always changing into something else. Pumpkins turn into carriages, frogs into princes, mermaids into girls. Nothing is ever what it seems. Nothing ever stays the same. And I guess that's the way it is in real life, too.

Gram didn't tell us she was sick until a couple of months ago. Not until she knew she was going to die. I still didn't believe it, though. Not until the sickness changed her, turning her into a weak old woman.

Then one day, she fell into an enchanted sleep.

That's the part fairy tales get wrong, see. In Gram's stories, things usually come out right in the end. Sleeping Beauty wakes up. Little Red Riding Hood gets to go home.

Gram did not wake up. Gram is never coming home.

And with her gone, I don't know how the story is supposed to go.

2

After the service, Gram's ashes are buried next to Grandpa's, under an old oak tree. Their grave is just one row up from the grave of a woman named Isabella Fortune, who was born eight years before Gram but died when she was only twenty-four, which doesn't sound very fortunate to me. I asked Gram about her once, and she said that Isabella had been one of her favorite teachers before she'd gotten sick and died. Now the grass around her grave is overgrown and dotted with weeds.

People keep saying we should be grateful that Gram led a long and happy life, and I guess that's true. But as we stand over the gravestone she will share with Grandpa, listening to Ruth blow her nose, I imagine that the stone belongs to someone else. To two strangers. I pretend that Gram is standing right next to me, her whispered words crackling in my ear.

"What do you reckon?" she would say. "What carried these poor souls away?"

"Maybe he came home when his wife was doing one of those face masks," I'd murmur back. "The kind that Lily and Mom do. And the sight of it was so scary it gave him a heart attack."

"Yes. And he was lonely in the grave, so one night his ghost got up, walked back to the house, and whispered, 'boo,' in his wife's ear. Scared her right to death."

"And now they're even."

The minister clears his throat, and the image of Gram fades away. I realize that a smile has snuck onto my face and wrestle it off.

Most people follow us back to Gram's house once we're done in the graveyard, although some of them go their separate ways.

Lanternwood has only one main street, High Street, which curves in a slow horseshoe, sandwiched by the river on one side and farmland on the other. From Gram's front yard, you can see the church—with its wobbly steeple and ancient bell—to the left, and the village hall—with its cheery red brick and bulletin board—to the right. In between the two are old, pretty houses that seem to shine in the sunlight like charms on a giant bracelet, linked together by the flower gardens that spill over their neat picket fences.

And Gram's house is the best of them all.

Actually, it's called a cottage—kind of like how Lanternwood is technically a town, but everyone calls it the village. There's even a white sign that hangs just over the fence outside the house that says "Morning Glory Cottage" in big handwritten letters. It's named for the morning glory vines (I know, big surprise) that have climbed around the door, all the way up the white walls to the sloping roof.

Mom, Dad, Lily, and I officially moved in at the beginning of the summer, when Gram finally told us how sick she was. We used to live forty miles away, but Gram needed to be taken care of, and Mom wanted a bigger house. So now we live here, in Morning Glory Cottage, where six generations of my family have lived before us, including Gram's father, who was once the mayor of the village.

Six might sound like a lot of generations to you, but Lanternwood is old. Like, really old. It was founded in 1747, and not much has changed since then. The church is the original one. People come to take pictures of it and of the village hall. They pick apples and have lunch in the old apple orchard, where there's a little café now, or they take picnics down to the meadow beside the river. They say coming to Lanternwood is like stepping back in time. Like something out of a fairy tale.

Dad used to drive me here pretty much every weekend to stay with Gram, so I've always had my own bedroom, and I've explored every corner of the village.

I also know everyone who follows us back to the cottage from the funeral. Dad knows them all, too, since most of them have lived here forever and still talk about what a fat baby he was.

Old Joe (who is Gram's age) and Older Joe (who is about a thousand) hit the buffet table and then strike up a conversation with Dad about corn prices. They run the farm that wraps around one side of the town. If you ever visit Lanternwood, odds are you'll get stuck behind Old Joe driving his tractor down High Street, chugging from one end of the horseshoe to the other.

Gloria and Ruth—Gram's best friends since childhood—make a beeline for me as soon as they walk in the door.

"Oh, Emma," says Gloria, opening her arms and enveloping me in a crushing hug. "We miss her already, don't we?"

I shouldn't be surprised by Gloria's strength. She's only five feet tall, but she manages to string the holiday lights outside the village hall every year and has been known to use her huge handbag to hit people who ask how old she is.

"Yeah," I say. "We do."

"She had a good life," croaks Ruth, banging her cane against the wood floor for emphasis. "A good, long life."

When you come to Lanternwood, Ruth will be the one leaning on her cane in her yard next door to the church, waiting to complain about her aching bones to anyone who happens to pass by. Now she lets out a sob, and Gloria reaches into her enormous purse and hands her a tissue. Ruth blows her nose—actually she sounds like she's trying to blow it *off*—and brings all conversation to a halt. Then she catches sight of Mom.

"Excuse us, Emma," she says. "We need to have a little chat with your mother."

As Gloria and Ruth corner Mom and begin to pressure her into joining the garden club, I make my way over toward where Dad has gone to sit with Lily. In the corner of the room, standing in front of one of Gram's river paintings, I glimpse Professor Swann, who used to teach in town at Hampstead College. He's dressed in the same tweed suit and old-fashioned hat that he wears every day when he takes his morning and evening walks to the river.

You can tell by his British accent that Professor Swann didn't grow up here. Even though he's lived in Lanternwood for most of his life, he's still kind of an outsider.

He is standing alone right now, sipping coffee and staring off into space, his eyes misty with tears. Which is sweet, since I don't think he and Gram were particularly close.

"Gloria has extra tissues if you need one," I say.

Professor Swann looks startled to see me. "How kind, Emma," he replies. "But I've got a—no—where is it now?" Patting his pockets, he eventually produces a purple handkerchief.

"She was a wonderful woman, your gram," he says as he dabs his eyes. "Truly extraordinary."

I thank him and worm my way through the crowd toward Dad, wanting to tuck myself under his arm.

"Isn't anyone in this village under the age of ninety?" I hear Lily ask him.

Lily doesn't approve of old people. Or people who smell funny, wear sweatpants, or don't like her Instagram posts as soon as she uploads them.

Lily only approves of people like her. People with perfect shiny hair who go to Pilates classes on Saturdays and have the right shape of nose to look down on everyone else.

She's probably almost relieved that Gram is gone so she doesn't have to listen to her cough at night or kiss her soft, saggy cheek or pretend not to notice the crumbs that sometimes got caught between the folds of skin around her mouth.

Lily is good at noticing the outsides of people. She gets that from Mom, too.

Thinking about outsides makes me remember the spot between my toes again, and I'm just bending to examine it when Old Joe appears by my side.

"Between you and me, I don't think your gram would have liked that service too much," he says, one of his woolly eyebrows crooking.

"No," I say. "She'd have thought it was boring."

On my other side, Boomer thumps his brown-speckled tail, and Old Joe leans down to give him a good scratch behind his ears.

"Hey there, boy." He straightens again. "You know, it was me who gave Boomer to your gram."

"I know," I say, grinning. "She said you got him to help you on the farm, but all he did was scare the cows. And when you realized he wasn't much help at all, you left him tied on her stoop in the middle of the night."

He snorts. "That old bat," he says affectionately. "Never could believe a word she said to you. Anyway, some of us are heading to Gloria's house in a while. To give her a real send-off, you know? Why don't you ask your dad if you can come along?"

I think about accepting the offer, but honestly, I'd rather be alone right now. Or at least I'd rather not be around other people.

"Thanks," I say. "But maybe some other time?"

"Sure thing, Emma," Old Joe says, winking his good-bye. "You take care of yourself now."

When everyone is looking the other way, Boomer and I slip out the back door. Mom will be angry I didn't ask, but if I did, she'd probably want me to stay until all the guests are gone. Who knows how long that will take?

At the end of the yard, there's a crumbling stone wall with a red door in it that leads to a little passageway between two rows of houses so ancient I'm sure I can hear them creaking sometimes. Ruth's not the only one around here with old bones.

We run down the passage and turn onto High Street across from the church, then veer left. We gallop past the apple orchard and run down the gravel road that spits us out onto the wide meadow along the riverbank.

Once we reach the meadow, I let Boomer off the leash and he goes charging toward a line of unsuspecting ducks. I love the feeling of the long grass skimming my ankles as we speed past groups of picnickers.

Soon we reach the end of the meadow.

Lots of people come here to picnic and walk by the river. They all stop when they get to the line of elm trees with the single strand of barbed wire stretching between them.

But like I said, I know *every* corner of Lanternwood.

Boomer and I duck beneath the wire and weave between the trunks, keeping clear of the patches of poison oak. The leaves rustle their usual greetings as we pass.

We run deeper into the wood, until the ground rolls like a gentle wave down into a little valley, where there's a green glade cut cleanly in half by a diamond-bright stream. The water forms a small pool at the center of the valley, like it's stopping to take a breath before rushing on to meet the river.

This time of year, the valley shimmers with clumps of orange jewelweed and sapphire bellflowers that shoot up from a blanket of moss so soft you could lie down and sleep for a thousand years. Or at least an hour or two.

Wild rose vines climb the trees, their blooms turning the air to honey. An enormous sycamore tree stands higher than all the rest, dappling the valley floor with the shade of its leaves and making the whole glade feel like a secret, round room.

We fly down the hill, and I flop onto the moss, not caring that the damp of it will soak through my new dress. Boomer settles beside me, and I stroke his soft fur as I listen to the stream rippling slowly past.

I think about a day before I'd ever seen this place, when Gram and I had been sitting by the river. She was telling me the story of Rapunzel again. She told that one a lot, but I never minded hearing it.

That day, though, I interrupted her. I was only in second grade, but already the kids in my class didn't like fairy tales much anymore. They had started to say that magic was for babies.

I didn't want to be a baby. But not believing in magic? The idea filled me with dread.

And besides, when Gram told her stories, they felt so real to me that it often seemed that she must have been there to see them somehow. That perhaps brave knights had once roamed along our very river, and Lanternwood had been inhabited by secret princesses.

Still. I wanted the truth, and I knew Gram would give it to me. "Gram," I said, "do you really believe these stories? I mean, princesses trapped in towers and things like that?"

Gram lifted her chin. For a long minute, she just stared at the river, and her eyes had this sad, faraway look she sometimes got. I wondered what she was thinking about.

Then she turned to stare at me with her sharp green eyes and twisted the parasol she always carried to protect her daisy-petal skin. "Did you know, Emma," she said, "that the Greeks have their own version of Cinderella, much older than the one we tell today? And the Egyptians and the Chinese, too?"

"No," I said, puzzled.

"It's true. And the same can be said for many fairy tales. People living in different places and different times all came up with the same stories. Now, how could that happen if there wasn't some truth to them?"

I looked at her blankly.

"What I mean is, I think there's some truth in every story—every story worth telling, at least—but *especially* in fairy tales."

"Okay," I said slowly. "But what about the fairy part? Like magic, I mean? Is that real?"

She looked at me for another long moment, her gaze firm. "Let me tell you something, Emma Talbot. If there is one thing I believe about this world, it's that there is magic in it for those who care to see. Now, would *you* like to see some?"

My eyes widened as I nodded.

And the next morning, she brought me here. To the Spinney.

I still remember the first time I saw it. The way the light in the trees flashed mischievously, from green to gold and back to green again. And the wild roses seemed to twist just slightly on their vines to get a better look at me. How every corner of the place seemed touched by some unseen enchantment, shimmering just out of sight.

How it felt like my heart had been charmed into a

bird that soared inside my chest.

"You mustn't ever tell anyone about the Spinney," Gram had whispered, taking my hand and leading me down the sloping hill to the glade. She was the sternest I'd ever seen her. "It must always be our secret."

"Why, Gram?" I asked.

She leaned in closer, as if someone might be hiding nearby, listening to our every word.

"Because it's magic, of course. Full of the charmed folk. But they're very shy, you know. Imagine if you told someone, and they told someone, and before you knew it, crowds were stampeding through here, holding up their phones and trying to take pictures of the poor fairies and fauns. The creatures would have to leave, wouldn't they? There's hardly anywhere left for them to go these days as it is."

My eyes grew star bright, my heart flew higher. "Fairies?" I asked. "Are there really fairies here, Gram?"

"Of course there are," she said. "Look—they've already left you a welcome gift." She pointed to the hollow in a huge sycamore tree. I tiptoed closer and peered in.

"It's a book," I said.

"So it is," Gram agreed.

I blink, and Gram is gone. Boomer and I are alone in the glade. I glance over to the towering sycamore tree, the dark hollow. After all this time, the book from that first day is still there, but I can't bring myself to open it and look inside. Not now.

Instead, I get up from my bed of moss and climb to Throne Rock, two big boulders covered in yellow lichen that grow together in the shape of—you guessed it—a throne. And I clear my throat.

Before, I wasn't sure why I needed to come here so badly, other than to feel close to Gram. But now I know what I need to do. I need to give Gram the kind of funeral she would want. The kind she deserves.

"Charmed folk," I call, "citizens of the Spinney, I ask you to gather around me now in honor of this most solemn occasion!"

For a moment, all is still in the glade. Then Boomer's ears perk as something stirs from a patch of jewelweed.

And as I wait for them to come—the fairies with their soft-beating wings and the fauns walking on hooves silent as time itself, the elves with sparrows burrowing in the nests of their dark hair and the gnomes with their pointed hats pressed to their chests—tears begin to spill down my face.

Here is something you should know about Gram.

She wasn't just my grandmother. She was my very best friend.

3

Even though I feel really tired, I can't seem to sleep.

That happens to me sometimes. My brain feels like a carousel, spinning around and around and bobbing up and down, and the longer it spins, the harder it becomes to sleep.

Tonight, memories of Gram twist and whirl in my mind.

There's picking blackberries in the meadows Gram and baking oatmeal raisin cookies Gram and sitting by the fire reading Gram and throwing balls in the river for Boomer Gram.

All those memories make me feel like I've lost a thousand different people instead of only one.

Finally, I sit up and throw my covers off, then head

for the rickety stairs that lead to the kitchen.

Whenever I can't sleep at Gram's—I still think of it that way, even though she's gone and I live here now—I go down to the kitchen. Usually I find her there, stirring milk on the stove and heating up a slice of apple pie. Like she's been expecting me.

I do my best to tiptoe down the creaking steps. I don't want to wake Mom and start another fight.

My heart jumps to my throat when I see a light on in the kitchen and someone padding around the stove. And even though, deep down, I know it can't be her— that it can never be her again—it doesn't stop me from hoping. If anyone could return from the dead, it would be Gram.

It's not, though. It's just Dad in his red checkered bathrobe.

"Hey there, Butterfly," he says, casting a tired smile across the midnight kitchen. "You doing okay?"

I am too old to be called Butterfly, and most times I roll my eyes when he calls me that, but secretly I don't mind it. And tonight, it feels extra nice.

"No," I say. "Not really."

"Yeah. Silly question. Take a seat."

He nods to the round wooden table that has so many scars running through it you could almost believe it had once been a giant's battle shield.

"You couldn't sleep, either?" I ask.

"No," he says. "Thought I'd come down and heat up some warm milk and pie. That's what your gram always did for me when I was a kid."

"Me, too."

Dad smiles as he stirs the milk. Then he pours it out in two mugs and serves us each a piece of the blackberry pie Gloria brought after the funeral. It's not as good as Gram's apple pie, but it will have to do.

"Sorry about your mom," Dad says, halfway through his slice. "You know she's been stressed."

Mom was really mad at me for running off earlier. She said it was because I didn't ask her, and I told her I didn't ask her because if I had, she wouldn't have let me go. Then she said that was all the more reason for me not to go, which makes absolutely no sense. When she saw that I'd ruined my dress, her mouth folded into a thin line like it always does before she's about to totally lose it.

Things went downhill from there.

"She won't even miss Gram," I grumble into my pie. "She's just stressed about the move and the house and everything."

Mom designs houses that have "clean lines" and "open floor plans." Gram's cottage, with its comfy, overstuffed couches and tabletops cluttered with knickknacks, is probably her worst nightmare.

"We'll *all* miss Gram," Dad says, nudging me with an elbow. "But you had a special connection with her. There's no denying that."

I wince. I *had* a special connection? Now that Gram's gone, is that gone, too? An image flashes through my mind of the frayed tire swing rope over the river that snapped in two one summer when I tried to kick too high, sending me plunging into the water.

"To Gram," Dad says, raising his glass. I clink mine against his.

Dad's milk leaves him with a frosty mustache that makes me giggle, just a little. He leans over and plants a milky kiss in my knotted hair.

"I'm sorry she's gone, Emma," Dad says as he stands to go back to bed. "We'll miss her a lot, won't we?"

"Yeah," I say. "We will."

I stay at the table for a while after he leaves, thinking about how there are two kinds of missing.

There's the kind when you've lost something important and can't find it no matter how hard you look. Like when you can't find your homework and the teacher's walking around to collect it, and the closer she gets, the more you panic.

And then there's the kind when you know where something is, but you just can't get to it. Like after you come back from summer camp and you wish you could go back for just one more day. You wish so hard it makes your insides ache.

It sounds impossible, but I think I miss Gram both ways.

When I go back upstairs, I don't return to my own bedroom. Instead, I creep into Gram's. And I'm not the only one. Boomer is there, too, lying at the foot of her bed. When he sees me, he cries and thumps his tail at the same time, like he's both happy it's me and sorry it isn't Gram.

He scooches over as I climb under Gram's sheets, still unmade from the last night she slept here before she went to the hospital. The smell of her is so strong it makes my eyes water. It smells like wishing.

I burrow deeper as my eyes fall upon the book lying open on the velvet armchair beside the bed. It's framed in a square of moonlight, so you can see the cracks in the old spine.

I'm sure you've heard of *The World at the End of the Tunnel* by R. M. Wildsmith. It's one of those books like *Alice in Wonderland* or *Peter Pan*. Everyone kind of knows the story, but most people have never actually read it.

Just in case you've been living in a cave for the last fifty years, though, I'll summarize. It's about a brother and sister, Jack and Sarah, who go out to play one day and find this old train track in the woods. It leads to a tunnel, and they wind up going through it into another world, the Goldengrove. The Goldengrove is a giant forest where gnomes carve entire villages from the trunk of a single elm tree, fairies host grand balls in moonlit clearings, and wizards disguised as snowy owls keep watch from high branches. The afternoons in the Goldengrove are always perfectly warm and sunny and have been known to last for days at a time.

Except it's not the Goldengrove anymore, because the hobgoblin king and queen have captured the fairy princess whose laughter makes the sun rise. Now that she's their captive, the hobgoblin king has taken over the Goldengrove and turned it into the Dimwood. In the blackness of the eternal night, all the wickedest creatures—the trolls and banshees and ogres—have driven the good creatures into hiding.

Anyway, Jack and Sarah journey across the forest, defeat a troll army, rescue the fairy princess, battle the evil hobgoblin king and queen, and return the world to the sunshine.

Sorry for ruining the ending, but if you didn't see it coming, you really should read more stories.

The World at the End of the Tunnel happens to be my favorite book in the entire world.

The first time Gram read it to me, I was eight, and it was snowing. Like, hard. The roads were so bad that school was canceled for a week, and Dad couldn't come get me from Lanternwood.

There was too much snow to go to the Spinney, and anyway, it was too cold for walking around outside, which meant Gram and I spent most of our time bundled up in Morning Glory Cottage.

I didn't mind it, but Gram, who hated being cooped up inside, went a little stir-crazy. She finished about twenty paintings in her studio, cleaned the whole house, and cooked enough soup to last all winter.

One morning, I opened the door to her room and found her lying in her bed, looking out the window, crying. There was an old green shoebox on her lap.

"Gram?" I asked. "Are you okay?"

She turned to me and frowned, leaning down to shove the shoebox under the bed.

"Emma," she said. But it was like someone else was saying my name. There was a coldness in her voice I wasn't used to, like the icy weather had climbed inside her. "You should have knocked."

My eyes started to well. I couldn't have been more surprised if Boomer had lunged over and bitten me. "I'm sorry," I said. "I didn't mean to—"

But her scowl had already evaporated. "No, I'm sorry," she said, shaking her head. "I didn't mean it. Come here, darlin'."

I scrambled up onto the bed with her, staring out through the old foggy panes at the snow-covered garden.

"You know you don't have to come here, don't you?" she said. "I love having you, but I don't want you to ever feel like you have to come, do you understand? I want this house to be a happy place for you. A place you *want* to visit."

I nodded, even though I didn't understand. And still don't. Morning Glory Cottage was and is my favorite place in the world, besides the Spinney. "I love it here," I said. "It's pretty in the snow."

Her face twitched into a smile. "Yes, it is, isn't it?"

It was then that I noticed the old book lying on her lap. "What's that?" I asked.

"Ah," she said. "*That* is a very old, very interesting story. Would you like me to read it to you?"

And she did. The sound of R. M. Wildsmith's words filled up the world that had gone silent in the snow, so that for the next few days, it felt like the only world that existed was the one in the book.

As soon as we finished, I asked if we could read it again.

The last few weeks before Gram died, when she'd gotten really sick and couldn't leave her room, I would come in to find her staring out her window with the same pained look on her face as I'd seen that snowy day.

And I knew she was thinking about how she wanted to be outside, living, instead of in her room, dying.

This time, *I read The World at the End of the Tunnel* aloud to her. But we were only halfway through before she went to the hospital and never came back.

Now, I reach over and pick the book up. Then I turn to the beginning, careful not to damage the old pages. On the title page, there's an inscription from my grandpa, who must have bought the book for Gram.

For my muse and best friend.

Below these words is Grandpa's illegible signature. I trace the writing with my fingers, thinking that I could have written the very same thing about Gram.

Then I flip the page and start to read.

> *The adventure all began with a glass of milk being overturned by an elbow and Jack and Sarah being turned out from the house for the morning in punishment. An inglorious way to begin an adventure, perhaps, but then we can't control when or how adventure may find us.*

I hear the story in Gram's voice, and after a while, she lulls me to sleep.

4

The next few days pass by in a fog.

No, I mean an actual fog sails in off the river and settles over Lanternwood, like a giant ghostly ship dropping anchor.

The fog doesn't stop me from spending most of my time outside, though. Morning Glory Cottage is just too full of emptiness, even with us all living there now.

So I take Boomer for long walks, from the cornfields on one end of the village to Briar Hollow Lane on the other. Briar Hollow Lane is a little gravel road just before the bridge that marks the town limits. There's a No Trespassing sign at the top of the road because it leads to a water-filtration shed or something like that. Gram told me once when I asked why we couldn't walk down there, and the answer was boring enough that I quickly lost interest.

Somehow, life in Lanternwood has carried on pretty much the same as it did before Gram died. Boomer chases Old Joe's tractor and tries to attack it as it chugs down High Street. Ruth stands by her gate, groaning about her old bones, or else hovers over Gloria as Gloria prunes the garden for her, complaining loudly about everything she's doing wrong.

Boomer and I walk along the river, too. I throw his ball in and laugh when he belly flops into the murky water. He runs through the last summer picnickers, who come despite the fog, and I pretend to be angry with him when he steals a block of cheese or a bag of Goldfish.

I can almost see Gram beside me, twisting her parasol overhead, wearing one of her old-fashioned long dresses and a frown on her lips that doesn't quite match the mischief in her eyes. "Now, Boomer. Manners, please."

The Thursday before school starts, Mom creeps into Gram's room and wakes me up. Boomer grumbles at her. He still thinks Mom, Dad, and Lily are intruders in his house.

I don't blame him. I hate the way Lily complains about the shower going cold and the noises the house makes at night, and how Mom walks around with a measuring tape, eyeing pieces of Gram's furniture like they're

30

naughty children. Sometimes I wish they would all just pack up and head back to our old house. Though I guess it would be okay if Dad came to visit on the weekends.

I pull the covers up and shimmy down beneath them.

"Come on, Emma," Mom says. "We're going into town today. Just you and me. Special treat."

I peek out at her. As usual, she's already dressed nice with her hair done and lipstick on.

Sometimes I'm sure Mom and I are from different planets, but there's no denying I'm her daughter. Where Lily has Dad's buttercream skin and Gram's green eyes, I've got Mom's much darker complexion and curtains of inky hair. But while Mom's hair falls in silky plumes around her face, mine is more like a knotted nest. I usually pull it back into a ponytail so I don't have to deal with it.

"What's the treat?"

"You'll see," she answers helpfully. "Get up and get dressed."

Mom has felt bad about yelling at me after Gram's funeral, so I think maybe she's taking me to the movies or something.

But no. Once I'm in the car, I find out she has kidnapped me to go back-to-school clothes shopping.

In other words, I've been had.

"But I've already got clothes," I plead.

"I think we've established that you need new tights.

And a backpack. Your winter jacket will definitely be too small now, so we'll need to get a new coat, too."

I cross my arms over my chest.

Mom sighs. "*And* we'll go to the bookstore when we're finished."

"Bookstore first," I say hopefully.

"Fine, fine," Mom says, shooting me a little *you win* smile.

We park a few blocks from the bookstore. The streets are jammed with people running errands or licking ice cream cones and soaking up the last days of summer.

We pass a man making dollar bills disappear and re-appear again in strange places. I want to stop and watch—see if I can figure out his trick—but Mom pulls me right past the big church, past the gallery where Gram used to sell some of her paintings, down to the quiet part of the street, where we duck into the bookshop.

I take a deep breath through my nose. I love the smell of bookshops—all those pages waiting to be turned. I speed past Mom, heading toward the kids' section.

As usual, I go straight to the place where I know *The World at the End of the Tunnel* will be. I always look there, just in case R. M. Wildsmith has suddenly decided, after fifty years, to write a sequel.

As always, he hasn't.

I know it's silly to hope that he would write a sequel

after all this time, but I can't help it. I don't want the story to be over.

I pull out one of the copies on the shelf and turn to a random page.

> *Jack galloped into the trees, thinking only of bumpy toads and buried treasure and other things that hide in forests, waiting for children to find them. Sarah paused at the forest's edge. She felt as you do when you have just left home for a long journey and you're sure you have for-gotten something very precious behind. But she only paused for a moment, and then she shook the feeling away and set off to find her brother.*

I shut the book and browse the rest of the shelves slowly, pulling out the interesting-looking books and reading the back covers and jacket flaps. Which is fun but also strategic. The more time I spend here, the less time we'll have for clothes shopping later.

Any moment now, I know Mom will walk over, look at her watch, sigh impatiently, and tell me it's time to go.

Except she doesn't.

Finally, when I have a tower of books so high I can't add even one more, and I'm actually a little worried Mom might have had a heart attack, I pick up my teetering stack and waddle toward the front of the shop.

I see her standing there, laughing at something the man she's talking to has just said. The man is tall and has a baseball cap tugged low over his face. He wears a leather jacket, even though it's way too hot for that today. As I draw nearer, Mom waves at him and he kind of glides from the store.

"Who was that?" I ask.

Mom takes half the books from me, and I see her eyes are glinting with excitement. "*That* was Arnold O'Shea."

I raise an eyebrow.

"He's a big-time journalist," Mom says. "You see him on the news all the time. Anyway, he's just bought a new piece of property—right on the river—and he's looking for an architect, so I gave him my card. Of course, he may already have someone in mind, but we'll see."

I've never seen her so starstruck before. I don't care in the slightest about Arnold O'Whatever. But maybe I can use Mom's good mood to my advantage.

"That's awesome, Mom," I say. "Oh, and I'm ready. This is all I want."

"This is *all*?" Mom says, floating back to earth. Apparently, my reverse psychology trick has not worked as well as I'd hoped. "You must have fifteen books here."

"But there's a really good sale. Buy one, get one half off. So it's really like I have only . . . not as many."

You should know that math is not my best subject. It is, in fact, my worst.

"Oh, all right, then."

"Thanks, Mom," I say sweetly, holding tighter to the stack of books—*my* books now—almost not believing my good luck.

After we leave the shop, both of us in a good mood now, we go for burgers, another thing Mom doesn't usually like to do. She and Lily are "salad people." When I'm done with my fries, she slides half of hers onto my plate and studies me as I eat.

"I'm sorry that things have been hard on you lately, Emma," she says. "I know you miss your gram a lot."

I meet Mom's gaze, her eyes that are mirror images of my own, and feel a swell of love for her. Even though I've never said it, I'm actually really glad that I take after Mom in the looks department. I'm glad we have that in common, at least. Something she and Lily don't.

In fairy tales, kids almost always have terrible moms. Like Hansel and Gretel's mom, who leaves them in the woods so she won't have to feed them anymore. Or else their moms have died and left them with a wicked stepmother, like in *Cinderella*. Mom and I might not always get along, but I know she loves me. I can see it in her eyes right now. So I guess things could be worse.

"Yeah," I say. "I miss her all the time."

"Things will get easier," Mom replies, leaning back in her chair and blinking, "once you start school and make some friends. To be honest, I was always a little worried that spending so much time with your gram, wonderful as she was, wasn't the best thing for you. It'll be good for you to have friends your own age."

Leave it to Mom to ruin the moment.

She makes it sound like I didn't have friends at my old school. Like Gram *kept* me from having them. But Lucy and Isla and Delia were my friends since kindergarten. We sat together at lunch, went to one another's birthday parties, hung out after school most days.

It's just that when I started coming to Lanternwood more on the weekends, I missed a lot of stuff. And I couldn't tell them about the Spinney or anything, because (a) it's secret and (b) they probably would have thought it was stupid.

Anyway, they all started to change last year. Like, instead of going to play board games at Delia's house, everyone else wanted to stay at school and watch the boys' basketball game. I still don't understand how watching someone else play something could be more fun than actually playing yourself.

Then I moved here at the end of sixth grade, and after a few weeks, we stopped texting each other so much. We had already kind of drifted apart, I guess.

After Mom pays the bill and we start toward the mall, I am still thinking about what she said about making friends.

I haven't actually given my new school much thought, but now I'm wondering if Mom is right. *Will* I make friends? Because kindergarten was a long time ago. Making friends now is probably much harder. Especially when you don't know anyone. I wonder if there will be any other new kids.

I follow Mom around the department store, lugging my two bags of books as she leads me to the accessories section. We pick out tights first ("I expect you to take better care of these, Emma") and a hat with matching gloves that I like because they're purple—Gram's and my favorite color. I find a fleece jacket that's really soft and warm. Then, just when I think we're done, Mom finds a rack of jeans that are on sale and forces me to take two pairs to the dressing room.

The lights are bright as I wiggle out of my shoes. It's when I'm pulling the jeans off that I glance at my foot and I see it.

The white spot.

It's not that I've forgotten about it since Gram's funeral. It's just that I've been hoping if I ignored it, it would go away. I've been wearing my socks around the house so Mom won't see and I don't have to look at it.

It hasn't gone away, though. It's still there and bigger now, but less round. It's kind of . . . shapeless. Like a snowball that's started to melt.

There's something else, too. A new spot in the same place as the first one, just on the other foot. It can't be a coincidence.

I scrunch back out of the jeans and gaze at myself in the mirror, checking my body for more spots. I don't find any more on my legs, but as I gaze at my arms, I see a little cluster of them by my elbow, like white freckles. And when I peer very closely at my face under the bright lights, I'm sure that I can see pale pinpricks above my eyebrows. Were these little spots already there? Or are they new?

My palms are sweating, and my mouth goes suddenly dry. What's happening to me?

"Emma?" Mom calls. "Do the jeans fit? I was thinking we should look at shoes before we leave."

"No," I say. "No, they don't fit. I don't want to look at shoes, Mom. I'm tired."

She must hear something off in my voice, because she walks closer to the dressing room. "Is something wrong?"

"No," I say again, because the last thing I need is her freaking out right now. "It's fine. Everything's fine."

Except I think I might be lying.

5

I let Mom buy me a terrible pink backpack so that she'll let us leave the store. When we get home, I run upstairs with my bags of books and clothes and throw them all in a heap onto my bed. Boomer has followed me, hoping that I'll take him for a walk.

"Just a minute, boy," I say, patting him hastily on the head.

Then I open up my laptop, search for "white spots on skin," and click on the first result. I skim through the text, which seems to be describing exactly what's happening to me. Then I come to the pictures.

I scroll down, only letting my eyes rest on each image for a second before I close my laptop.

I don't have what the people in those pictures have.

I can't. I just have a couple of white spots that are probably there because Mom switched detergents or something. They'll be gone in a day or two.

Trying to shake the images from my mind, I scurry down the hall to the bathroom. I lock the door behind me and turn on the bath tap.

When the water finally gets hot, I slip in and I stare at the blobs of white on my feet.

Then I grab Lily's loofah, pour soap over it until it's good and foamy, and begin to scrub at my toes. I scrub the spot on my right foot for at least a minute, but when I splash water over it, the spot is still there, so pale it almost glows. I scrub the left one next.

After a few minutes, the doorknob begins to rattle.

"Emma!" Lily calls, rapping on the door. "Emma, let me in. I need to get my straightener."

"Go away!"

"Seriously, Emma. Open the door!"

She pounds harder.

"Just give me a few minutes!"

I scrub harder.

"I'm getting Mom!"

She stomps off down the hall, and I look at my feet. The spots are still there.

I pull myself out of the bath, shivering, wrap a towel around me, and open the door just as Lily is marching back down the hall, Mom behind her.

"Girls," Mom says, "we've talked about—"

But she stops short, glancing from my face down to my feet. "What's wrong?" she asks. "You're bleeding!"

I look down. I've scrubbed my toes so hard that little droplets of blood have started to bead between them.

"Nothing," I mumble. "I just—"

But Mom has already leaned down to examine them. "What are these spots?" she asks. "These places where your skin is white?"

Lily scowls back and forth from me to Mom, like she's disappointed that I'm not getting the scolding I deserve.

"I don't know, Mom," I say. I put my palms to my face and I begin to cry. Then Mom is there, wrapping me up in her arms and making calming noises.

And I know she's trying to make me feel better, but all I can think is that I wish she were Gram.

6

The next morning, I wake up when the light is still thin and silver. It's one of the last days of summer. I should go back to sleep.

But then yesterday comes rushing back to me, and I'm wide awake.

Right after she saw my spots, Mom called the doctor, who told her that she should make an appointment to see a dermatologist. Mom got one for next Friday.

"Dr. Crenshaw also told me that we shouldn't worry in the meantime," she said, squeezing my shoulders.

But I could feel Mom hovering over me all night. Worrying.

Half of me wants to pick up my computer and do more research. The other half is itching to go stare at myself in the bathroom mirror, examine every inch of my body for more spots.

"Come on, Boomer," I say instead, nudging him awake. "We're going for a walk."

The air is cool outside. It's still so early that we have the village and the meadows to ourselves.

The only other person I see is the Apple Lady, wearing her usual headphones and carrying a basket away from the orchard. I don't know her real name. I only really ever see her going to church on Sundays and walking around the village in the morning. It seems like she usually comes out to pick apples from the orchard or wild blackberries from the brambles that grow along the edges of the meadow. It must have been apples the first time I saw her, though, because I've always thought of her as the Apple Lady.

As we pass her, she looks right through me without saying hello.

That's normal for her. I asked Gram about her once, and she said some people just keep themselves to themselves. But I bet it gets lonely, keeping yourself to yourself.

Boomer races up to her, wagging his tail and nipping at her apple basket. She flinches, lifting her basket higher.

"Sorry," I mutter, pulling him away. I push Boomer forward, and he keeps galloping right past the end of the meadow and into the trees. I run behind him, calling his name, but he's probably already halfway to the glade.

I hesitate for a moment. The Spinney is my favorite place in the world, but the day of Gram's funeral was the first time I've been in a while.

Today, though, I feel drawn there again. I need a distraction from my own skin. And besides, I have to find Boomer. So I slip under the barbed wire and into the woods.

From the meadow, the Spinney looks narrow—nothing more than a few rows of trees. But once you get inside, it feels vast. Like the Goldengrove, which is enchanted and grows bigger the farther in you go.

The trees are quieter than I remember, and my scuffed boots thunder as they hit the forest floor. The shadows are deep as wells. It's a relief to reach the edge of the valley and see Boomer down below, lapping water from the stream.

I make my way into the glade, under the shelter of the sycamore tree, and then settle myself on Throne Rock.

It feels so strange to be here without Gram. Without anyone.

When I was here the other day, I was so sure that if I had looked up, I would see the charmed folk like I used to. But now the glade is empty, and I can't remember the last time I saw them. Like *really* saw them. When did they slip away? How did it happen without me even noticing?

"Hello?" I call softly. "Is anyone there?"

But no matter how long I sit there, no matter how quiet I am (Gram always told me that the charmed folk are terrified of loud noises), no one comes. Not a single fairy flitting over my head or a gnome out collecting acorns. Not even a plain old robin. They are nowhere to be found.

On that very first day Gram took me here, she told me that the charmed folk used to be *everywhere*.

She sat down in a patch of jade grass by the edge of the stream, and the sun coming through the sycamore branches made it look like she was sitting in a tiny field of golden flowers. I sat opposite her, clasping the book I had just found inside the sycamore hollow.

"But that was a long time ago," Gram explained, "back in Ireland and England and Germany, before the time when people decided they were afraid of magic."

"Why were they afraid?" I asked.

"People are always afraid of things they don't understand, darlin'," said Gram. "Being afraid is easy. It's understanding that takes work."

"So what happened?" I asked, from my place beside her. "What did the people do?"

"They hunted the charmed folk," Gram said, eyes narrowing to a knife's edge. "They hunted them almost into extinction. They chopped down the trees of the old-growth forests so the charmed folk would have nowhere to hide. So the poor creatures came here as stowaways on passenger ships. They hid in steamer trunks and hat boxes. They came hoping for forests deep enough to hide them. Old forests, like this one, with enough tree magic to protect them."

I considered this. It *did* seem to make sense that if there were such a thing as the charmed folk, they would live here in Lanternwood, a place that seems forgotten by time.

"If they're all in hiding, how do you know they're here?" I asked.

"Well," she said thoughtfully, "I used to play here as a little girl, too. And one day, I came across a fairy who had flown too close to the stream." She skimmed her paint-crusted fingers over the water's surface, and the stream seemed to skip at her touch. "Her wings had gotten wet, and she was drowning. So I plucked her from the water and wrapped her in fern fronds to dry."

"Was she okay?" I asked.

"She was," Gram said. "And very surprised, because almost nobody can see fairies and other charmed folk anymore. They've all forgotten how."

"How did you see her, then?"

"Well, they say it takes one to know one, don't they?" she mused. "Perhaps I could see her because I have a drop or two of magic running in my veins, leftover from long, long ago." She gave me a little wink at this. "Anyhow, the next time I came back to the wood, the fairy queen was here in the sycamore hollow, her ladies-in-waiting holding gifts of honeysuckle nectar and buttercup jam. It was her daughter, the princess, I had saved, you see. The queen told me that as long as I kept their existence a secret, I was welcome to the wood anytime.

"After that, whenever I came here, I would find that the fairies had left me something in the sycamore hollow. In time, the fairies themselves came out to join me in my games, and then the other creatures began to emerge from their dens and burrows, too."

I looked down at the book I had just found, the one Gram said the fairies had left me in the sycamore hollow, trying to decide whether or not I believed her. "But haven't you broken your promise now?" I asked suspiciously. "You told me the secret."

"Ah, but only because the fairy queen herself gave me permission."

"Will I be able to see them, too?"

Gram cocked her head. "Why don't you try? There, look. There's one just over your shoulder."

I spun around, but all I saw behind me was a stubbly holly bush. "Where?" I demanded.

"Right there," Gram said. "Just look for a moment. See what could be. Look *through* your eyes, Emma, not with them."

I screwed up my face and stared at the bush. But it was still just a bush. I closed my eyes and let my mind fall open, like a book.

And then I tried again.

Gram and I never could quite agree on what the fairies looked like.

When I saw them, they had wings spun from spider's silk and clothes stitched from flower petals and leaves.

When Gram saw them, they had butterfly wings and hats and tunics made with bits of thread and spare buttons they had managed to pluck from unsuspecting humans who wandered too close to the forest.

It was part of their magic, she said, that they appeared different to different people.

Today, though, no one appears at all. It's just Boomer and me, alone in the glade. I didn't really expect anyone to answer my call. I'm starting to think that the charmed folk were only ever real because Gram said they were.

Now that she's gone, they've gone, too.

I slide from the rock to the ground and walk softly over to the sycamore hollow to pull out the book inside. The very same book I found that first day in the Spinney.

It's stayed dry enough out here over the years, because the hollow is deep. But inside its leather cover, its pages are soft and worn. I open it to the first page, on which are written a few spidery words:

The Spinney Chronicles

And underneath, in my terrible second-grade handwriting:

BY: EMMA TALBOT AND GRAM

I flip through each page, watching my handwriting get smaller and neater as the years go by. Gram's handwriting, meanwhile, never changes.

This book is a record of all the afternoons the two of us spent in the glade together with the charmed folk. The first stories are devoted to the fairy clans. Then come the ones about the elves, and then the forest troll, and after that the gnomes.

Whenever we finished a story, Gram would tell me to read it to her in the glade. "Stories are like spells," she said. "They never work properly unless you tell them aloud."

Whenever I told one of the stories we'd written, all the charmed folk would gather around to listen as I read from my perch on Throne Rock. They loved to hear stories about themselves, Gram said. And after I was done, I would run around the wood with them, all of us acting out the story I had just read while Gram watched and laughed. The charmed folk love make-believe, too.

That's how I remember it, anyway.

Three-quarters of the way through the book, the pages go blank.

The empty sheets sting my eyes and claw at my throat.

Gram and I should have filled this whole book together. The idea that the pages will stay blank forever now is unbearable.

There is still a pencil nestled in the journal, and I find myself picking it up. It feels good in the crook of my thumb. Like it belongs there.

I'm not ready to go back home, but I don't want to be here in the Spinney alone, either. I want to be somewhere else entirely. I want to climb into the journal and the world that Gram and I created and never, ever leave.

So I begin to write.

Once upon a time, there was a small cottage that sat halfway between a village and a great wood, as if it could not decide to which it belonged. And inside the cottage lived a girl named Ivy and her grandmother, whom she called Gran.

Ivy had lived with her grandmother ever since she was a baby, and her grandmother had lived in Poppy Cottage since any living soul could remember. Ivy loved her grandmother more than anything in the world, and she loved the cottage second-best.

There was not always enough firewood to stay warm nor food to stay full, but even on nights when they were hungry and cold, Ivy and Gran were always in good cheer. They huddled close together and Gran whispered the stories of olden times, before magic had been stamped out and magical creatures driven to extinction. The more Gran spoke, the warmer Ivy's cheeks felt. The more her belly seemed to fill, even if she had only a crust of bread for supper.

Each day, Ivy and her grandmother walked in the great forest, where Gran collected herbs and leaves that she made into remedies to heal the villagers of their aches and pains. As they went, Gran taught Ivy the names of all the plants and trees that grew there until she knew each like it was her own.

Some days, they walked so deep that Ivy for-got there was anything beyond the forest's borders, and she emerged from its shadows puzzled to find Poppy Cottage standing just where she'd left it that morning.

The villagers whispered dark things about the forest, but it held no fear for Ivy. And yet, she sometimes saw things there that she could not understand. One instant, her grandmother's skirts would brush against a dead cottonwood tree, and the next, its branches were covered in tender green leaves. Towers of dappled foxglove bells blossomed wherever she walked. And if Ivy and Gran happened to shut their eyes in a bed of ferns, when they awoke, a red fox would often be curled up next to Gran, its pointed face resting in her lap.

Sometimes Ivy awoke in the night to see her gran treating the forest animals by the dim light of the cottage's fire. She dressed their wounds and gave them remedies, just as she did for the villagers in the daylight.

If Ivy didn't know magic to be gone from the world, she might wonder if Gran had a drop or two running in her veins.

Perhaps it was that magic that strung the days all together, like holly berries on a winter garland, into one long ripe ruby afternoon. Ivy felt certain it would go on forever and ever, and she and Gran would be together always.

7

When my alarm goes off on the first morning of school, Boomer lets out a small groan and burrows deeper into the covers as I drag myself out of bed. Today is my first day as a seventh grader. First day at a new school. I should be excited, but all I want to do is stay right here with Boomer.

In the bathroom, I study my face in the mirror. There are dark circles under my eyes. I haven't been sleeping well the last couple of nights. And is it just my imagination, or are the spots on my elbow getting bigger?

I look away but not before my stomach does a belly flop. At least school will give me something else to think about until my appointment.

Back in Gram's room, which I have now officially

taken over, I glance at the tower of new books sitting on the bureau, but instead I grab *The World at the End of the Tunnel* and drop it into my terrible pink backpack.

"Emma!" Mom calls. "You'll be late for your bus!"

"Coming, coming," I mutter, shooting a last jealous look at Boomer, whose nose is still twitching with dreams.

As I'm passing Gram's studio, I hesitate. I haven't been inside since before she died. I don't want to see the paintings that she was still working on, that she'll never get to finish now.

I push the door open, though, and instead of looking at the paintings, I search the floor until I find what I'm looking for. The old leather satchel that she used to carry her paint supplies in. The leather is frayed and splattered with paint, but it's still a million times better than the backpack I already can't believe I let Mom buy me. Quickly, I dump all my school supplies and books out of the backpack and transfer them into the satchel.

This way, I'll have a little bit of Gram with me.

I grab one of her old cardigans that's hanging on the back of the door, too. It's not cold enough for sweaters yet, but at least the spots on my elbows will be all covered up.

I race down the stairs, brushing past Mom. "Emma! What are you—"

"Sorry, Mom. I'm going to miss the bus!" I say.

"Well, have a good first day, sweetheart," she replies. I just have time to hear her sigh before I whip through the door.

The bus stop is right outside our house, and I reach it as the school bus is pulling up. Gloria waves from outside the village hall, where she's weeding the garden beds. "Knock 'em dead, Emma!" she calls out. I shoot her a quick smile, hoping no one on the bus heard.

As I walk up the stairs and tell the driver my name, I start to feel all wobbly. I've never felt this way on the first day of school before. Is it because it's a new school? Or because I'm still thinking about my spots?

The front seats are mostly occupied by kids who are squirming so nervously, they must be sixth graders. I hope I don't look as anxious as they do. In the back, there are two boys, both wearing headphones, who look up at me and away again. And in the middle are two girls sitting next to each other who stare at me. They seem like they might be seventh graders, too. They've painted their nails the same color blue, and one of them has the exact backpack I dumped a few minutes ago. She starts whispering to the other, and they giggle. I take a seat two rows in front of them and on the opposite side of the aisle.

The bus pulls away, passing Morning Glory Cottage and Ruth's house and Professor Swann as he walks past the graveyard. Past the leafy orchard and Briar Hollow Lane, and suddenly we've left Lanternwood behind. I feel a nervous twist in my stomach, like there's an invisible string connecting me and the village, and the farther away we go, the tighter it pulls.

Relax, I tell myself. *It's just school.*

A few minutes later, we turn into a neighborhood where some kids who definitely look like eighth graders get on and go straight to the back of the bus. Behind them walks a girl with strawberry-blond hair that's perfectly straight. When she looks at me, I can tell she's wearing mascara, but not because she's done a bad job putting it on. She drums her fingernails against each of the seat backs as she walks down the aisle. The nails are painted blue.

"Edie!" calls out one of the two girls who stared at me earlier.

Edie's eyes fall on Gram's bag, laid across the seat next to me, and her eyebrows arch before she moves on. The bus jerks forward, and she gives a little screech of laughter that's echoed by the other two girls.

At the next stop, there's only one girl waiting. She's got frizzy red hair and an impressive collection of freckles, and she keeps her eyes on her shoes as she walks. When she glances up at me, I smile—to let her know she can sit with me if she wants—but she has already looked away again. She takes an empty seat behind the sixth graders.

A few minutes later, we're pulling up at school, where the assistant principals are waiting inside to sort us all into our homeroom classes. Kids rush around me, laughing and calling out to one another.

I squeeze the strap of Gram's bag and pretend it's her hand.

Once I have my homeroom assignment, I burrow my way through the crowds straight to class, where Mr. Owens, a bald man with a walrus mustache, checks my name off his list with a sleepy sweep of his hand.

By the time I've been to math and health, I don't feel so nervous anymore. Instead, I feel bored. It seems like every teacher has memorized the same first-day-of-school speech about citizenship, hard work, and "building a strong school culture." My thoughts start to drift back to my skin, and I make myself think instead about the story I started, the one that's waiting for me in the sycamore hollow.

It felt so good, writing in the journal again. The thing is, I have no clue what to write next.

When I first got the journal, I told Gram I didn't know how to write a story on my own, so we always wrote them together. I would write a chapter over the weekend, and when I went home for the week, Gram would read what I had written and write the next chapter, until we finished the whole story together.

I think about Ivy and her gran all through social studies, but by the time the bell rings, I still don't have any good ideas.

Thankfully, there's only English left before lunch.

In the first stroke of luck I've had all day, my English teacher actually seems to be an interesting human being. She doesn't look that much older than Lily. She's wearing trendy glasses with frames too big for her face and chunky leather boots.

"Cool bag," she says as I walk in. "I'm Ms. Singh."

"Emma," I say, smiling for the first time all day. "Cool boots."

Behind me, I hear a familiar laugh and turn to see Edie walking in. I sit down, and to my surprise, she takes the seat next to me. Her friend with the pink backpack has followed her in and sits down on her other side.

"I like your bag, too," murmurs Edie, flicking her hair over her shoulder. "Where'd you get it? The dumpster behind the Salvation Army?"

"Must have been right next to that ugly sweater," her friend adds.

I feel my cheeks go hot as they both start to giggle. "No," I say. "They were my gram's."

Edie opens her mouth to say something else, but

before she can, a new girl slides into the seat in front of me. "Vintage," she says. "Nice."

She has dark curls and a wide smile, and glasses like Ms. Singh's.

Edie shoots me a last smirk. And I think maybe I was right to be nervous about today.

8

Ms. Singh hands out our syllabus, and I flip through it, scanning for all the titles we're going to read this year. Some of them I don't recognize, but some I do. There's one by Sir Arthur Conan Doyle, who wrote all the Sherlock Holmes stories, and Gram's favorite Shakespeare play, *A Midsummer Night's Dream*.

"And we'll be doing lots of reader's theater," Ms. Singh is saying. "So brush up on your elocution!"

"Electrocution?" yelps a boy in the back, whose name is Austin, I think.

A few other boys giggle.

"*Elocution*," says Edie. "It means pronouncing things clearly."

Darn. I was kind of hoping Edie would be an airhead. It would make it easier not to care if she made fun of me.

"That's right, Miss . . . ," Ms. Singh says.

"O'Shea. Edie O'Shea."

O'Shea. O'Shea. Why does that name sound so familiar?

I whirl halfway around to look at her. She can't be, can she?

But she has the same wide brown eyes, the same confident gaze, as the man Mom was talking to in the bookstore the day she took me shopping.

"O'Shea like Arnold O'Shea?" I blurt before I can stop myself.

She studies me coolly. "Yes," she says. "He's my father. But I don't like talking about him at school. I don't want people trying to be my friend just because my dad is famous."

The way the corners of her lips curl with satisfaction tells a different story.

I blink at Edie for another moment before turning back to face Ms. Singh, cheeks burning again. I don't think I would want to be friends with Edie if her dad were the King of England.

"I'm sure everyone here will judge you on the merit of your character, Edie," Ms. Singh says. "Not your father's job. Now, moving on."

She assigns us to write an acrostic of our names, which is a poem where, for each letter of your name, you describe yourself with a word or phrase that starts with that letter. Then we have to share.

The girl who said she liked my bag offers to go first. "I'm Fina," she says.

> *"F: From California*
> *I: Imaginative*
> *N: Not a morning person*
> *A: Adaptable."*

A few people whisper excitedly when she says "California," and when Fina is done, Austin calls out, "Gnarly, bro!" in a terrible surfer accent.

Since she volunteered to go first and I'm sitting beside her, I have to go next. "I'm Emma," I say.

> *"E: Easy to get along with*
> *M: Messy*
> *M: Moved here this summer*
> *A: Always reading."*

Fina smiles and nods at me, and Ms. Singh says, "Wonderful! A reader!"

I also came up with another one while I was waiting for everyone else to finish their first. One that I'm not about to share with anyone.

E: Eager for this day to be over
M: Missing Gram so much
M: Might have something wrong with my skin
A: Anxious about my appointment on Friday

After me goes Edie. She clears her throat and takes a deep breath, like she's about to read some great work of art.

"E: Eloquent
D: Determined
I: Intelligent
E: Entertaining."

I roll my eyes. Edie might not be an airhead, but she is definitely full of herself. While the rest of the class shares their acrostics, I write a new one in the margin of my notebook, shielding it with my arm so no one can see.

E: Egotistical
D: Disagreeable

I: Irritating
E: Evil

Okay, so maybe evil is a *little* bit dramatic. But I couldn't think of anything better for the last *E*. Next to it, I draw a devil face with long, stick-straight hair. As I'm putting on the finishing touches, I look up to see Ms. Singh staring at me. It's funny how some teachers know how to scold you without using any words, like a superpower or something.

I put my pencil down and mouth, "*Sorry.*" I like Ms. Singh—I don't want to get on her bad side. At least there's no way she could have seen what I was writing.

Once the whole class is done sharing, it's time to go. As I reach back to grab my satchel, I bump my desk, and my pencil rolls onto the floor. I lean down at the same time that Fina reaches for it.

"Oh, here you go," she says, grabbing hold of it first.

"Oh, thanks," I reply.

"Um," she says. She's looking past me.

I turn to follow her gaze, and to my horror see Edie leaning over her desk, staring at my notebook. I slam my arms down on top of it, but not before her cheeks go past red to an "icebox plum" shade of purple. Then she stands up and walks out of class without another word.

But I have a feeling I haven't heard the last of this from Edie.

In fact, I have just thought of a much better word for the last *E* in her name.

Enemy.

9

When I get home that afternoon, Mom is sitting at the kitchen table, wearing her reading glasses and typing away on her laptop. She glances up as I trudge in and drop Gram's bag. There are circles under her eyes that match mine, which is weird. Usually even when Mom is stressed, she doesn't look it.

"How was your first day?" she asks, turning on her potential-new-client smile.

"I don't want to talk about it."

"Are you sure? I got you a treat." She pushes forward a plate of double chocolate cookies from my favorite bakery in town.

I *am* hungry. I couldn't face the thought of the lunchroom after the Edie thing, so instead I went to the

66

library, ate half my sandwich under the table, and then tried to read. But mostly I thought about the Edie thing. Why hadn't I closed my stupid notebook?

I sit down and bite into the cookie. Boomer wags his way into the kitchen, and I stroke his head as I eat.

"Tell me *something*, at least," Mom says. "Did you make any friends? What about your teachers?"

"I like my English teacher," I reply. "And that journalist you met, his daughter goes to my school."

The instant I've said it, I realize it was the wrong move.

"Arnold O'Shea?" Mom asks, her eyes widening. "Did you make friends with her?"

"Not exactly," I mumble, getting up to pour myself a glass of milk.

"Well, I'm sure—"

Mom stops when she sees me glancing at her laptop. For a second, we both freeze. Then she lowers the screen and I look away, and we both pretend we haven't seen the website she was just looking at.

It's only then that it occurs to me that Mom has never in my life bought me an entire plate of cookies as a treat. Or to wonder *why* she has those dark circles under her eyes.

It's because she's done the same Google search as me, of course. She's been on the same website. Seen the same pictures.

She thinks I *do* have what those people have.

"I'm going to take Boomer for a walk," I say suddenly, turning from the kitchen before she can reply.

This time, instead of heading for the Spinney, we walk toward the church. The air is ripe and heavy and smells like the end of summer. As soon as we reach the sidewalk, Boomer leaps toward a squirrel, which scampers up a nearby oak tree. Across the street, Ruth stands at her fence, leaning against her cane. She calls me over when she sees me and invites me in for lemonade.

"These old bones aren't good for much anymore, but they can still squeeze the lemons and stir the sugar," she says.

"No thanks," I reply. "We're on our way to the graveyard."

"Going to visit your gram, eh?" she crows. "Well, send her my regards. The garden club just isn't the same anymore. We all still think about those margaritas she would bring."

She stares wistfully in the direction of the graveyard as the church bells ring, five minutes late, like usual.

"Me, too," I say. "Except, you know, the margarita part."

I wave goodbye and head for the gates of the graveyard, where a few yellow leaves have already fallen onto the grass. Boomer and I walk between the old gravestones—crooked and slick with moss, some of them so old you can't even read the names on them anymore—until we come to the newer ones.

The grass around the grave behind Gram's—the one belonging to Isabella Fortune, Gram's teacher who died really young—has been tidied up recently, and someone's planted a little rosebush by it. It makes me happy to think there must be somebody left to remember her, even after all this time.

I kneel on the ground in front of Gram and Grandpa's grave.

My grandpa died of a heart attack when I was too little to remember him, but I think I love him anyway. I know from the way Gram used to talk about him that he was a really good husband. The kind who gave her books and inscribed them, "For my muse and my best friend."

Today, though, I'm almost jealous enough to hate him, because she's with him now and not here with me and Boomer.

The grass is uneven at the place where they buried Gram's ashes. Unlike on the old tombstones, the lettering on this one is sharp—sharp enough to cut me all up inside. Where there used to be only one name, now there are two.

"Hi, Gram," I whisper, pressing my palm to her name.

Boomer whines before flopping down beside me.

"It's weird being in the cottage without you," I go on. Just because Gram can't answer doesn't mean I can't keep on talking to her. It makes me feel a little less lonely anyway.

Boomer lays his head in my lap, and I rub his ears, tugging them gently the way Gram used to.

"I guess *every*thing's been kind of weird since you died, Gram. It's too lonely in the Spinney. And there's this thing that's been happening to my skin. It's turning white. I think . . . I think I might have this condition."

Until now, I haven't actually said the word out loud yet. Maybe I'm worried that if I say it, I'll make it real. Like an incantation.

But maybe the opposite will happen. Maybe it's like in Rumpelstiltskin. Maybe if I say the name, I'll take away its power, and I won't feel so scared about it anymore.

"It's called vitiligo," I say.

I know. It doesn't sound like a big deal. It sounds more like something you would order at an Italian restaurant than a skin disease.

"It isn't dangerous or anything, which is good, but it makes your skin turn white. And it can spread all over your body. Weird, right?"

A few more leaves float down to the grass. I bite my lip.

"Also, I started school today, and it was awful. There's this girl there. She was really rude to me, so I wrote a mean poem about her, and she saw it. She'll probably tell everyone, and now they'll think *I'm* the mean one."

Boomer spots another squirrel and goes bounding off, but I stay where I am, trying to picture Gram next to me, trying to hear what she would tell me to do.

Instead, I see us at the village fair when I was seven.

Gram had abandoned her parasol to the side of the tent and was dancing with Old Joe, her long dress skimming the grass as she spun on bare feet. Nearby, Ruth led Professor Swann in a waltz, and he kept looking over at Gram like she might be able to rescue him.

I was sitting under the dessert table, nibbling at an oatmeal raisin cookie and wiggling a loose tooth with my tongue, when two boys walked up.

"That pale lady dresses funny," said one boy.

"That's because she's a witch," the older one said knowingly.

"Is not."

"Is too. Just like the ones in the stories who do spells and have cauldrons and warts and eat little kids for breakfast."

Fuming, I reached out and pinched the boy who had just spoken, hard on his leg.

"Ow!" he howled as I darted away, ducking under the

back of the tablecloth, so that when he raised it to look under the table, there was no one there.

"It was her, it was her!" the younger boy yelped. "The witch put a . . . a . . . a *curse* on you!"

That night, I couldn't sleep, and when I came downstairs, Gram was there, already putting a slice of apple pie on a plate for me.

"What's keeping you awake tonight, darlin'?"

I repeated what I'd heard the boys say.

"And did that bother you?" she asked. She sat across from me in her white nightgown, her hair in a long silver braid, the way she always wore it to sleep.

"The parts about you eating little kids and having warts," I said. "Not the part about being a witch. I wouldn't mind if you were a witch."

It *was* kind of witchy, the way she always knew when I couldn't sleep. And she *had* said that she might have some magic in her blood.

"Well, that is certainly comforting," she replied.

"Doesn't it bother you, Gram? That those kids think that stuff?"

"Goodness, no," she said. "If I spent my life being bothered by what other people thought of me, I'd never get anything else done, would I? Besides, there's no point in worrying about things you can't change, and you can't change what people think of you."

"Why not?" I asked.

"Well, because what people think of you usually tells you much more about *them* than it does about *you*. For instance, I think you are the smartest, best, most wonderful little girl in the world. Now what does that tell you about me?"

I giggled. "Um, that you love me?"

"Very much," Gram said.

The memory ends abruptly as Boomer flies up to me, skidding to a halt just as he reaches my chest. I hug him tight as he pants, looking over his back at Gram's gravestone.

"I know there's nothing I can do to change my skin," I say, "and maybe I don't even have this vitiligo thing. I'll try not to worry. *And* I'll try not to care about what people think of me."

But secretly, I bet it's easier not to care what people think of you when you're Gram's age than when you're twelve.

And anyway, when I was with Gram, it was like I lived in a different world—one made of old books and warm milk and sprinkled with fairy dust. A world where Gram could fix anything with a twinkle of her eye. But now that she's gone, the spell has broken. And I'm not sure if her advice can fix things in the world I live in now.

I think about the last thing that little boy said after I pinched his friend. About Gram putting a curse on him.

I feel a tear snaking down my cheek.

Gram always said that there was magic in the world for those who cared to see it.

And if magic is real, then I guess curses must be, too.

10

Instead of turning for home when we leave the graveyard, Boomer and I walk to the meadows, duck underneath the barbed wire strand, and slip into the Spinney.

When we reach the middle of the forest, I sink into the moss. It's a relief to be here after spending all day at school. I lie there for a while, breathing in the smell of the wild roses and looking up at the branches of the sycamore tree.

For now, most of the leaves are still green, but in a couple of months, they'll be amber and orange and gold. Then they'll fall and sunlight will take up the whole sky.

Change is coming, the trees whisper.

That's the thing about transformations. You think you're looking at one thing, but it's already on its way to being another. Just because you can't see it changing right in front of you doesn't mean it's not. And there's usually nothing you can do to stop it.

I squeeze my eyes shut and try to sink deeper into the moss, stretching out my arms and imagining they are tree roots. I listen to the stream trickling toward the river, which will take its water to the ocean, where someday it will turn into clouds and come down again as rain.

Everything turns into something else eventually.

I hear a twig snap nearby, and I shoot up.

"Hello?" I call. "Is someone there?"

The glade is deserted. But I can't shake the feeling that I'm not alone. Or that someone was just here, right before Boomer and I slipped under the barbed wire.

I look around for another minute to assure myself that the forest really is empty. Then I stand to go. It's only as I brush my palm against the trunk of the sycamore tree, wanting to feel its smooth skin against my own, that I see it.

The journal is not where I left it, deep in the hollow. A corner pokes out, like someone left the book there in a hurry, without taking the time to push it in properly.

A chill rushes over me. Has someone been here, reading my journal?

I pull it out from the hollow and flip through the pages, looking for signs of an intruder, until I come to the end of the chapter I wrote last week. When I flip to the next page, it is filled with words.

Words I didn't write.

As she grew older, Ivy was allowed to roam the great wood by herself. She delighted in its secret thickets and in weaving between the trees as fast as her feet would carry her.

One winter's day, Gran sent Ivy into the village to buy a loaf of bread from the baker. As Ivy waited in line, she overheard two children talking in low voices.

"There's no moon tonight," said the first, a boy with laughing blue eyes and dirt on his cheek. "You know what that means."

"The witch will wander the forest," said the second, a girl with eyes that matched the boy's, though hers seemed afraid.

"That's right," said the boy, "and all those who look upon her are lost, for one glance from her red eyes will turn any man to stone."

"But what about a child?" asked the girl.

"Not a child," said the boy. "One look from the witch will put a child under her spell. Then the witch can take her back to her cottage and—"

But just what the witch would do, Ivy did not hear, for at that moment, the children's mother called them away, and it was Ivy's turn to order.

As she made her way back through the snowy lanes to Poppy Cottage, clutching the warm bread to her chest, Ivy wondered at what she had heard. Was it true? Could there be a witch in her forest? She had the feeling that the boy was only teasing the girl, but she had to know for sure.

So that night, Ivy crept from the cottage and into the heart of the forest. She climbed into the crook of her favorite cottonwood tree and pulled her blanket tight around her shoulders. Then she waited, watching the shadowed forest below for any sign of the witch.

But the night was long and the blanket warm, and soon Ivy found herself drifting off to sleep.

When she awoke, it was still night and, though she couldn't say why, her heart was racing. Blearily, she looked around until she saw something that made her blood run cold as snow.

Not a stone's throw away, there was a silent figure gliding across the forest floor. She wore a white cloak that fell to her feet, with a hood that was lined in fur. She carried in one hand a large wooden staff. The way she moved was unnatural, as if she floated rather than walked. Suddenly, the figure stopped and then, as if she could sense Ivy's gaze, slowly turned her head toward the cottonwood tree.

"No!" cried Ivy, remembering what the boy had said about the witch's gaze entrancing children. She jumped from her tree and ran, faster and faster, all the while feeling the witch's breath like a cold wind on the back of her neck. Just as she was sure the witch would catch her, she broke free of the forest and into the clearing where Poppy Cottage stood.

Her gran waited in front of the cottage, and Ivy threw herself straight into her arms.

"Where were you, my girl?" her grandmother asked. "I've been ever so worried."

Ivy told her about the witch. When she was done, her grandmother shook her head.

"That was no witch, Ivy," she said.

"Then who was it?" Ivy asked.

"A dream, I should think," Gran said. "Come, let's go in and get you warmed up. I've a pot of stew on the fire."

They spoke no more about the strange woman that night, but long after Ivy was asleep, her grandmother sat awake, staring into the fire. Trying to read the shape of the future in its dying flames.

11

When Ms. Singh's class lets out the next day, I head for the library again. My journal is tucked safely into Gram's satchel, and all day, I've been itching to pull it out and examine the new chapter. I walk faster, until I round the corner and get stuck behind Edie and Fina, the nice girl from California.

"Are you from LA?" Edie's asking. "My dad goes there sometimes."

I've been waiting for Edie to get her revenge for yesterday, but she hasn't so much as looked my way all day.

They head straight, toward the cafeteria, and I turn right to the library as Edie tells Fina to sit with them at lunch. I guess being from California makes you automatically cool. Meanwhile, it's halfway through the second day of school, and I still haven't made *any* friends.

The library is empty besides two kids sitting at the computers. I take a table in the back and pull out the journal, followed by my lunch. I try to nibble quietly at my carrot sticks (which, it turns out, is pretty much impossible) as my fingers trace the shape of the words, each spike and dip of the pen forming its own question.

Who wrote them? Who knows about the Spinney? Hadn't Gram told me never to tell anyone else about it? And how could anyone know about the journal inside the sycamore hollow, and how Gram and I took turns writing our stories there?

For a wild minute yesterday, I thought Gram must have found some way to write to me from beyond the grave.

But then I flipped back and saw that the handwriting didn't match hers at all. It looks kind of familiar, but it's not Mom's or Dad's or Lily's, either, unless one of them was trying to disguise their handwriting so I wouldn't be able to recognize it.

I can't really see any of them writing this chapter, though. Mom hates the woods. No offense to Dad, but he could never write this. He doesn't even like to read. Gram told me that as a little boy, he was never interested in hearing fairy tales or reading books together like she and I did. Not even *The World at the End of the Tunnel*. And Lily . . . well, Lily just doesn't care enough about me to do something like this.

But there is something about the chapter that feels so familiar. Probably because it's exactly the kind of thing Gram would have written. And maybe that's the reason that I'm not creeped out by it.

Because it feels like, for the first time since she died, I've gotten a tiny piece of her back.

It feels a little bit like magic.

"Hey," says a voice.

My head snaps up as I slam the journal closed.

Fina is standing beside my table, fidgeting with her backpack straps.

"Oh, hi," I say, voice lifting with surprise.

"Can I sit with you?" she asks.

I glance behind her. "I thought you went to sit with Edie."

Fina takes this as an invitation to sit and slides into the chair beside me, dropping her backpack on the floor. "No," she says. Then she leans in closer. "I don't think I like her very much, actually."

"Even though her dad is a *famous* journalist?" I ask.

"She was so mean to you yesterday about your bag.

I don't like hanging out with people like that, even if their dads *are* famous."

I am starting to think Fina and I are going to get along just fine.

"Actually," she goes on, "I was looking for you in the cafeteria yesterday, but you weren't there. And when I didn't see you again today, I thought you might have come here."

"How'd you know?" I ask, scooching my lunch over as she pulls out her own brown bag.

"Emm-A," she says. "*A* for 'always reading,' right? I like reading, too. That's why I wanted to sit with you. Plus, us new kids gotta stick together."

"And you're Fin-A," I say. "*A* for 'adaptable.'"

She smiles. "It's short for Josefina," she says. "Josefina Ramirez."

"Emma Talbot," I say. "I like your name."

"Thanks! It's my grandmother's name, too."

"Does she live back in California? Or did she move with you?"

"She's in San Diego," Fina says. "We lived outside of LA, but we used to go see her a lot. I really miss her. What about your grandmother? You said yesterday that your bag is hers, right?"

"My grandmother—Gram—she died," I blurt out.

The words still feel wrong—silly, almost—coming out of my mouth. I wonder if they'll ever feel real. "Just a few weeks ago."

"Oh, no!" Fina says, eyebrows furrowing behind her glasses. "I'm sorry, Emma. That majorly sucks. My grandfather—Abuelito—died a few years ago, and it was awful. I still miss him. Sorry, that probably doesn't make you feel any better."

"No, it's okay," I say. "I don't think I'll ever stop missing Gram."

Fina nods. My eyes start to well, and I decide we need a change of subject. "It must be really different here from California."

"It is," Fina says. "It's much greener. And the air is so, like, thick! The air in California isn't like that at all."

"I bet it's really boring here compared to there."

"I think the place where you grow up is always really boring," she replies. "It's not like I went to red-carpet premieres or fancy clubs or anything. Mostly I just went into LA for field trips and stuff."

I giggle. "Edie would be really disappointed to hear that."

"I bet she would," Fina replies, grinning. "Anyway, what were you reading?" She peers down at my lap, where I'm still gripping the journal.

"Oh, that's not, um, what I'm reading," I say, stuffing the journal into Gram's satchel and pulling out *The World at the End of the Tunnel*. "This is."

Fina almost jumps out of her chair. "Oh, my gosh, I *love* that book!" she says. "It's one of my favorites!"

"Really?" I say, but it's more like a squeal. Because like I said, even though most people have heard of the book, not that many people have actually *read* it. "I've read it like a thousand times."

"Same here." She reaches into her backpack and pulls out a notebook. All across the cover, there are quotes written in silver Sharpie. She points to one that I recognize immediately.

It's from a scene in the book after Jack and Sarah reach the Dimwood. They have the feeling that something is following them, but it's not until they rescue a gnome from becoming an ogre's midnight snack that a snowy-white owl swoops down and reveals himself to be an old wizard called Maradel. He rewards them for their kindness with a basket full of fresh bread and butter that magically replenishes itself and a hollow stone with a flame inside that never burns out. When Jack and Sarah thank him for his magic, he says they have themselves to thank. Then he says the thing that's written on Fina's notebook.

"*Kindness is its own kind of magic.*"

"I check the bookstore for a sequel every time I go," I say.

"I used to have a refrigerator box that I pretended was Fernlace. I made a flag and cut a door and everything."

"Cool." Fernlace is the fairy palace in the book, in case you don't know. On the outside, its walls are made of the strongest river stones, but inside, they are woven from threads of soft cloud.

Fina grins, but then she pulls out a ziplock bag full of vegetable chips and pulls a face. "Ugh. My mom knows I don't like these."

"In that case," I say, digging into my satchel once again until I root out two of the double chocolate chip cookies Mom got me yesterday, "want a cookie?"

She giggles. "I really do. My mom never lets me take cookies to school. She's way into healthy food."

I hold up my carrot sticks. "Same," I say. "I don't usually get cookies, either."

I hope Fina doesn't ask me why I have them today. Ever since I found the journal, I've had something else to think about besides my white spots. And I'm not ready to tell anyone else about those.

Fortunately, she breaks a big bite off and sticks it straight in her mouth. "Mmmm," she groans. "This is amazing."

Ms. Singh walks down the hall and catches sight of us in the library window. She waves and gives a thumbs-up.

"She thinks we're reading," I say. "Doing something educational."

"This *is* educational!" Fina insists. "We're having book club. You know what I love about that book? Every time I read it, it feels like the first time."

"I know what you mean," I reply. "It feels like it all happened a really long time ago, but also like it's happening right as you read it."

"Exactly."

"Uh-oh." Mr. Yardley, the librarian, has spotted us and is headed our way, looking disapproving. "We aren't supposed to have food in the library."

Fina glances at the cookie, then stuffs the rest of it in her mouth. She holds up her hands innocently. "What 'ood?" she asks through her mouthful of chocolate.

I laugh so hard I almost spit out the rest of my own cookie.

"The library is a place for reading, not eating," Mr. Yardley says in a disapproving voice, just as the bell rings.

"Sorry, Mr. Yardley," I say. I try to sound serious about it. The last thing I need is to be banned from the library. We gather our things to go.

"What do you have now?" I ask.

"Math," she says. "What about you?"

"Science," I say.

She makes a gagging motion. "Blurg!"

"Anyway, that was really fun."

"Same time tomorrow?" says Fina hopefully. "Except maybe we can go to the cafeteria and eat first?"

"Definitely."

Fina waves goodbye and sets off. I start walking in the opposite direction, feeling lighter than I have since before Gram died.

12

It's funny how much different school is when you have a friend. Wednesday goes by really fast. And I don't mind it that much when I hear Edie and the Graces (*both* of her minions are named Grace, if you can believe it) whispering my name and laughing as I pass them in the hall.

Fina and I eat lunch together before heading back to the library, just like we planned. We talk about our families. I tell her about how Mom always wants everything to be perfect, like one of her architectural drawings, and about how I've been really lonely since Gram died. I learn that Fina's mom got a job teaching history at Hampstead College, which is why they moved. Her dad is a professor, too, but he's on something called sabbatical.

"It just means he has a *lot* of free time on his hands," Fina says with a roll of her eyes. "So he's been the one doing all the cooking and cleaning. He's really bad at cleaning, but Mom and I don't want to hurt his feelings. Yesterday, he put bleach in the laundry instead of detergent. He turned all of Mom's shirts white!"

Part of me is dying to tell her about the journal. I need someone to talk to about the new entry and who wrote it. Also, *is* the woman in white that Ivy sees in the forest a witch? Or is she someone else, or just a dream like Gran said? And how do I decide what to write next?

But the other part of me knows I can't tell anyone. If I did, I would have to tell about the Spinney.

So instead, I tell her about the poem I wrote about Edie. Fina's eyes go wide.

"So *that's* what she was looking at when you leaned down to get your pencil! No wonder—her face went all red and pruney."

She lets out a little giggle.

"It's not funny!" I insist. "She's probably plotting to murder me or something."

Okay, maybe I was joking about the murder, but Edie *does* bump into me extra hard during a basketball game in gym later that day. Coincidentally, she manages to do it right when the coach is glancing down at her phone.

I don't tell on her. I've been waiting for her to do something to get back at me, so it's almost a relief when it finally happens.

On Thursday, Fina and I have just sat down in the cafeteria when I see her waving someone over.

"I hope it's okay," she says. "I told her she could sit with us. She's in my math class, and she's new here, too."

I turn around to see a short redheaded girl with masses of freckles bobbing toward us with her tray. She sits down and introduces herself as Ruby.

"Hey!" I say. "I remember you. You were on my bus the first day of school!"

She's the one who looked really nervous, who I smiled at.

"Oh, yeah," she agrees after studying me for a moment. "I remember you, too! I made my mom drive me the last couple of days. I hate the school bus."

"Well, I officially call the first meeting of the New Kids Brigade to order!" Fina says, banging her fist on the table like a gavel. Ruby and I glance at each other and laugh.

"Are we a secret society?" I ask.

"Like with nicknames?" Ruby says eagerly.

Before Fina can answer, I look up to see Edie scowling

at us as she passes by. Ruby sinks into her seat, but her eyes follow Edie all the way to a table across the room, where she sits with the two Graces and a pair of boys, Sean and Austin.

"You know Edie?" I ask.

"Not really," Ruby says. "Only that when I had to say my name on the first day of school, she laughed."

"Why?" Fina asks blankly.

Ruby points to her freckled face with one hand and holds up a lock of hair with the other. "Red hair, red freckles, red name," she says. "The kids at my old school thought it was funny, too. I wasn't exactly, um, popular there. But I thought maybe now we're older . . ."

She stares wistfully at her PB&J.

Secretly, I don't think it was very nice of her mom and dad to name her Ruby. But maybe the freckles came later.

"Don't mind Edie," I say. "Having a famous dad has given her a big head."

Ruby's eyebrows shoot up. "Her dad is *famous*?"

"Famous-*ish*," Fina corrects.

"Point of order," I say. "I would like to vote for a change in discussion topic."

"I second that motion," Fina says, grinning. "Ruby, where'd you move here from?"

Ruby hesitates, like she actually wasn't done talking

about Edie yet, then says she moved from Virginia. By the time she's done telling us about all the pets she brought with her—three dogs, five cats, two chickens, and a hamster—lunch is over.

"Wait, wait!" Fina says as we start to get up. "I now officially declare this meeting adjourned!"

She bangs her fist against the table again. "Our next meeting shall commence tomorrow, lunchtime. The topic: Mr. Owens giving detention out just for talking in math class. It's a total infringement on our First Amendment rights!"

"You guys will have to tackle that on your own," I say, thinking about my doctor's appointment tomorrow afternoon. "I have to leave school early. . . . I have a thing."

Fina shoots me a quizzical look, but I don't really want to tell anyone about the appointment. Or my spots, either. At least not until I know what the doctor is going to say. My stomach turns a somersault.

Friday can't come soon enough.

13

Dad picks me up on Friday afternoon to take me to my appointment. Mom had an important client call, so she's meeting us there.

On the way, we listen to the radio for a few minutes before Dad punches it off.

Then, "Your spots could be lots of things, you know," he says. "A fungus or something."

"Ew, Dad."

"It's not a big deal. People get them all the time. When I met your mom, she had this terrible fungus on her toenails. Didn't let me see her feet for months until it was all cleared up."

A nervous giggle escapes my lips as I imagine Mom's face when the doctor told her she had a *fungus*. She probably went berserk. In case you haven't noticed, Mom is not really the fungus type. "She's never told me that."

"She's never told *anyone* that," Dad says. "So you can't either."

As we pull into the parking lot of the doctor's office, my heart jumps into my throat. Dad turns off the engine but doesn't move from his seat.

"Whatever happens, Butterfly," he says, "you know we love you, right?"

"Right," I say.

"Okay. Let's go."

Mom is already in the waiting room when we walk in. She gives me a hug and kisses my head and tells us she's already checked me in. Then she crosses one leg over the other and swings her ankle back and forth, back and forth, which makes me feel even more nervous than I already was.

We wait for approximately a year before the nurse calls us back to the consultation room, and for about a lifetime before a short woman in a big sweater dress appears through the door.

"Hi there," she says. "I'm Dr. Howard."

She shakes Mom's and Dad's hands, then looks at me and smiles. "You must be Emma," she says. "How are you today?"

"Okay," I say, because according to Mom that's what you say when someone asks how you are, even though (also according to Mom) you are also not supposed to lie.

Sometimes you just can't win.

Dr. Howard gestures to the table, covered in crinkly white paper, and I sit down on it. Dad and Mom both stand beside me, ignoring the chair in the corner. "So," the doctor says, "what seems to be the problem?"

"Well, um, I started to notice these spots," I say. "Like, white spots."

"On her toes first," Mom says. "Right, Emma? And then on your arms."

"And I think there are some really tiny ones above my eyebrows," I add, not looking at Mom. I haven't mentioned those to her.

Dr. Howard blinks. "And when did you start noticing them?"

I think back to Gram's funeral. "A couple weeks ago. But there was only one then. On my left toe. And then a week or so later, there were a lot more. Or at least that's when I noticed them."

I see her studying the skin around my eyebrows. Her face is impossible to read.

"Right," she says. "Well, how about we give you a bit of space to change into a robe, and then I'll look at those spots, okay?"

She hands me a robe and tugs the curtain around the bed. As quickly as I can, I take off my jeans and shirt, then shrug into the robe.

"Ready," I call.

Dr. Howard pulls the curtain back. She examines the right leg first, then the left. She even looks at the bottoms of my feet before doing my arms and stomach. As she runs her fingers along my shoulders, I wonder if she can feel how hard my heart is beating. Every now and then, she hesitates over an area and looks at it through a magnifying glass. She runs her fingers through my scalp and finishes by studying my face again.

While she examines me, she asks me questions in a bright voice, about school and stuff. It's almost enough to distract me from the tiny frown I see creep up her face.

"So, what's wrong with me?" I ask when I feel like I can't stand not knowing for even one more second.

"You are a perfectly healthy young lady," Dr. Howard says. "Why don't you get dressed again, and then we'll talk? Mr. and Mrs. Talbot, maybe we can step out into the hall for a moment."

Notice how she didn't exactly answer my question?

Yeah. Me, too.

I get dressed as fast as I can. Everyone is still gone when I pull the curtain back again. The door is open a crack, though, and I peer out.

They're all standing in the hall. Dad's arms are crossed against his chest as Dr. Howard speaks. Mom's eyebrows are knitted tightly together. Then Dr. Howard says something, and I see Mom's mouth drop into a little round O.

I can read that shape as easy as words.

It's O as in Oh, No.

O as in Uh-Oh.

Or like *vitilig-O.*

14

Frequently Asked Questions about Vitiligo

My hands shake as I read the pamphlet for the third time. Rain beats down against the windshield, and Dad has the wipers going full speed as we turn off the highway.

What Is Vitiligo?

Vitiligo is a common condition that causes depigmentation of the skin. It occurs when an overactive immune system begins attacking the cells that create pigment, or color, in the skin. The condition generally begins as small pale spots, often on the hands, feet, or face. These spots can grow into larger spots and merge with others to create patches of pale skin. Spots or patches often form symmetrical patterns on the body, so a person with vitiligo on her right arm is likely to have it in roughly the same place on her left.

Dr. Howard said I was right about the spots on my toes and around my elbows and also above my eyebrows. She found one on the back of my neck that I hadn't noticed before, too. My face is the part I'm most worried about. I can hide my knees behind jeans for most of the year and my neck behind my hair. And arms are just arms. But my face . . . is my face. *My* face.

Except it doesn't really feel like mine anymore.

How Did I Get Vitiligo?

As with many autoimmune diseases, it's unknown what causes some people to develop vitiligo, though it is suspected that there can be a genetic factor, and it can be triggered by stress.

Dr. Howard explained that a "genetic factor" means that vitiligo can sometimes run in families. Dad reaches a hand over and rubs my back. He doesn't have vitiligo. *Nobody* in my family has vitiligo. And Lily's the one who is stressing over all her college applications, not me. So why am I the one who got it?

Is Vitiligo Dangerous or Painful?

Vitiligo rarely causes symptoms besides skin whitening. It is not painful, dangerous, or contagious. However, the condition causes many sufferers psychological distress, which can lead to social anxiety or depression. Therefore, it should not be considered simply a "cosmetic" condition.

My eyes keep floating back to the sentence about psychological distress. *(Which can lead to social anxiety or depression.)*

I really wish they'd left that part out.

I know what depression is because Gram said Gloria was depressed for a long time after her husband, Bill, died. She was so sad that she started sleeping all the time and skipping garden club meetings. She even forgot to string the Christmas lights in front of the town hall.

Gram told me she and Ruth had to drag Gloria to the doctor, where she got medication and therapy to help her feel happier again.

I don't want to ever be that sad.

But then I think about the pictures I saw online. People whose faces were two totally different colors. People with white patches all over their bodies. I bet they get stared at a lot. Like when Lily broke her foot skiing a few years ago and had to be on crutches afterward. Wherever we went, people would always follow her with their eyes, like they were wondering what was wrong with her.

Lily loved the attention.

But Lily only had to deal with it for a couple months. I bet having people stare at you your whole life *would* make you sad and anxious. You would probably want people to just treat you like everyone else.

What Is My Prognosis?

The path of vitiligo is impossible to predict and occurs differently in every patient. Your spots or patches may stay small and be confined to one area of the body, or they may continue to spread, covering much or even all of the skin. Spreading can occur rapidly and stop abruptly, or it can occur slowly over a long period of time.

If my white patches keep spreading, people might be staring at *me* for the rest of my life.

If I spent my life being bothered by what other people thought of me, I'd never get anything else done, would I? Gram says in my head.

But Gram had perfectly even, dove-pale skin. Snow White skin. People only looked at her funny sometimes because she *chose* to dress differently, with her long dresses and her parasol. I don't have any choice about whether my vitiligo spreads or where it goes. I'm like a tree with vines wrapping their way slowly around me, and nothing I can do to escape their grip.

What Are My Treatment Options?

There is no cure for vitiligo, but there are treatments that can slow its progression and can help some patients to regain pigment. These include creams and light treatments. Your doctor will help you determine the best course of treatment for your condition.

As soon as Dr. Howard had officially diagnosed me, Mom started quizzing her about treatments.

"Many people decide not to treat this condition at all," Dr. Howard told her, glancing at me. "But certainly, there are treatments to explore if Emma would like to."

Then she and Mom talked for a long time about all these different creams and light treatments where I would go into this stand-up booth and have a specific type of light shined on me. Something about that kind of light can sometimes help bring color back to people's skin.

I knew I should be paying attention—it's my skin, after all—but it was kind of hard to because they started speaking Science instead of English, and Mom kept interrupting with questions every time Dr. Howard was starting to get somewhere.

She and Dr. Howard finally decided that twice a day, I will put this cream on my white spots to help the color come back and try to keep the spots from spreading too fast. And I'll come back to the office twice a week to stand in the light-box thingy.

Then Dr. Howard stood to go. "Do you really think this stuff will work?" I asked suddenly. "I mean, make my skin normal again?"

"I'm not going to lie to you, Emma," she said. "For some people, treatments work really well. For others, vitiligo is tougher to treat. Sometimes it takes a while to find what works. But maybe . . ." She hesitated, thinking. "Maybe you can start by rethinking what you mean by 'normal.' Between you and me, I think normal is pretty overrated anyway."

I mustered a small smile because she sounded a lot like Gram.

Still, I think I'd rather have my old skin back.

But that's the thing . . . I don't really get to choose.

15

Dad clears his throat from the driver's seat. "Are you okay, Butterfly?" he says, voice raised over the rain.

"I could be better," I reply honestly.

"Well, I know it's not what we were hoping for," he says, "but I have to admit I feel kind of relieved."

"*Relieved?*" I ask, turning to stare at him.

"Relieved," he says again. "Like Dr. Howard said, you are perfectly healthy. Your vitiligo isn't going to make you sick. You're going to be just fine."

"I guess that's a bright spot," I say. "Actually, there are a lot of bright spots."

I point to white speckles on my elbow. "Get it?"

Dad hesitates, then chuckles. "That's my girl," he

says. "With that attitude, you'll be feeling great again in no time."

Except I mostly just made the joke for Dad. And despite what he says, I *do* feel sick. My insides are all trembly, like I'm coming down with the flu.

When we get home, I go straight upstairs to change my clothes. Mom, who beat us there, watches me track mud up the stairs and doesn't say a thing.

Boomer is on Gram's bed, and I think he has finally given up on her coming back again, because he doesn't cry when he sees that it's me and not her. He just lifts his head and wags his tail. I close the door behind me and change into my pajamas, even though it's still just afternoon. I nuzzle my face into Boomer's fur and shut my eyes.

But that's no good, either, because when I close them, all I see is the sad shape of Mom's face, standing out in the hall with Dr. Howard. I don't want to make Mom sad. And I don't want people feeling sorry for me, or staring at me.

I want to be Emma, the girl who reads a lot. Who lives in Lanternwood. Emma who hangs out with Fina and Ruby.

I don't want to be Emma, the girl with vitiligo.

I take a huffy breath, try to tell myself that I'm being stupid. It might not get any worse. It might have already stopped spreading, even. And if it does keep spreading, well, it's like Dad said. It's just skin, isn't it? I should feel lucky it's not something really bad, like cancer or some rare flesh-eating bacteria.

Except I don't.

I open one eye, pull my feet to my chest, and examine the white spots on my toes. They aren't exactly spots anymore—more like patches. And the patches aren't exactly white. Not white like a fresh piece of paper. They're creamier than that. Mom would probably call it eggshell or pearl. But the color is still miles away from the rest of my skin. Like a puddle of milk spilled on Gram's kitchen table.

I've always liked my skin just the way it is.

You, Emma, are the color of afternoon light settling on the trees in the Spinney, Gram had told me, and I had been proud. But now, for the first time, I almost wish I hadn't inherited Mom's complexion. That I'd inherited Gram's skin color instead. Then you would barely be able to see a difference between my spots and the rest of me.

I squeeze my eyes shut again and try really hard not to think for a long time. So long I must have fallen asleep, because the next thing I know it's getting dark outside, and there's a knock at my door.

"Emma?"

It's Lily.

"What?" I call.

"Can I come in?"

The last thing I want is for perfect Lily to walk in here and rub her perfect skin in my face. (Seriously, she's never even had a pimple.)

"No," I say. "I'm getting dressed."

"Oh," she replies. "Okay. Well, um, dinner's ready."

I'm not hungry, but I know Mom will just barge in and make a fuss over me if I don't eat any dinner, so I drag myself out of bed.

Downstairs, Mom has already piled my plate high with chicken parmesan and garlic bread. My favorite dinner.

"How are you feeling, sweetheart?" she asks as I slump into my usual seat.

"I'm okay," I say. "My stomach doesn't feel very good."

I force down a mouthful of pasta.

"Well, I don't want you to worry, all right?" Mom says. "I read that treatments work best on younger people. And there are other options, too—"

Dad clears his throat and shoots Mom a warning look.

Have you ever heard the expression "if it ain't broke, don't fix it"?

Yeah, well, not my mom. I don't think she ever saw something she didn't think needed fixing.

And now that something is *me*.

I can already feel her getting all obsessive like she does sometimes. Like she is about Lily's college applications, which she asks about every night.

Part of me is really thankful for Mom, because I *do* want my old skin back, and I know not all kids have parents who would pay for those treatments. Not all moms make chicken parmesan when their kids have a bad day. I know that.

But part of me just wants her to say that no matter what happens with my vitiligo, I'm going to be perfect, at least to her.

"All I'm trying to say is that we're not going to let this thing get the better of us, all right?"

"Sure, Mom," I say. Across the table, Lily is staring at me hard. I glare back at her, and she drops her gaze.

Mom smiles at me. "That's my girl. Now, Lily, how's the personal statement for Yale coming? Is your new draft done?"

I eat in silence until I've shoved down as much as I can stomach. Boomer sits beside my chair, looking hopefully at me. I sneak him a piece of chicken. A giggle escapes my lips.

"What?" Dad asks, raising an eyebrow.

I lean down and stroke Boomer's head, black dappled with spots of ivory.

"Nothing," I say. "It's just, I guess I'm going to look a lot more like Boomer from now on, huh?"

It's not funny, really. I just needed to laugh about something or else I'm going to start crying. I thought making a joke might help lighten the mood, like it did in the car with Dad.

Instead, Mom puts her fork down on her plate. "Oh, Emma," she says quietly. "That's not very funny. And don't feed the dog from the table, please."

Then she gets up and sweeps our plates away.

I guess dinner is officially over.

16

The next morning, I wake up early. I lie there until the first crescent of sunlight appears on the floor of my bedroom, like a seashell washed in on the tide.

I can't go back to sleep, so I make myself get dressed and brush my teeth without looking at my reflection once. Then I grab the leather journal and slip out the door, Boomer tip-tapping close behind me.

We walk down High Street, passing the silent church. The first birds are starting to twitter sleepily in the branches above us, and the only color so early is the first bits of scarlet dappling the trees.

For the first time this year, I feel autumn in the air, hanging just out of reach. A chill crawls up my arms. Of course I didn't think to bring Gram's sweater.

I break into a run as we pass the orchard, like if I pump my legs fast enough, I can outrun this thing that's happening to me. We fly down to the meadows, and by the time we reach the Spinney, I'm not cold anymore, and Boomer is panting happily.

The moss under my scuffed boots glitters with dew, and there is a threadbare carpet of golden leaves beneath the sycamore tree. A raven caws from its branches.

I creep up to sit on Throne Rock, flipping through the journal to the new chapter and rereading it once again. Ivy in the moonless forest, keeping watch for the witch. The woman in the white cloak appearing below her.

I still don't know what to write next. I only know that I want to disappear into the pages of the journal, to escape the pit in my stomach that's been there since Mom took me back-to-school shopping but that has become much heavier since yesterday.

So I turn to the first blank page and pick up the pencil again. I tap the eraser against the page for a few minutes, thinking.

Slowly, I write down a few words.

Then a few more.

And then the pencil races along the page, the Spinney flickers out of sight, and I find myself back in the story.

For many weeks, Ivy refused to set foot in the forest. Though it hurt her to be away so long, she was too frightened to return. For though her gran insisted that the woman in the white cloak had only been a figment of Ivy's imagination, Ivy knew what she had seen.

After the winter's snows had melted away, Ivy awoke one morning to find a weight on her feet. She looked down to see a bundle of fur.

"I came across him begging for scraps in the village," said her grandmother.

Gran insisted the creature was a dog, but Ivy thought he looked more like the pictures of wolves she had seen in fairy books.

"He's yours," Gran said. "He won't let any harm come to you. Now you can return to the forest, you see?"

Ivy decided to name the creature Shilling, for his coat was silver as a coin. It shone so brightly that sometimes Ivy suspected it was made of starlight.

With Shilling by her side, Ivy soon felt brave enough to return to the forest, where the wolfdog's ears and eyes always stayed alert, as if he were searching for any signs of danger. Ivy was overjoyed to feel the pull of the wind through the trees once more, and the embrace of the sunlight that glittered in the glades.

The seasons stretched into years like saplings into great trees. Shilling grew from a pup to an enormous creature that made the villagers hiss and whisper behind their hands.

But still they came to the cottage for Gran's remedies. And when the villagers left Poppy Cottage, they spoke in serious voices of how the child, Ivy, had herself grown from a small girl into something else. Something equally wild.

Ivy never heard this gossip, for she spent each happy day in her beloved forest, climbing the trees and memorizing from above the location of every thicket and clearing and rock and burrow. She spent each contented night by the fire, learning from her gran to prepare and mix remedies.

And, like a stone dropped into a deep pool, Ivy's memory of the woman in white slowly faded away into nothing at all.

Until one moonless summer's evening, Ivy and Shilling stayed late in the forest, picking dandelions to make a remedy for aching bones. When Ivy glimpsed the stars appearing between the branches of the trees, she knew it was past time to head for home.

Together, she and Shilling galloped through the trees, each racing the other and both racing the wind.

But just as Poppy Cottage came into view, Ivy's breath caught in her chest and she stopped short.

For there, gliding from the cottage, was the woman in the white cloak, carrying her wooden staff. Although it was summer, her fur hood hung across her face, hiding it from view. Shilling began to growl, but Ivy motioned for him to be quiet. Together, they hid behind a great oak tree. Nearby, Ivy could hear the sound of the woman's cloak sliding across the forest floor. Fear spread like a dark ink stain across her heart.

She waited until the sound faded away, then sprang out from behind the tree. For she had just realized the importance of what she had seen. The woman in white, leaving Poppy Cottage, where Ivy left her grandmother tending the fire.

"Gran," she whispered.

And then she took off running once more.

17

When Boomer and I return from the Spinney, the sun hangs in the watery blue sky like a juicy golden apple, ripe for the picking. And somehow, I feel a little bit lighter. Because for a whole hour, I wasn't thinking about my skin and my maybe-spreading-even-now vitiligo.

And now that I've written a chapter, it's somebody else's turn. Will they like what I wrote? Will they write again?

I'm so lost in thought that I nearly bump into Professor Swann, out for his morning walk.

"Morning, Emma," he says, tipping his hat at me.

"Hi, Professor Swann," I reply.

"A beautiful day," he says, his accented words crisp as crunching leaves, "isn't it?"

"Yeah, it is."

"The kind of day you want to share with someone," he says, squinting up at the sky. "You know, we will miss your gram terribly around here. She always made me feel welcome in Lanternwood, even when other people treated me as an outsider. Always had a kind word to spare. She was a wonderful person. But you know that better than anyone, of course."

"Yeah, she was," I say, feeling a bit taken aback. I didn't realize that she and Professor Swann knew each other that well. But I guess that explains why he seemed so upset after her funeral.

He wipes a bit of lint from his suit. "Well, I'd better—"

"Professor?" I interrupt. "Do you think— I mean, does it get easier? People say it does, but I don't think I'll ever stop missing Gram."

He flashes me a sad smile. "You won't," he says. "But it will get easier."

It's just, there's something in his eyes that makes me feel like he doesn't quite mean it.

The last garden roses are blooming in the corner of Gram's yard, forming a little crowd of pink, cheerful faces to welcome me through the white gate. Inside Morning Glory Cottage, it's toasty warm, just the way Gram liked it, and Lily is sitting at the kitchen table.

"What were you doing outside?" she asks. "Mom and Dad think you're still sleeping."

"I went for a walk," I say. "Why are you up so early anyway? Don't you need your beauty sleep?"

Lily usually sleeps until at least ten on the weekends.

"I have to work on my personal statement. Mom will be mad if she finds out you left without saying."

"She'll only find out if you tell her."

Lily hesitates, then shrugs. "Better take your sneakers off." She picks up her phone with one hand, a Yale brochure in the other, and snaps some "applying to college" selfies.

I wriggle my feet out of my shoes and kick them over beside the door just as Mom and Dad come downstairs.

"Oh, you're awake," Mom says.

"I, um, just came down."

Lily doesn't correct me. She's probably being nice because she feels sorry for me, and I decide that maybe I don't mind that so much. Because what is the point of contracting a life-changing skin condition if your sister isn't at least going to be a little nicer to you?

Later that morning, Fina texts me and asks if I want to hang out.

I reply and tell her I do as long as it's not at my house.

Because I swear, every time I look up, somebody is staring at me, like if they look hard enough, they can actually see my spots getting bigger. It's starting to make me paranoid.

Fina tells me to come to her house, and Dad drives me into town, which is crowded since it's Saturday. Fina lives practically across the street from the main Hampstead College gates, in a little lavender house with a neat square of grass in front.

I barely have time to knock before the door flies open.

"Fina?" I say dubiously.

She stands in front of me, wearing some kind of crazy helmet with bars across the face and holding a baseball bat.

"Emma!" she says. "Come in!"

"Um, okay."

I take an uncertain step into the house as a woman appears from the kitchen. She has bright brown eyes, a smile with dimples, and chestnut hair with purple tips. I try to imagine what it would be like to have a mom cool enough to dye her tips purple. Awesome, most likely.

"Hello there," the woman says, holding out a hand. "I'm Ana Ramirez. You must be Emma."

"Hi," I say. "Nice to meet you."

"Fina's told us wonderful things about you," she says.

"Mo-om," Fina warns, "don't be awkward."

Just then, someone else comes down the stairs, a man in a baseball helmet holding a vacuum cleaner. He's walking funny, kind of like a crab, and he keeps looking around like he's waiting for something to jump out and attack him.

"Are you guys playing some kind of game?" I ask.

"Kind of," Fina replies.

"It's not a game," insists the man, who must be her father. "It's life and death."

"Don't worry," Fina says. "It's only death if you're a spider."

"Hi, Emma," says the man, taking off his helmet. "I'm Luis Ramirez. Fina's dad and deputy spider catcher."

"You're hunting spiders?"

"Yes! We have an infestation of them. And they're huge!" Fina creates a circle a little bigger than a quarter with her thumb and pointer finger.

"They're more like animals than spiders," Ms. Ramirez says, shivering.

"And this here house ain't big enough for the both of us," Mr. Ramirez drawls in a funny voice. "It's us or them."

Ms. Ramirez rolls her eyes. "And *I'm* the awkward one. Right."

"When I went to the bathroom this morning, there was one in the tub," Fina says, grimacing. "It just sat there, *watching me*."

"See, Emma? We can't go on like this." Mr. Ramirez offers me the helmet and vacuum cleaner. "And besides, I have to make some lunch."

"Did they have a red dot on them?" I ask.

Fina shakes her head. "No. They were black."

"Then they aren't black widows. And if they're big, then they aren't brown recluse spiders. So they're probably harmless."

Gram taught me about spiders. She said it was smart to know what the poisonous ones looked like, especially spending so much time in the woods. She wasn't bothered by the other kinds, though.

Fina is staring at me like I've just told her I can fly. "*Harmless* spiders?" she repeats. "There's no such thing as a *harmless* spider. I'll need years of therapy to get the image of that tub spider out of my head."

"You know what this means, don't you?" Mr. Ramirez says to her. "Emma's working for *the other side*."

"You mean she's Team Spider?" Fina asks, clutching her hand to her heart.

I think we can agree by now that the Ramirez family is extremely weird. In an extremely awesome way.

I look from Fina to Mr. Ramirez and grin before

jamming the baseball helmet on my head. "I'm not a spy," I say. Then I lower my voice to a whisper. "I'm a *double agent.*"

"Excellent," Fina says.

The two of us go around the house, sucking up all the cobwebs from the corners and checking under the furniture for more spiders. Every time we move a chair to look underneath, I lift the vacuum nozzle and say, "I'm going in." Then Fina raises the bat over her shoulder and says, "Copy that. I'll be your cover."

By the time we're done, we have found forty-eight cents, half a chocolate bar, one of those little umbrellas you put in fruity drinks ("I've been looking for that everywhere!" Fina says), and zero spiders.

"I think we scared them all away," Fina says, taking off her mask (a baseball catcher's mask, I've figured out) and flopping down onto the sofa, panting.

"I think your parents tricked us into cleaning your house," I reply.

Fina's eyes go wide. "Outsmarted again!" she says, shaking her fist.

"It's okay. Your parents seem so cool. Mine would never let me run around the house swinging a baseball bat. And your mom's hair! I love the purple."

"She promised me that after my Quinceañera, I can get blue streaks."

"What's a Quinceañera?" I ask.

"It's this big celebration that happens for a girl's fif-teenth birthday," Fina explains. "There's a mass and then a big party. Everyone gets dressed up and dances a lot. It's supposed to mark the transition to womanhood. My grandmother has been planning mine since I was, like, two."

"Cool," I say. "I bet my sister would have loved to have one. She made Mom get a room in a fancy hotel so she could have a slumber party for her Sweet Six-teenth."

"That sounds fun."

"I wouldn't know. I wasn't exactly invited."

"Well, maybe for *your* Sweet Sixteenth, you can have a hair-dye party!"

"Not likely. My mom would kill me if I dyed my hair," I reply, "no matter what age I was."

"But at least you would be a very stylish corpse."

We both laugh. Then Fina's phone chimes.

"Oh, Ruby's almost here!" she says. "I invited her, too."

After a minute, there's a knock on the door, and Fina opens it to reveal Ruby. "Hi, guys," she says. She wrin-kles her nose. "Have you been playing baseball?"

Ms. Ramirez comes out before we can answer and waves hello to Ruby. "Lunch is ready, girls!"

All that spider hunting has made me really hungry, and whatever is cooking in the kitchen smells great.

It turns out that Mr. Ramirez has made enchiladas. Highly delicious enchiladas. Only Mr. Ramirez doesn't seem to think so. He shakes his head as he bites into his.

"Still not right," he mumbles. "Darn."

"All his students love his enchiladas back home," Fina explains. "But he can't get the recipe right here."

"The tomatoes are different!" Mr. Ramirez protests. "Or maybe it's the peppers."

"It tastes really good to me, Mr. Ramirez," I offer.

"Me, too," says Ruby. Then she turns to Fina. "So, what was it like in LA? Did you know any movie stars?"

"We didn't actually live in LA," Fina says. "We were in this college town called Claremont that was like thirty miles from there."

"And unfortunately, we didn't know any movie stars," Ms. Ramirez says.

"But we knew lots of history stars!" Mr. Ramirez adds brightly.

"History stars?" Ruby asks.

"You know, stars of the history world. In fact, last year, I was at a conference with Da—"

Fina elbows him just hard enough that he gets the point and goes back to eating his enchiladas.

"What's your book about, Mr. Ramirez?" I ask. "Fina said you were writing one."

"No," Fina replies. "I said he was *supposed* to be writing one. But I don't think watching Netflix all day really counts."

"Last week, I caught him watching *Pretty Little Liars*," Ms. Ramirez says, shaking her head. Ruby and I giggle, and Fina lets out a groan.

"I wanted to know what all the hype was about!" says Mr. Ramirez.

"You are so embarrassing, Dad," Fina groans.

Maybe so, but by the end of lunch, I'm pretty sure I've had more fun with Fina's family than I've had with mine since before Gram died. And that makes me happy.

But kind of sad, too.

18

When I look in the mirror on Monday morning, I get a shock.

I've been trying to stay away from mirrors all weekend, but I'm sure my face has changed since last week. The spots above my eyebrows, which were the size of pinpricks last time I checked, have now grown into real spots. Some of them are closer to the size of thumbtacks.

Is this what it's going to be like from now on? Waking up every morning to find someone new staring back at me from the mirror? Before, you couldn't notice the tiny pale flecks unless you looked really closely. But now the spots above my eyebrows are like a sign that says:

EMMA TALBOT HAS VITILIGO.

If only I could cover my face like I can cover my toes and elbows.

Which actually gives me an idea. I start pulling open the cabinet drawers, frantically searching through all of Lily's nail polishes and lip glosses until I find what I'm looking for.

Five minutes later, I'm staring at myself in the mirror once again. A groan escapes my lips.

Somehow, I've made everything *worse*.

"Emma!" Mom calls. "You're going to be late! And don't forget your sunscreen!"

Over the weekend, Mom bought me this special sunscreen. SPF 1000 or something like that. When your skin loses the pigment, it apparently also loses its ability to protect itself from the sun, which means I can get burned really easily. The last thing I need is for the spots on my face to turn bright red with sunburn, so after I put on my treatment cream, I squeeze some sunscreen from the bottle and slap it on my face.

I take a deep breath at the top of the steps. Then I bolt down them as fast as I can. Because I cannot deal with Mom seeing what I've done just yet.

But of course, she's waiting at the bottom of the stairs, probably so she can smell me for sunscreen. When she sees me, she gasps and says, "Emma, what did you do?"

"I have to go."

"Wait! Emma—"

But I'm out the door and running. Ruth and Gloria call good morning to me from across the street, and I wave at them without looking up. I keep my head down as I get on the bus and stare at my feet as I trudge to my usual seat. Then I pull out *The World at the End of the Tunnel* and bury my face in it.

> *After several hours of swinging from the oak tree in their netted trap, Jack and Sarah heard the leaves stirring and then the sound of a saw meeting rope. Before their eyes had time to grow wide, they suddenly found themselves falling to earth.*

The bus stops, and Edie gets on. I keep my eyes glued to the book.

> *Rubbing their backsides and scowling, Jack and Sarah looked around to find themselves surrounded by stubby creatures with gray skin and pointed ears. Clover elves. Each set of long twiggy fingers held a bow, and each of the bows held an arrow. All of these arrows, Sarah noticed with alarm, were pointed directly at—*

Just as we pull away from Edie's stop, I feel something hit me in the back of the head, and—thinking of elves with their bows at the ready—I instinctively spin around.

Too late, I realize it was just a balled-up candy wrapper that Edie threw at me, and now I'm staring at her and the Graces, and all three of them are staring back at me, mouths agape.

"Oh. My. *God*," Edie says, a joyful smile spreading across her face. "What. A. *Freak!*"

"She's like a zombie or something," says Grace One.

And because I have the worst luck ever, Grace Two already has her phone out. In the instant before I turn around, she snaps my picture.

I whip forward, cheeks on fire. I mean, I knew it was bad, but are my new bangs really *that* terrible? And how do they make me look like a zombie?

I sink lower in my seat and fumble in Gram's satchel for my phone so I can get a look at myself. Before I find it, though, we reach Ruby's stop and she climbs up. Relief fills me as she sits down next to me.

"What's with Edie and her friends?" she whispers. "They're all looking up here and laughing."

"I think it's my bangs," I say. "I did a really bad job cutting them."

Ruby stares at me, her cheeks going even pinker than usual. "Um, I don't think it's just the bangs," she says. "It's your face? It's all white."

My heart plummets. I thought my bangs covered the spots. Could they have somehow spread even farther since I looked in the mirror a few minutes ago? Do I have some kind of super strain of vitiligo or something?

Ruby lifts her hand to my face and rubs at one of my cheeks with her thumb. "I think it's sunscreen."

I turn my phone camera lens toward me and see that Ruby's right. The sunscreen Mom got me is like chalk against my skin. I look like I'm about to go to a mime convention.

"It's this new stuff my mom's making me wear," I say, breathing a sigh of relief. "It's really high SPF."

"Oh," Ruby says. "It must be the mineral kind. My mom makes me wear it, too, because I burn like crazy. You have to rub it in really well. Otherwise it does, you know, *that*."

"Thanks, Ruby," I say as the bus pulls up to the school. "I'm gonna go to the bathroom to fix this. See you at lunch."

"Do you want me to come?" she asks in a small voice.

"No. No, it's okay."

I keep my eyes on my shoes as I weave through the halls and into the first bathroom I see. I look at my chalky face under my ridiculously crooked bangs in the mirror, then grab a handful of paper towels, soak them in water, and begin to scrub.

"Emma?"

I whirl around to see Ms. Singh standing in the doorway.

"Did you know you're in the staff bathroom?" she asks gently.

I shake my head. "I'm sorry. I had a sunscreen emergency."

"A sunscreen emergency," she echoes, nodding. "Right. Are you good now?"

"Um, yeah," I reply. "Except my bangs. But I can't really fix those."

Ms. Singh takes a few steps toward me and brushes lightly through my bangs, studying them. "It's not so bad," she says. "Hold on a minute. Stay here. If anyone else comes, tell them you have my permission. All right?"

I nod, and she disappears through the door. A few minutes later, she comes back holding a small pair of scissors. "Trust me?" she asks, holding them up.

"Should I?"

"My mom was a hairdresser. I learned some things."

Trying not to think about how weird it is to get a haircut from your teacher in the bathroom at school, I close my eyes.

I feel the scissors snip through my hair, but not in the same way I did it this morning. Ms. Singh has a lighter touch and cuts kind of upward instead of straight across.

"Um, Ms. Singh?" I say, eyes still closed. I feel like this will be less awkward if one of us is talking.

"Yes?"

Snip.

"You're an English teacher."

Snip, snip.

"Can't get anything past you, can I?" she says with a little laugh.

"Do you like to write? Like stories or poetry or anything?"

The snipping stops for a moment. "Sure," she says. "Sometimes. Why do you ask?"

"Well, how do you decide what your story is supposed to be about?"

Snip, snip, snip.

"That's tricky," says Ms. Singh. "But I guess I would say that you should write about what's in your heart. About something that's important to you."

"Yeah. That's good advice."

Snip.

"Are you writing a story?"

"Kind of. Yes."

I decide to leave out the fact that I have a mysterious pen pal who is helping me write it.

"That's wonderful! There, now look," Ms. Singh says, squeezing my shoulders.

I open my eyes and look in the mirror. The bangs are *much* better than before. They're straight now, and cover everything above my eyebrows. You can't see my spots at all. If Ms. Singh noticed them while she was cutting—and I don't see how she couldn't have—she doesn't say anything.

"Thanks," I reply. "It doesn't look like I cut them myself anymore."

"You're welcome," she says, smiling. "Now, get to class, and good luck with that story. And Emma?"

"Yeah?"

"You look nice with bangs. But you looked nice without them, too."

When I arrive in English class later that morning, Ms. Singh gives me a thumbs-up, and I smile back at her.

"What happened to your zombie freak face?" Edie says as she sits down.

"What happened to your twin?" retorts Fina, appearing behind her.

"What are you talking about?" Edie asks, eyes narrowing.

"I just figured the only explanation for being so rude is that you're someone's evil twin." Fina crosses her arms over her chest. "So what'd you do with the good one?"

I laugh, and Edie starts to say something, but Grace Number One jerks her head toward Ms. Singh, who looks like she's about to come over. Edie smiles sweetly at her.

"Are you okay?" Fina whispers. "Ruby told me what happened on the bus."

"I'm fine," I say. Honestly, it was almost worth it for Edie to call me a zombie freak just to see Fina defend me like that. It makes me feel all warm and fuzzy.

"Good. Why'd you cut your hair anyway?" Fina asks. "I mean, the bangs look good on you, but what inspired you?"

"I don't know," I say. "I guess it was just time for a change, you know?"

19

At the end of the week, I tell Fina and Ruby I'm going to be late to school the next Monday because of a dentist appointment, but really I'm going for my first light treatment at Dr. Howard's office. I'll have to get good at thinking up excuses if I'm going to have to do these treatments twice a week.

A nurse takes me back to a room with this really tall box that looks a little like a spaceship. Then I have to close my eyes and put on goggles and go stand inside the box. She counts down from three. When she gets to one, a light flicks on so bright I can see it with my eyes closed—and there's a whirring noise. Then I just stand there like that for a whole minute, pretending that I'm being beamed up into space.

"That's all?" I ask when the light switches off. I didn't feel anything. It seems kind of crazy that just a little bit of light could bring the color back to my skin.

"That's it," says the nurse.

Dr. Howard told me that even if the light box works, it will take a few months to start seeing any improvement, but I still glance down at myself afterward. The patches on my feet are bigger than quarters now. Looking in the mirror, I hold up my hair and turn to see my neck. The spots there haven't joined together yet, but there are a dozen or so sprinkled around. Next, I pull back my bangs and study the spots underneath. There are even more now than last Monday, following the angle of my eyebrows. I pat my bangs firmly back down so that the spots are hidden again.

Here's something I haven't really been honest about until now. I've started noticing other people's faces. Like, *a lot*. I study their skin colors. Give them names like the ones on the backs of Gram's paint tubes. *Summer sands* for Lily and *wild honey* for Fina. I stare at Ms. Singh (*driftwood*) during class and look at how smooth and even her face looks, even on the days when she has little baggies under her eyes.

And sometimes I feel jealous of them. All those one-colored people who don't even know how lucky they are because they're too busy thinking about how their noses are too long or their eyelashes aren't long enough, so they never stop and take a second to be thankful for their skin. Even Ruby has an even layer of *fresh cream* underneath her freckles.

I always wear my hair down now to cover the spots on my neck and long-sleeve shirts and sneakers to cover my other ones. But I won't be able to hide the spots on my forehead if they decide to creep down past my bangs. And what happens if all my treatments don't work and the spots keep growing, and more and more of the color gets sucked out of me until I have none left at all?

I read online that it happens to some people with vitiligo. They lose *all* their color. Then there are some who have patches all over their body and actually have their doctors give them a depigmenting cream to get rid of the rest of their color. Because at least that way, they're one color again. And people probably don't stare at them anymore, because they just look really pale (*magnolia blossom*). So maybe it wouldn't be so bad.

But the idea of losing the rest of my color makes me wrap my arms tightly around my waist, like if I just squeeze hard enough, I can keep it from draining away.

Every afternoon that week, Boomer and I run through the village and down to the meadows after school, always heading for the Spinney. On Thursday, we race

Old Joe's tractor as it rumbles down High Street. It's not much of a race, to be honest.

"How's school going?" Old Joe calls as we slow down by the tractor cab. "What grade is it again?"

"Seventh," I say, tugging on Boomer's leash to get him to slow down. "And it's good."

A car honks. There's a long line of them behind Old Joe. He grins at me and winks.

"Seventh grade is a head-scratcher, that's for sure," he says. "You be good now. Make your gram proud."

"I will."

Then he kicks the tractor into full speed, by which I mean about ten miles an hour. Boomer and I peel off past the orchard, where families are picking apples from the trees, then through the meadows and into the Spinney. We rush down the hill toward the glade and the sycamore hollow to see if my pen pal has written the next chapter of our story.

Every day, the carpet of leaves on the forest floor has grown thicker and brighter, and today I actually slip on them and go sliding down the slope. When I get to the bottom, Boomer pounces on me and starts drenching my face with kisses. For the first time since Gram died, I laugh so hard my stomach hurts.

There's this part of *The World at the End of the Tunnel*—after Sarah and Jack are taken in by the clover elves and have started training to defeat the troll army—when Sarah suddenly realizes that she can't remember the last time she thought about home.

Did things like bedtimes and hot baths and setting the table for supper still exist somewhere? When Sarah thought of such things, it was as if she were recalling details of a long-ago dream.

When I step into the Spinney—or roll into it, for that matter—I feel the same way. Like the rest of my world doesn't exist at all. Like the forest is the only thing that's real.

Even though I didn't say it to Fina, I think that's the other reason I love *The World at the End of the Tunnel* so much. I always felt like Sarah, Jack, and I all shared this secret. They had the Goldengrove, and I had the Spinney.

Every day this week, I've checked the journal for a new chapter, and every day, there's been nothing. It's been almost two weeks since I wrote about Ivy seeing the woman in white leaving Poppy Cottage.

I thought it would be a good cliff-hanger, but maybe my pen pal doesn't agree. Or maybe they have writer's block. Or maybe they've forgotten about the story altogether.

But as I dust myself off and look inside the sycamore hollow today, I feel my heart leap. I'm sure the journal isn't quite at the angle I left it. And sitting atop it is a new pencil, freshly sharpened.

I grab the journal and skip breathlessly over to Throne Rock. I nestle myself into the nook of the cool boulders and turn through the pages, impatient to find out what happens next in the story.

Ivy ran across the clearing and burst through the door of Poppy Cottage, Shilling galloping beside her like a shooting star.

Inside the cottage, Gran sat upon a stool by the little fire, whittling something that looked like a crutch. She looked up in surprise as Ivy rushed in.

"Gran!" Ivy cried, running to her grandmother and flinging herself at the old woman's feet. She laid her head in her grandmother's lap. "You're safe!"

"Of course I am, child," said Gran. But her face looked pale in the meager firelight.

"The woman in the white cloak," said Ivy. "I saw her leave. Are you all right?"

"I am," Gran replied. But a tear slipped from the corner of her eye.

"What did she want?"

"Dearest Ivy," said Gran, setting down her whittling. "There is so much I wish I could tell you."

Ivy shook her head, confused. Shilling whined.

"What do you mean, Gran? Why can't you tell me?"

Gran smiled. But her breath rattled in her chest.

"Are you sick, Gran?" Ivy asked, noticing how her grandmother's color seemed to be fading further, like the sun fleeing the evening sky. "Did the woman in white do something to you?"

Her grandmother lifted a cold hand to Ivy and brushed it against her cheek. "I am an old woman, my girl. It is time I take my leave of the world."

Ivy clutched at Gran's skirts. "You can't!" she cried. "You mustn't!"

"You are strong," said Gran, passing the half-whittled crutch to Ivy. "You are ready. Be well, my girl."

Gran took one last breath that seemed to go on forever, and then in an instant was gone.

Ivy and Shilling tilted their heads up in unison. Their howls pierced a hole through the moonless night.

20

I don't go back to the Spinney on Friday afternoon, or even over the weekend.

By the time I finished reading the new chapter, hot tears were burning down my cheeks.

And the more I thought about it, the more I felt like I'd been betrayed. It was *my* story, after all. It was supposed to be something to take my mind off my problems. A fairy tale that started with "once upon a time" and ended with "happily ever after."

I had to watch my grandmother die, but Ivy was supposed to save hers. Wasn't she?

I'm still stewing about it on Monday, when I arrive at school late from my light treatment.

"You're quiet today," Fina says at lunch. "Is every-thing okay?"

"Yeah," I reply. "Totally fine."

"Did you have another dentist appointment this morning?" Ruby asks. "Do you have a cavity or some-thing?"

"No," I say slowly, trying to decide what to tell them. "I—"

But just then Fina's head cocks to the side. She's star-ing at me.

"What's that?" She points to my mouth.

"What's what?" I ask, running my fingers over my lips, feeling for sandwich crumbs. But there's nothing.

"You have this little white spot," she replies, "right there at the corner of your mouth."

My heart stumbles, then falls, like a runner who's just been tripped.

"Um," I murmur, "I don't know. I—I need to go to the bathroom."

I whip out of the cafeteria, down the hall, and into the bathroom. *Please, no*, I think. *Please let it be a spot of sunscreen.* I check to make sure no one else is there, and then lean close to the mirror above the sink.

There it is. My newest spot, hovering just above the left corner of my lip.

Tears spring to my eyes.

I can't hide my mouth with a strategic haircut—unless I want to become a bearded lady. Why is the vitiligo spreading so quickly? Why does it have to be on my face? Why me at all?

A really mean thought crosses my mind.

Which is that I wish this were happening to someone else. Anybody else but me.

"Emma?" calls a voice. Fina is standing in the doorway, Ruby right behind her. "Are you okay?"

For some reason, her question makes my tears multiply. "Um," I say, my chin all wobbly, "I don't really know."

In an instant, Fina is there with her arm around me, hugging me tight. Ruby stands just to the side, watching wide-eyed and biting her lip as I cry.

"It's okay, Emma," says Fina. "Whatever it is, it's going to be okay, I swear!"

I'm not sure how she knows this, because she doesn't even know what's wrong yet. But it still helps me to stop crying. And then instead of tears spilling out, it's words.

I tell both of them about seeing the first spot at Gram's funeral and then the next ones in the dressing room at the mall. I tell them about seeing Mom's face out in the hall with Dr. Howard, and how I knew then that I really did have vitiligo.

Fina nods as I talk, and Ruby's frown grows deeper and deeper until she wears a panicked look, like I've just told her that I'm dying.

"Oh my god," she says when I'm finished. "That's awful, Emma. I'm really sorry."

"It's not *so* terrible," Fina protests. "I mean, I'm sure it's really hard getting used to it, but I think it's kind of cool. Most people just get to be one color, but you get to be two!"

I shoot her a watery smile. Leave it to Fina to think that being one color is boring.

"So it's not contagious?" Ruby asks.

"Right," I say.

"Then how'd you get it?"

I shrug. "I don't know. It just happens to some people. That's the way autoimmune diseases are."

I see Ruby shiver a little, and I'm pretty sure she's worrying about what it would be like if *she* got it. Which is kind of annoying, actually.

"Don't worry," I say to her. "Only like one in a hundred people get it."

That was something else Dr. Howard told me at our appointment.

"One in a hundred?" Fina echoes, handing me a paper towel to blow my nose on. "I know way more than a hundred people. How come I've never heard of it?"

I shrug again. "Maybe because some people get it when they're older? And not everyone gets it on their face, so some people can cover it up with clothes and stuff. Or they wear makeup."

"Oooh," breathes Fina. "Your bangs. Is that because—"

I lift up my bangs so they can see underneath.

Fina's expression doesn't change at all. She just looks at my forehead and nods. "And your appointments?"

"Light treatments," I say. "I stand in this box that fills up with a certain kind of light that's supposed to help me get color back in my spots."

"Whoa. Cool," Fina says, looking genuinely impressed.

"Is it working?" Ruby asks.

"I'm not sure. It takes a while to know."

"Emma," Fina says, "this must be really tough for you, but Ruby and I are here for you no matter what. We don't care what color—or *colors*—you are. And I will personally kick the sorry butt of anyone who does."

She pulls me and Ruby into a group hug, embracing us tightly.

"Thanks," I reply. "That makes me feel a little bit better."

And I'm not lying, either.

21

My friends are really good about keeping me busy after school for the next few weeks. Fina invites me and Ruby over a bunch, and Ms. Ramirez takes us to the bakery in town for cake, or if she's busy, Mr. Ramirez takes us to the movies or bowling.

Fina and Ruby are also really good about not talking about my vitiligo. I mean, I know they would if I wanted, but right now, I kind of want to talk about anything else. Especially since I've started thinking about it all the time when I'm at school.

Now that I have spots where people can see them (another one showed up a few days after the last one, this one on the right side of my mouth), I've started being really careful about keeping my head down in the hall and making sure that in class my hair is always hanging loose around my face so you can't see the spots from the sides. If I have to talk to someone up close, I rest my chin in my hands, so my fingers cover them up.

Fridays are the best because I get to go home for the weekend, where I don't have to worry about hiding all the time. Even better, Mom's been so preoccupied with reviewing Lily's college applications that I think she's forgotten to be so worried about me.

One Friday night, I'm in bed reading *The World at the End of the Tunnel*. Sarah and Jack and the clover elves are just about to celebrate their victory over the troll army when an ogre kidnaps Jack and sweeps him off to the hobgoblin king's castle. Before Sarah can follow them, there's a knock on my door.

"Come in," I say.

I have to hide my surprise when the door opens to reveal Lily standing there, holding her huge makeup bag. This is a surprise because (a) I have no idea what Lily wants from me and (b) Lily never stays home on Friday nights. Though now that I think about it, she hasn't been going out nearly as much as she used to. I guess because Mom's been keeping her so busy with applications.

"Hey, Emma," she says, smiling.

"What's up?" I ask.

She comes in and sits down on the bed next to me, making the springs creak. She glances at the book lying open on the bed, and I wait for her to say something about it.

Last year, Lily told me that since I was in middle school, I should be reading "real" books. *Classics.* She thinks books like *The World at the End of the Tunnel* are for little kids.

But she doesn't understand how the pages in my books leave space for you to crawl into them and dream up your own stories, instead of trying to cram your head so full of big words there's no room for you at all.

I don't think you could ever be too old for a book like that. Gram never was. Grandpa must have known it, or else why would he have given her *The World at the End of the Tunnel*?

But Lily doesn't say anything about the book at all. Instead, her eyes drift back to me. "I haven't really asked," she says, "um, how you've been doing with, you know, everything?"

I search her face for signs of the Lily I'm used to, the one who usually only notices me long enough to forget about me again. But I have to admit, she actually seems kind of . . . *sincere.*

"Well," I say, still cautious, "I've been better."

"Yeah. This vitiligo thing must be kind of tough to get used to, huh?"

"Kind of," I agree. And then, because for the first time I can remember, Lily is showing an interest in me, I add, "Thanks for asking."

"I was actually thinking maybe I could help," Lily says, holding up the makeup bag. "It's totally up to you, but if you wanted to cover up your, um, you know, spots, I could teach you how."

"Really?" I ask, eyebrows shooting up behind my bangs. "You would do that?"

Lily looks stung, like she offers to do nice things for me all the time. "Of course," she says. "I actually watched a couple of tutorials on YouTube about how to do it. Do you want me to?"

"Um, yeah," I say. "That would be great, actually."

Last night, I read this blog that Fina sent me about a supermodel who has vitiligo. She has really dark skin (*twilight falls*), so her vitiligo patches stand out a lot. And she has them all over her body. In the blog, she talks about how she's really proud of the way she looks and how her vitiligo makes her unique and beautiful.

She's right, too. She is really, really pretty and totally different looking from basically anyone else I've ever seen before. I think it's awesome that she loves her patches.

And I wish I felt the same way about mine. Maybe one day I'll think they're cool, like Fina says she does. But that's not how I feel about them now.

Lily is sorting through the bottles and sticks and containers that she's spread out all over my bed, her hair tucked neatly behind her ears.

"I borrowed some of Mom's stuff," she says, "since your skin tone is pretty similar to hers. But we'll buy you your own. I can take you if you want."

She puts a few bottles up to my face and studies the colors before making her choices. "You're going to want to start with a concealer," she says, showing me this tube that looks like lipstick except inside, the stick is skin-colored.

She hands me a mirror that I can watch myself in as she holds up my bangs and rubs a thick line of the concealer stuff over the pale spots above my right eye, which have now joined together in full patches—like a pale caterpillar crawling along my forehead. She rubs it in with her thumb. Already my skin looks much more even. Then she tells me to practice on the left.

After that, we put concealer on the spots by my mouth, and then a liquid foundation that's cold and silky against my skin.

"So, how are your applications going?" I ask. Since we're being all interested in each other now.

To my surprise, Lily sighs, and her spine slumps. "I'm really not sure," she says. "Yale is crazy competitive, you know?"

I've *never* heard Lily talk like this before, like she's anything less than perfect. Honestly, it's kind of nice to know that even my sister has doubts about herself. It means she's probably not an alien robot clone, something I have suspected from time to time. She's an actual human being.

But the second I hear her getting down on herself, all I want to do is reassure her.

"You'll get in," I say. "And even if you don't, there are other good colleges."

She shrugs. "It's a lot of pressure," she says. "And honestly . . ."

She trails off, biting her lip as she rummages around the makeup bag.

"What?"

"You can't tell Mom, okay? She's driving me nuts about the whole college thing."

The surprises just keep on coming. I've never heard Lily complain about Mom before. I thought since they had so much in common, they always got along. "I promise," I say.

She takes a deep breath. "Well, I was kind of thinking it might be nice to take a break from school. After graduation, I mean. Do something different for a while."

"Like what?"

She wipes at a smudge on my nose. "I'm not sure," she says. "Travel or something? Go off the grid and meet new people?"

Okay, seriously. Who is this girl and what has she done with my sister? Or is it really possible that she's been inside Lily this whole time, zipped up behind all that perfection?

"*You?*" I ask. "Ditch college? And *Instagram?*"

Lily laughs. "I know," she says. "But Instagram isn't as much fun as it used to be. My friends from home are kind of . . . lying low recently. And the kids at my new school don't really know me."

Is that why Lily has been home so much recently? Not just because she's stressed about applications but because she's having trouble making new friends?

For the first time, I think about how hard it must have been for Lily to move right before senior year. And how weird it is that I haven't heard her complain about it. But maybe Lily knew that us moving in to take care of Gram was more important than where she finished school. Maybe she cared more about Gram than I thought.

"You shouldn't worry about *all* the kids at your new school," I say. "You should just find a couple who like you for you. That's what I did."

Lily is done with the foundation now, and has moved on to brushing a powder over my face. I close my eyes. The brush tickles in a relaxing way. "That's good advice, Emma," she says. "You're really smart, you know? About some things."

"*Some* things?"

She laughs as she sprays my face with this cold stuff that she says is to keep the makeup from coming off.

Then, "Voilà!" she says, sitting back and nodding with satisfaction. "What do you think?"

I open my eyes and hold the mirror up so I can see my whole face. No patches. No spots. My skin is one color again. "Whoa!" I breathe. "They're gone! I look almost like I did before. Except . . . I look so—"

"Grown-up?" Lily finishes.

"Yeah," I say. "Exactly. Thanks a lot, Lily."

"No problem," she says, gathering up all her stuff. "I'll make a list of what we used, and we can go buy some this week. Remember, no telling Mom what we talked about."

"I won't," I say. "Or that we stole her makeup."

"Oh, don't worry about that. This was her idea."

I feel my smile fall flat. "What was her idea?"

"Me teaching you to do your makeup. She told me to offer to do it. She said you would probably like it better if I helped you."

154

Translation: this whole thing has been a setup. Lily is only helping me because Mom told her she had to.

She's probably going to march right down the hall to Mom and give her a full report. And Mom will be relieved. Relieved not to have a daughter who's covered in spots anymore. I feel suddenly queasy.

"Hey, you okay?" Lily says.

"I am *so* sick of people asking me that," I grumble.

She frowns. "Emma, I—"

"Close the door," I snap. "On your way out. Please."

Lily starts to say something else, but I've already picked up *The World at the End of the Tunnel*. I hear the floorboards creak beneath her feet, then the door shutting softly behind her.

I would be *okay* if I could just have my old life back. A life without vitiligo. Or one where Gram was still here. I know she would have found a way to make it better.

But I can't wish myself back to my old life—the one *with* Gram and with*out* spots.

Maybe that's what my pen pal was trying to tell me in the last chapter of our story. Gram can no more help me now than I could have saved her from her cancer.

And this thought makes my heart ache with loneliness.

22

The next morning, I head straight for the Spinney after breakfast, stopping to say hello to Gloria—on her way to meet a friend at the orchard café.

"Emma, sweetheart," she says. "Stop by for some tea soon, will you? I've barely seen you since, well, the funeral. What is it, six weeks now? Hard to believe it. It feels like yesterday."

I glance up toward the graveyard, where the Apple Lady is just emerging from the church, head down and headphones on. It *is* hard to believe it's been six weeks since the funeral, but whether it's because the time has gone by slow or fast, I'm not sure. It just feels weird that I've gone six whole weeks without Gram. And that I'm only ever going to get further away from her.

A knot rises in my throat.

"Sure, Gloria," I reply. "I'll come soon."

When Boomer and I slip under the barbed wire a few minutes later, it's to find squirrels scurrying back and forth, gathering up the acorns that have fallen everywhere. Boomer goes barreling after them. I walk behind, leaves crunching beneath my feet. Leafmeal, Gram said the charmed folk called it, when the autumn leaves started to shatter into dust.

Before today, I wasn't sure if I even wanted to keep writing Ivy's story. But when I woke up this morning, I found myself thinking about what Ms. Singh said when I asked her for advice about writing. *Write about what's in your heart. About something that's important to you.*

And maybe she's right. Maybe instead of trying to escape from the darkness I feel inside me, I can write about it. Maybe I can write it *out* of me.

Together, Ivy and Shilling made a place for Gran to lie in her favorite glade, where the ground was soft and covered in clover, and nearby ran a gentle river. Ivy marked the spot with a pile of river rocks, smooth and gray and solemn looking.

Then they returned to the cottage, and Ivy tucked herself into bed. For many days, she did not move.

Not when hunger rumbled her belly or when cold

crept in through the dark chimney or when the villagers who had come to seek Gran's remedies knocked upon the door.

She only slept and wept and thought of Gran. Of how she had once believed that they would be together always. And of how she had often wondered if Gran had magic running through her veins.

Now, she knew, there was magic in the world. A magic that was frightening and cruel.

For Ivy was sure of one thing: the woman in the white cloak was a witch after all. A witch who had killed Gran.

And then one gray morning, Ivy woke up thinking of revenge.

She flung the sheets from the bed and dressed herself. Then she set off into the forest.

She left Shilling behind, as she knew he would never let her find the witch. He would sense danger, take hold of her cloak with his sharp teeth, and pull her all the way back to safety.

On and on she walked, until it felt like she had been going for years. Finally, she came to a place where the trees were spiked with thorns, where they grew so tall she could not see their ends and where their leaves were so thick that daytime became night.

And there, in the center of the trees, was a dark cottage.

Ivy hid herself away behind one of the trees and watched. Was this where the witch lived?

Just then, she heard a voice behind her. "Child, what are you doing so deep in the woods? Have you become lost? The forest is not safe for a girl so young."

Ivy turned around to see a beautiful woman with rosy cheeks and a basket of herbs. She stood behind Ivy smiling.

"No," Ivy said. "I am not lost. I have come looking for a witch. I mean to kill her."

"Well, then," said the woman, "you'd better come with me, for killing a witch is no easy thing. Still, I might be able to help. And to give you a bite to eat, for my, how hungry you look! I've got a stew simmering on the fire."

In fact, Ivy could not remember the last time she had eaten, and she felt half-starved. And she knew she would need help to defeat the witch. So she followed the beautiful woman toward the dark cottage.

"And why, might I ask, do you hope to kill the witch?" asked the woman as they walked.

"She killed my gran," replied Ivy.

"Ah, yes," said the woman. "That is a nasty thing to have done."

As they drew nearer to the cottage, Ivy began to feel dread stirring in her belly.

"Are you not afraid," Ivy asked, "to live in such a dark corner of the forest?"

"Not in the least," said the woman merrily. "I keep the fire burning brightly."

But when Ivy looked up, no smoke curled from the chimney. "I thought you said you had a stew simmering."

In answer, the woman's hand shot out and grabbed Ivy's arm. Too late, Ivy realized she had been tricked, for suddenly, the rose-cheeked woman was gone, and the woman in the white cloak stood before her, holding Ivy tightly with one gnarled, clawlike hand, and gripping a wooden staff in the other.

"You!" cried Ivy. "You killed my grandmother!"

The witch threw her head back and laughed. When she did, her hood fell away so that Ivy could see her face—cruel jet-black eyes and a wicked smile. "Indeed I did," she snarled.

"I'll get you back for it, I swear!"

But in her fury, Ivy had stared straight into the witch's eyes, and suddenly, she found herself unable to struggle against the old woman's grip. For the village boy in the bakery all those years ago had been right—one glance from a witch is enough to put even the most determined child under her spell.

"I could kill you, too, my girl," said the witch, "but I think I have an even better idea." She released her grip on Ivy and waved her staff through the air, cutting it like a knife cuts butter. "I shall simply make you disappear."

23

October slips by quickly, like a twig being carried downstream by the stream in the Spinney.

Lily turns in her Yale application, and Mom decides we have to go out for a special dinner to celebrate. I've pretty much been giving Mom and Lily the cold shoulder ever since my ambush makeover. Lily has offered to take me into town for makeup a couple times, but when I shake my head the second time, she rolls her eyes.

"Whatever, Emma."

So, basically, things are back to normal between us.

At dinner that night, I listen as Lily and Mom go on and on about Yale and how great it will be and all the classes Lily is going to take. I think about what Lily told me about wanting to take a year off, and I don't understand how she can be so fake with Mom. Why doesn't she just tell her the truth?

I start spending even more time at Fina's. It's Fina and Ruby who finally go with me to buy some makeup at the drugstore. Ruby decides she wants some, too— mascara and eyeliner—and we take it all back to Fina's. Ruby experiments with doing her eyes while I show Fina what Lily taught me.

I practice at home, too, until I get good at it, and I'm pretty sure that no one will be able to notice my vitiligo at school.

I have to admit that even if I am mad at her, I am also really glad that Lily showed me how to do my makeup, because the spots beside my mouth spread even faster than any of the others have done. A few weeks after I first noticed them, they look like a thick set of parentheses around my lips, and every time I see them, my stomach drops. Once I've covered them up, though, I can usually pretend they aren't there at all.

I start visiting the Spinney again most afternoons, but every time I check the journal, there's nothing new there.

But there *are* other changes. Whenever Boomer and I walk through the village, we see new signs of fall spreading across Lanternwood. The air always seems to taste slightly of cinnamon, and the trees are red, yellow, and gold, like fireworks frozen just as they burst in the air. Huge piles of leaves start appearing on the sides of the road, and Boomer makes it his job to run through every single one.

The trees in the orchard are crammed with apples, and the café hosts apple bobbing competitions every afternoon. Gloria and Ruth seem to be competing to see who can pack the most pumpkins on their porch, while ghosts made from torn white sheets appear in the trees, and fake cemeteries sprout up in people's front yards. Even Mom, who doesn't really like stuff like that, buys a big orange wreath crawling with plastic spiders and a doormat that says *BOO!*

One day toward the end of the month, Fina, Ruby, and I are sitting at our usual table at lunch. Fina hasn't said much since we sat down. She keeps twirling her spaghetti around and around with her fork.

"Are you okay?" I ask.

"Hmm?" she says, her head snapping up. "Oh, yeah. I'm fine. Just a little homesick, I guess."

"What's October like in California?" Ruby asks.

"Well, it doesn't get cold. Not really. And my family back there is getting ready for Día de los Muertos."

"What's that?" Ruby and I ask together.

"It means Day of the Dead. It's a Mexican celebration," Fina explains. "It goes for three days, but it starts on All Hallows Eve, when the spirits of the dead can come back to visit the people they've left behind."

Ruby's eyes widen. "So you celebrate *death*?"

She shakes her head. "We celebrate the lives of people who are gone. We keep their spirits alive by remembering them."

"I like that," I say, imagining how much I would give to be able to spend just one day a year with Gram.

"Not all Mexican people celebrate it, but my grandmother has her whole life," Fina says. "So my family always goes to San Diego to stay with her and visit my grandfather's grave. Abuelita makes a big altar for him with marigolds and pictures and his favorite foods, and she and my dad and my aunts all tell stories about him. But this year . . . I don't know what I'll do."

"You guys could come over to my house," I say.

Since I've been trying to avoid home as much as possible, I haven't invited either of them over to Morning Glory Cottage yet. But Fina has been so good about taking my mind off my vitiligo. The least I can do is help her feel better about not being with her family. And besides, I think she'll like all the spooky village decorations.

"Well, we're too old to trick-or-treat," Ruby says firmly.

I'm not exactly sure I agree, but I decide to go along with it. "Then we can hand out candy and stuff and have a sleepover."

A grin spreads over Fina's face. "Totally," she says. "I'm in."

Since I am still giving Mom the cold shoulder, I wait after school until Dad gets home to ask permission for my Halloween sleepover. But annoyingly, he just tells me I have to ask Mom.

"Sure you can," Mom says brightly. "But you'll have to clean your room. And set the table for dinner, please. Which friends are you having?"

"Fina," I say, shuffling over to the silverware drawer. "The one from California, whose mom works at Hampstead. And Ruby. She's new at school, too."

"Not Edie?" Mom asks, her voice all sweet and innocent.

"No, Mom," I say. "Edie and I aren't friends. She's not a very nice girl."

Mom looks up from the stove, brow creasing. "Really? But her father is so lovely!"

"You don't even know her dad," I protest. "You met him once, for like a minute."

"Actually," Mom says, drawing out the word. *Act-u-a-lly*. "Arnold called me this morning. He wants to meet with me to hear my ideas for his new house. Isn't that wonderful?"

"Congratulations, hon," Dad says, brushing past me

on his way to the fridge. "A client like that will do great things for your portfolio."

"I *know*!" Mom squeals. She actually squeals. "We have a meeting set up next week. I have a lot to do before that, though. And it's only a preliminary interview."

"You'll knock his socks off," Dad says. I look at Boomer and stick out my tongue like I'm gagging. He thumps his tail appreciatively.

As it turns out, I'm not the only one with the bright idea to have a Halloween party. The next day at lunch, Edie and the Graces go around handing out invitations to a party Edie is throwing. It seems like they hand out about a thousand.

When they get to our table, Edie stops and looks at me. For a second, I wonder if she knows about my mom meeting with her dad.

Then, "Something's different about you," she says, studying my face. In my lap, my hands clench together. Does she know about my vitiligo somehow?

"What do you want, Edie?" Fina asks.

"You're wearing makeup," says Edie, eyes still fixed on me. "Are you trying to look good for someone? Oh, my god. Do you have a *crush* or something?"

My hands loosen in relief. I look down at the fat stack

of invitations in her hand. "I'm really not the one trying too hard," I say smoothly.

She scoffs. "Jealous much? Sorry, I seem to have misplaced your invitations. Oh, well."

"Like we would come to your party anyway," Fina says. "We're having our own party. It's *way* more exclusive, and it's going to be *so* much more fun."

Maybe it's just my imagination, but I think I see Ruby sink an inch in her seat.

Edie smirks. "You keep telling yourself that—"

"Everything all right, girls?"

Ms. Singh is suddenly standing behind Edie. Edie turns on her heels and pastes on a sweet smile. "Of course, Ms. Singh," she says. "Emma was just telling me she won't be able to make it to my party, and I was saying what a shame that is."

"Oh, yes," Ms. Singh replies. "I'm sure they're really missing out. Better get back to your table and finish up now. The bell's about to ring."

Edie flashes another fake smile. I may be hiding my spots beneath my makeup, but Edie could be hiding *anything* behind that smile.

And I kind of hope I never find out what it is.

24

Halloween is on a Saturday, and all day, my stomach flutters with excitement when I think about the sleepover.

Finally, I see Fina's car pull up outside, and I bound through the door to meet her. She gets out and looks around like she's just been dropped off on Mars or something. Dad walks over to say hello to Mr. Ramirez as Fina meets me in the drive.

"*This* is where you live?" she asks, staring up at Morning Glory Cottage. I see her take in the white fence and the messy garden, then the rusted weather vane atop the ever so slightly lopsided roof.

"Yeah," I reply uncertainly. "I know, it's really old."

"Yeah. Like something out of a fairy tale," she says, grinning.

I try not to smile too big. Even though lots of people say that same thing about Lanternwood, I feel pride lighting me up inside. I want Fina to think it's as great as I do.

"My dad got us those to carve if you want," I say, pointing to the three pumpkins squatting on the doorstep.

"Nice," she says. "We can do them when Ruby gets here."

Except Ruby never texted me back this morning when I asked if her mom had said she could come, and I'm kind of starting to worry.

Finally, we decide we have to start our jack-o'-lanterns if we want to get done before dark.

"Oh, I brought sugar skulls we can decorate, too!" Fina says as we carve. "I make some for Abuelito every year."

By the time we're putting the final touches on our jack-o'-lanterns, little bands of trick-or-treaters have started pinballing around the village. But there's still no sign of Ruby.

"Maybe she has the flu or something," I say. "She seemed kind of quiet on Friday."

"Does she have thumb flu?" Fina asks. "Because otherwise she should still be able to text us."

We put our candles into our pumpkins. "They look so good!" I say, stepping back to study the flickering orange faces. Fina's is a unicorn with an only slightly crooked horn, and mine is a scary scream face.

Then both of our phones ding at the same time. I pull mine out from Gram's sweater pocket to see a text from Ruby. A quick glance at Fina's phone shows that she's gotten the exact same one.

Can't make it tonight.

Another message appears after the first, this one just for me.

I'm really sorry, Emma.

We go inside after that and decorate our sugar skulls with glitter Fina brought and brightly colored icing that Mom helps us mix up. I can tell both of us are trying not to pretend like it's any big deal that Ruby isn't coming.

But once we're done with our skulls and the trick-or-treaters stop coming, we eat pizza and watch a scary movie. And instead of paying attention, I keep thinking about that second message and getting a funny feeling in my stomach. Why apologize just to me? Because the sleepover is at my house? And why not answer Fina, who texted Ruby back to ask if she was okay?

I don't know. It seems weird.

"So, what's next on the agenda?" Fina asks once the movie is over and we've eaten all the pizza and most of the leftover candy.

I shrug. "What do you want to do?"

Fina looks out the living room window. Orange lights flicker up and down the street. "Is there anywhere creepy in the village?" she asks in a low voice. "You know, that we can explore?"

"Well, there's the graveyard," I say.

Fina grins. "I like the sound of that."

We go to my room and wait until I've heard everyone else come up. Then I bribe Boomer with a bone to stay quiet and creep onto the landing to make sure everyone's lights are out. It's eleven thirty when we sneak down the stairs. I lead the way, pointing to the creakiest steps so Fina will know to skip them.

The lock on the front door is really loud, so we slip out the back instead.

"Brrrr," Fina chatters. "It's cold!"

We link arms to keep warm as we walk swiftly toward the church. In the dark, with candlelight flickering from all the porches, it's easy to pretend that we really *are* in a fairy-tale village from a long, long time ago. That goblins and trolls might be hiding in every shadow.

"Do you think we'll see any ghosts?" Fina asks, her words making little white clouds. "There have to be ghosts in a place this old."

"Have *you* ever seen one?" I ask, pushing open the gate to the churchyard. "You said some people believe that spirits can come back on Halloween, right?"

The graveyard is completely silent, and a thin fog hovers just off the ground, making the tombstones look like they're floating in clouds.

Fina thinks for a moment. "Well, yeah, but that's not exactly the same as ghosts. Like, I've never *seen* a spirit. But there was this chair in their house where Abuelito always sat. A rocking chair. And one Día de Los Muertos, I swear it started rocking all on its own."

"Spooky," I say, weaving through the stones toward Gram. Suddenly, my heart is beating fast.

"Not really," Fina replies. "If there *was* a spirit, it was just Abuelito."

I point to Gram and Grandpa's stone. "This is where my grandparents are buried."

"Hi, Emma's grandparents," Fina says, giving a little wave.

"Is it okay if we stay here for a minute?" I ask.

"Sure." We both sit down, our knees disappearing into the fog.

"So, what was your gram like?" Fina asks, drawing her arms around her knees.

"Well," I say, not knowing where to start, "she was a really good grandmother. *More* than a grandmother, really. I always used to stay with her on the weekends, and she made the best apple pie. She was a painter, and

I would sit with her while she painted and she would tell me fairy tales. She's the one who got me to read *The World at the End of the Tunnel,* too. I think she's the reason I love books so much."

"Same with me and Abuelito!" Fina says. "Every time we went to visit, he would be sitting there in his rocking chair when we came in, and he would have a new book for me. Abuelita would go get me some food, and I would climb up onto his lap and he would start reading."

We go back and forth for a long time, trading stories about Gram and Abuelito.

I tell Fina about how Gram always carried a parasol and wore these long flowy dresses and how that made kids in the village think she was a witch but she didn't mind.

Fina tells me about how her grandfather fought in the Vietnam War and lost one of his legs there and how sometimes he swore he could still feel it. He said it felt like it was dancing, and then he would have to get up and dance, whirling her grandmother around the kitchen until they were both exhausted.

When the church bells begin to chime, both of us jump.

Fina looks at me. "Midnight," she whispers. "The time that spirits come back."

We listen to each ring, counting. My stomach begins to flutter.

Six, seven, eight . . .

I find myself staring at Gram's stone. I meant to take Fina to the old part of the graveyard, which is much spookier than this part. But instead I brought her here.

Nine, ten . . .

My heart is beating kind of hard, and I don't know if it's because I'm scared or because I'm hoping something will happen. Fina clutches my hand.

Eleven . . .

I look around the graveyard to check for any signs that we aren't alone, but there's nothing.

Twelve.

The bell goes still, and Fina and I stare at each other for a long moment.

"It's over," she says.

"Yeah," I agree, trying to hide my disappointment. I'm not sure what I was expecting. Gram taught me to believe in magic, not ghosts. And anyway, the bell is always five minutes late, which means it's already a few minutes past midnight.

Then suddenly, just on the other side of Isabella Fortune's grave, I see a darting movement. As soon as I turn my head it's gone, but I know it was there.

My heart skips a beat.

Fina and I are not alone in the graveyard after all.

25

Fina hears the little gasp I make. "What?" she says. "What is it?"

"I saw something by the church."

"Should we go investigate?"

My heart is pounding again.

"Yeah," I say. "Let's go."

We stand up and start walking, still holding hands. Whatever I saw, there's no sign of it now.

Then, as we're rounding the church, Fina squeezes my hand tighter and points. We watch, frozen in fear, as the figure slips through the gap in the brick wall that leads to the old part of the graveyard.

If it is a ghost, it's a very substantial one. And it is definitely not Gram. This person has stooped, narrow shoulders and a prowling kind of walk. Just before the figure disappears through the opening in the wall, it turns and gazes over one shoulder.

And even though we can't make out the figure's eyes, I *know*—I can *feel*—that they are staring straight at us.

Terror darts through my heart, and the next thing I know, we're running out of the graveyard, back across the street, and down the lane behind Morning Glory Cottage.

"What . . . was that?" Fina asks, still panting as I close my bedroom door behind us. "A ghost?"

"It looked more like a person to me," I say. Adrenaline buzzes in my ears.

"Or a vampire," Fina adds, somewhat hopefully.

We're both shivering, so we climb under the covers. For a minute, neither of us says anything, and I wonder if Fina is waiting for her heart to slow, too.

"I feel like we just had a real adventure," she says.

"Me, too," I reply.

"It's funny," she whispers. "Sitting there and talking about your gram and my grandfather, it kind of felt like they were with us, just for a few minutes, didn't it? I think that's exactly what Día de los Muertos is about."

When I fall asleep that night, I dream that I'm in the Spinney. All the charmed folk are there, and I'm leading them in some kind of game that involves hopping from rock to rock down the stream. I'm barefoot, and when I glance down, my feet are all one color again. I look up, and Gram is there, sitting on Throne Rock, reading *The World at the End of the Tunnel*. She catches sight of me and smiles, sunlight dappling her skin.

By the next morning, Fina has decided that the figure we saw was not a vampire but was, in fact, a cult leader about to perform a satanic ritual, possibly involving human sacrifice.

And despite the fact that the figure seemed to run away from us, she is also sure that we made a narrow escape from certain death.

I have a feeling this is one of those stories she's going to be telling forever, the kind that gets bigger and crazier the more time goes on.

It's not until I get up to brush my teeth that I remember that I don't have any makeup on. And my bangs are all funky, too, so you can see the patches above my eyebrows. But Fina didn't say anything about it. She didn't look at me weird. She treated me like there was nothing different about me at all.

And I start to wonder if maybe this whole time, I've been overreacting about having vitiligo. Because if everyone reacts the way Fina does to my patches, then all that's going to change is the reflection I see in the mirror. And I know I could get used to my patches if I knew everyone else would, too.

I walk Fina out when her mom arrives, and then I decide I'm not ready to go back inside yet. Last night was the first night I haven't felt lonely in Gram's house since she died. I don't want it to go back to the way it was. Not yet, at least. I run inside just to grab the sugar skull I made last night. I think I'll go and leave it for Gram. She would love the colors.

It smells like a wood fire outside, which means Old Joe and Older Joe are probably burning brush on the farm. Ruth's curtains twitch in her windows as I walk by, and I give them a wave. It was raining when Fina and I woke up, but now the air is clean and there's a breeze whipping around the bright morning like Boomer zigzagging after a squirrel.

Just as I'm about to cross the street, I hear a crunching sound—someone walking down the little gravel path that leads from the graveyard to the gates. I pause behind a parked car. Through its windows, I see a familiar figure, wearing the same tweed suit and hat as always.

Professor Swann looks both ways, then pulls his hat a bit lower over his forehead before stepping out onto the sidewalk. Like he's hoping no one will spot him here.

I wait until he's out of sight before crossing the street, wondering why the professor seemed so strange, and who he was visiting. I've never noticed any Swanns in the graveyard before.

There's nobody else in the graveyard now. My shoes are almost soaked through with leftover rain droplets by the time Gram and Grandpa's grave comes into sight, still clutching my sugar skull to lay against their stone.

But then I see that there's already something bright lying there on the grass in front of the grave.

It's a beautiful bouquet of flowers.

26

I stay at Gram's grave for a few minutes before walking back to Morning Glory Cottage. All the while, I'm thinking about those flowers. When I bent closer to look at them, I saw that their stems were uneven, and they were tied with twine, like they were hand-cut instead of from a store.

Could Professor Swann have left them? I remember the conversation we had in the meadows a few weeks ago—how he talked about missing Gram. The way he'd been crying after her funeral.

"The Hollidays' house was TPed last night," says a voice as I step out onto High Street. "You wouldn't know anything about that, would you?"

It's Ruth, who has assumed her usual position just inside her gate. She's still wearing her fuzzy bathrobe and pink slippers.

"No," I say. "It wasn't me."

"Bah, I'm just kidding," she says, swatting the air and—I think—trying to wink. "Want to come in? I've got a pot of coffee on."

"No thanks," I reply. "I don't really, um, drink coffee. Since I'm a kid and all."

She shrugs. "Well, you tell your mother we're expecting her at the garden club next month. No excuses this time."

She turns to hobble back to her house.

"Ruth?" I say suddenly, an idea popping into my head.

"Eh?" she grunts, looking at me expectantly. "Speak up, Emma. My hearing's not what it was. That'll be the first to go after your knees, mark my words."

"Right," I say, loudly this time. "Well, I was wondering— did Professor Swann ever have, like, a family? Kids or a wife or anything?"

Ruth squints her eyes, then shakes her head. "There was a wife once, but it didn't last. I seem to recall he had a flame for someone else. But that didn't work out too well—he's been a bachelor ever since." She lets out a bark of laughter, though I don't really get what's funny.

"So he wouldn't have anyone to visit in the graveyard?"

"He only moved here when he started work at the college. His parents aren't buried there, if that's what you mean. What are you getting at, hmm?"

I smile and try to look casual. "Oh, nothing," I say. "I just—I just wondered about him. Anyway, have a nice morning."

Then I walk away, my mind buzzing so loud with thoughts I'm sure even Ruth can hear them.

And the flowers aren't the only surprise I get on Sunday. Later that afternoon, Boomer and I run down to the meadows and slip into the Spinney to find that my pen pal has written again. As Boomer runs off to chase a stick floating down the stream, I draw Gram's sweater tight around me, settle into the nook of Throne Rock, and begin to read.

When the wicked witch was done with her wicked spell, she blinked, and Ivy found herself able to move once more. Thinking only of escaping with her life, she spun round and ran. To her surprise, the witch made no move to stop her but merely cackled louder. "You can run, my child," she cried, "but my curse will find you wherever you go!"

Back through the forest Ivy fled, and as she ran, a hard rain began to fall. It seemed to her as if every tree in the forest wept for her as she passed it by.

When she found herself once more at Poppy Cottage, she burst through the door and bolted it behind her. Shilling cried out when he saw her. Whether it was a cry of happiness or sadness, relief or fear, Ivy could not say, but perhaps it was all of these at once. The girl threw herself down next to him and buried her face in his fur. Then, finally, she began to weep.

It seemed to her that she wept for a very long time, but Shilling never moved, not even when his fur was soaked through with her tears. When finally Ivy could cry no more, she lifted herself up and looked around the empty cottage. It seemed smaller than it had before, darker and colder. Her eyes landed on the gloomy hearth, where the odd crutch her gran had been carving when she had taken ill still stood half-whittled. The little table was set for a meal Gran and Ivy would never share.

Ivy shivered. Her stomach pained her. She needed firewood and food to eat.

"Poor Shilling," she said softly. "You must be hungry, too."

And so it was that Ivy put her grandmother's cloak around her shoulders and opened the door, only to find a village girl standing on the stoop. She looked nervous, and she held a pie tightly in both hands.

Ivy recognized her as the little girl she had seen in the bakery all those years ago. It was from this girl's brother that Ivy had first learned of the witch. Ivy wanted to grab the girl by the shoulders, shake her, and tell her that her brother had been right, but he had been wrong, too. That the witch was far more wicked than he could have imagined.

"Yes?" she said instead.

The girl held out the pie. "It's for your gran," she said. "My mother is ever so thankful for the remedy she gave us. My brother's cough has all but gone now."

"Thank you," said Ivy, stepping out onto the stoop. "But my gran is dead."

The village girl looked at Ivy then, and her face drained of color. She pointed to the ground behind Ivy, but when Ivy looked, she saw nothing at all.

"What is it?" Ivy said. "What's frightened you?"

"You've got—you've got no—" The girl's voice trembled. "You've got no shadow."

Then she thrust the pie into Ivy's hands, turned away, and fled.

$\approx$ ~ **27** ~ $\ll$

When Monday morning arrives, I can't wait to get to school so Fina and I can talk about the flowers. Professor Swann left them for Gram, I'm sure of it. Could he have been the person in the graveyard on Halloween night, too?

When the bus pulls up to Ruby's stop, she's standing on the sidewalk. I wave to her.

But she keeps her head down and doesn't look at me at all. Not even once she's on the bus.

She walks right by me. Straight down to where the Graces are sitting on either side of the aisle. The Graces were particularly rude this morning, shaking their heads and staring at me with looks of disgust. Ruby hesitates, then slips into the seat beside one of them.

What is she thinking? I wait for the Grace she's chosen to look shocked, to shriek at Ruby to get out of her seat. But she doesn't. She gives Ruby a sideways look and simply shrugs.

The bus pulls away, and I turn my eyes forward, my stomach suddenly flipping over.

When we pull up at Edie's stop, she climbs to the top of the stairs. She pauses there, staring hard at me for a moment, and then her face does a funny thing.

One second, she's wearing her usual annoying smirk, and the next, her mouth and eyes are screwing up into this weird worried look. Her shoulders turn inward, and then she brushes past me as quickly as she can.

Totally confused, I perk my ears to listen to what she and the other girls are saying as the bus starts off again. I catch the words "sick," "not fooling anyone," and "so dangerous."

When I peek over my shoulder, they're all staring at me. Even Ruby.

Oh, Ruby, I think. *What did you do?*

I hurry off the bus at school, bumping into Sean—one of the guys who sits with Edie at lunch—as I step down onto the pavement.

"Watch it!" he barks, shooting me a dirty look. The kind that should really be reserved for the dog poop currently on the bottom of his shoe.

By now, the heat in my cheeks is like fire, and my hands have begun to shake. This feels like the dream where you show up naked to school. Except I'm wearing all my clothes. And I put makeup on like usual this morning to cover my spots.

So what is going on?

Fina's standing in our regular place in front of school. Head down, I scurry toward her. But even with my eyes on my feet, I can still see people parting around me, giving me a lot of space as I pass.

"Is that the girl?" someone to my left says.

"Oh yeah," says someone else. "I think so."

When I reach Fina, her eyes are full of thunderclouds. "Are you okay?" she asks.

"I don't know," I say. "What's—what's happening?"

"You didn't see it?"

"See what?"

"Come on," she says, linking her arm through mine and guiding me into school. We don't stop until we get to the library. I collapse into the chair closest to the door. My legs are all wobbly.

"What's going on, Fina?"

She has a look on her face like she's about to get a shot at the doctor's as she pulls out her phone and hands it to me. "I'm so sorry, Emma."

On the screen is a huge group message. ATTENTION!!! it screams. BEWARE OF EMMA TALBOT. SHE IS HIDING A RARE SKIN DISEASE THAT IS HIGHLY CONTAGIOUS!

Below the text is a picture of me that Edie took on the bus the day I hadn't blended in my sunscreen. The morning light glares off the white layer of sunscreen in an unnatural way so that I *do* look a little like a zombie freak, just like Edie said that day.

And now everyone thinks that's what I look like under my makeup.

There's another message, this one just a link. I click on it, and it takes me to this site about vitiligo. It's not one I've seen before. It's really more of a blog than a site, full of typos. It has all these horrible pictures, most of which I'm pretty sure have nothing to do with vitiligo, and says all these bogus things that aren't true. At the bottom, in bold, I read this:

Though rare, vitiligo is HIGHLEY contagious and can be life-threatning!!!

As I read, I feel my heart breaking into little pieces that go knocking around my chest like coins being rattled in a cup.

"This site says that I'm contagious," I say in a small voice. "It says I'm *dangerous*."

"Which is total crap," Fina replies. "Anyone with half a brain cell can figure that out."

But she's wrong. All those people moving away from me. They didn't want to "catch" my vitiligo. Tears bead my eyes.

"It was Edie," Fina says quietly.

I remember the way Edie smirked at me on the bus before her face went all scared and worried. And I realize that she *knows* my vitiligo isn't dangerous or contagious. And she sent this out anyway.

"Ruby must have helped," I say. "How else would Edie know about my vitiligo? That's why Ruby sent me that apology text."

Fina nods. "I heard some girls talking. Apparently, Ruby wanted to go to Edie's Halloween party. For reasons beyond human comprehension, she wants to be friends with that little brat."

"She wasn't popular in her old school," I mutter numbly. "Remember? She told us that first day at lunch."

"Being popular isn't the same as having friends," Fina says, scowling. "And Edie is never going to be a real friend to Ruby. She only let Ruby go to her stupid party so Ruby would give her dirt on you."

I don't say anything. I can't say anything. How could Ruby have done this to me?

"No one is going to believe this stuff," Fina says. "Seriously."

"They *do* believe it," I cry. "You saw how no one

wanted to get near me when I got off the bus. And look at this picture she took. People are going to think that's how I really look."

"People are probably just acting weird because they don't want to go against Edie," Fina says. "I swear, next time I see that girl, I'm going to—"

"Don't, Fina," I interrupt. "It'll just make things worse."

"But—"

"She's doing this because of that stupid poem," I say. "The one I wrote on the first day of school. She's been waiting to get back at me ever since then. And if you do something, she'll just come after you. Or she'll make things even worse for me."

Though, honestly, I don't really see how she could.

The first bell goes off, and through the windows, we can see kids hustling to get to class before the tardy bell. A girl I've never even seen before looks into the library and tugs at her friend's shirt to get her attention. The two of them stare for a second, then shriek and run away.

Like I'm a dangerous animal in a zoo.

A tear falls onto the table between me and Fina.

"Don't pay attention to them, Emma," she says. "They're jerks."

"They think I'm a freak, Fina," I whisper.

"No they don't," she replies firmly.

"Yes they do!" I cry. "And maybe they're right!"

Fina's jaw drops. "Emma, no!"

Mr. Yardley has spotted us and is striding over.

"I'll see you later," I say. Then I grab Gram's satchel and, clutching it for dear life, burst through the library door and out into the hall. Fortunately, there's a bathroom just around the corner. I run into it before anyone sees me, shooting into a stall and locking it behind me.

I don't think I'm ever going to come out.

28

I know I'm going to be in trouble for skipping first period, but anything is better than facing what's beyond the bathroom door.

Between first and second period, a group of girls comes in talking about me.

"I can't believe she would come to school," says one. I don't recognize her voice.

"Seriously. It's like she doesn't care that she's putting all of us in danger. *So* wrong."

I put my palms over my ears and press as hard as I can.

When I drop my hands, the girls are gone, but the door soon swings open again.

"Emma?" Fina calls softly. "Are you in here?"

I bite my lip and say nothing, and after a minute, she leaves.

A little while later, someone else comes in and knocks on the door of my stall. "Emma? It's Ms. Singh."

When I don't answer, she adds, "I know you're in there. Fina told me."

Fina must have recognized my shoes. Slowly I get up and unlock the door. Ms. Singh stands on the other side. "We have to stop meeting like this, Emma," she says with a hint of a smile that I can't return.

"Did Fina tell you why I'm here?" I ask.

Ms. Singh shakes her head. "Do you want to tell me?"

"No," I say. I don't ever want to repeat the things I read on that website, or the lies Edie wrote about me to everyone.

"Well, I can't let you stay in this bathroom all day," she says.

"I can't go to class."

She hesitates for a moment. "Then I'll take you to the office," she says finally. "And you can call your parents to come get you."

I nod, and let Ms. Singh lead me out of the bathroom and into the empty hall.

She waits while I call Mom from the office. I tell her I have a stomachache, and she says she'll be here soon.

Ms. Singh is frowning at me when I hang up. "A stom-achache, huh?"

I shrug. I feel exhausted all of a sudden.

"Are you sure you don't want to talk about what's wrong?" she asks. "I could help."

I shake my head. "Really, it's okay, Ms. Singh. Thanks for letting me call my mom."

"No problem, Emma. I hope you feel better."

Shooting me one last look of concern, she turns and walks out the office door.

When Mom arrives, I have to fight the urge to run to her and wrap my arms around her and cry into her shoulder. Instead, I focus hard on making up answers to the questions she immediately starts asking. Do I feel nauseous? Have I thrown up? Do I have any other symptoms?

When we get home, she sends me to bed and brings up some ginger ale and crackers. Boomer follows her and jumps onto the bed. Mom sits next to me and runs her fingers across my back the way she used to when I was little and woke up from a nightmare.

Things were so much easier back then, when night-mares were only in dreams.

I wish so bad I could tell Mom what is really wrong. But if I do, she'll stop rubbing my back. She'll want to know every single thing that every kid said, and she'll be horrified. Then she'll start strategizing.

So when she asks me if there's anything else she can do, I tell her I just want to sleep. Then I pull the covers up over my head and stay there the rest of the day.

29

I stay in bed on Tuesday, too. I tell Mom I got sick in the night.

Fina calls and texts me about a thousand times, so I set my phone to silent. I know she wants to talk about what happened, but I just want to pretend it didn't. Pretend that when I have to go back to school, things are going to be normal again.

The one person I *do* want to talk to about everything is Gram. I don't think I've ever missed her so badly.

There was this one time a few years ago when I was staying at Morning Glory Cottage and couldn't find a bracelet Mom had given me for Christmas. It had been Mom's growing up, and it was one of the few presents she'd ever given me that I hadn't asked for but had actually liked. It was made of silver links, and attached to one of them was a bell that rang when the bracelet shook.

"There, there, darlin'," Gram had said when she'd found me crying, pulling me into the flowy fabric of her long dress. "What is it?"

I told her what had happened and she listened, nodding seriously.

"Whenever I have a problem," she said, "I like to retrace my steps. Go back until I figure out where things started to go wrong. Or, in this case, where I might have lost the thing I'm looking for. So, when was the last time you saw the bracelet?"

I thought hard until I remembered hearing the church bell ring that afternoon, and looking down at the bell on my wrist, shaking it to make it chime along with the real one. I had gone with Gram to read while she painted a landscape of Old Joe's farm, and we'd been walking home through the fields.

We set out, retracing our route like Gram said, until I spotted something shiny in a muddy puddle in the middle of the bumpy farm road. The bracelet must have come loose when I'd shaken it and dropped straight off my wrist.

All I want now is for Gram to tell me how to fix things again. How to retrace my steps back to the way things were before Edie's texts, before my diagnosis, before Gram died.

"Just remember next time," Gram had said once the bracelet was safely around my wrist again, "that you've always got me, Emma. And with the two of us together, things can't be too bad."

But that wasn't true, was it?

Now, when I need her more than ever, I *don't* have Gram.

And it makes me wonder what else Gram said that wasn't true, either.

On Wednesday morning, I tell Mom I'm not ready to go back to school. Which is true.

When I get up to go to the bathroom, I hear her downstairs, talking on the phone in low tones, probably to Dad, who left early for work. I know I can't stay home forever. Eventually they'll take me to the doctor, who will see that nothing is wrong with me. Nothing she can fix, anyway.

But when Mom comes upstairs again, she doesn't mention the doctor. She brings me homemade pumpkin nut muffins and hot chocolate and nudges Boomer over so there's room for her to sit next to me on the bed. She leans over and kisses me on my head, then wraps her arms around me. I let my head fall to her shoulder.

I find myself staring at our arms, which are side by side. They're the exact same shade. The way we look is one thing we've always had in common. And I don't want my vitiligo to steal it.

"I'm sorry you don't feel well, sweetheart," Mom says quietly. "Is there anything I can do to make it better? Want to find something on Netflix to watch? I can take the afternoon off from work."

Actually, it might be nice to have some company. And weirdly, this feels like the first time since I got diagnosed that Mom is actually worried about *me* instead of my vitiligo. So we go downstairs and sit on the sleek blue couch she got to replace Gram's old lumpy one. We throw a blanket over ourselves and find an old cartoon movie I used to like when I was a kid. I don't want to watch anything serious.

In a little while, Dad comes home early and flops down next to us. It's really nice, sitting there with them, and I wonder why it can't be like this all the time. Or even just a little bit *more* of the time.

For a few hours, I even manage to forget about everything that happened on Monday. But when I close my eyes that night, I'm back at school again, getting off the bus to see a crowd of scowling faces. I see them over and over. And it never hurts any less.

The next thing I know, it's Thursday morning, and Mom is gently shaking me awake again.

"Emma, sweetheart? It's time for school. Do you think you're up to it?"

I hesitate. I have to go back sometime. And I'm worried that the longer I'm gone, the worse it will be when I do.

"You have a light treatment appointment in a couple of hours," Mom says. "How about you stay home until then, but after your appointment, I take you back to school on my way to meet Arnold O'Shea."

Hearing the name Arnold O'Shea makes me think of Edie O'Shea, which really does make me feel sick to my stomach.

But at least this way I won't have to ride the bus to school with Edie and the Graces and Ruby the Traitor. "Fine," I say. Who knows? Maybe I'll get lucky and the appointment will take so long I'll miss lunch, too.

Except, of course, I don't get lucky. Dr. Howard's office is actually running *early* today. So when Mom drops me off at school, fourth period has only just started.

At least Fina will be there. She'll hide in the library with me at lunch, and then there are just two more classes to get through. Still, it takes me a minute of standing by the school doors before I finally muster the courage to go in. And when I do, it's only because I can feel Mom staring at me.

I know she's really excited about her meeting with Edie's dad. She is looking even more perfect than usual in her best suit. But I can't manage to wish her good luck. I don't want her to get the account. I don't want her hanging out at Edie's house.

At the office, I pick up my late-arrival pass before going to English class. I'm tempted to drag my feet, but then I'll just run into someone in the hall. When I reach Ms. Singh's room, I stop outside to take a deep breath.

And I hear my name from the other side of the door, which is open a crack.

I hold my breath, listening.

". . . happening to Emma is something that happens to many people, including to some I know personally."

It's Ms. Singh. She sounds angry.

"Vitiligo is *not* contagious. It is *not* dangerous to you. If anyone had taken the time to research it—and I mean by looking at credible sources—you would know that. The only person this condition affects is Emma. Our job is to help make her feel supported, not ostracized. And no, Austin, it's not *ostrich-sized*. It means when you make someone feel different and unwelcome. And the next person I see ostracizing Emma will be doing detention with me until winter break. Am I clear?"

There are murmurings of agreement.

My heart is pounding. There's no way I can just waltz

into Ms. Singh's class now, so I spin around and begin speed-walking away.

I had wondered if Ms. Singh had noticed my spots when she cut my bangs. If she knows other people with vitiligo, maybe she realized I had it that day. But how does she know what Edie said about me? Has she seen the text? Or that stupid website?

I can't go back to locking myself in the bathroom again, so I go to the library and tell Mr. Yardley that Ms. Singh's class is in the middle of taking a quiz and I'm supposed to wait here until lunch. It's the first time I've ever lied about something like that to a teacher.

My stomach cramps when the bell rings and kids flood the hall. I glance up and spot Fina walking by. She sees me and heads straight for the library door.

"Emma!" she says, throwing her bag down and squeezing me in a tight hug. "You're here. I've been so, so worried about you. I was going to come to your house today if you didn't show."

"I got here a few minutes ago," I say. "I went to Ms. Singh's room."

Fina stiffens just a little as she sits down across from me.

"I heard what she was saying. About my vitiligo."

"It's a good thing, Emma," Fina says quickly. "Now that people know the truth, everything will go back to normal."

"But how did she know what happened?"

Fina bites her lip. "I, um, might have told her."

"Why?" I ask. "Edie's going to think *I* told her. She's probably going to do something else to me now."

Fina shakes her head and pulls nervously at her ponytail. "I thought of that. So I didn't tell Ms. Singh who sent the text," she says. "I'm sorry if it wasn't the right thing to do, but, well, you weren't here, Emma." Her voice goes mouse quiet. "I couldn't just let people say— I had to do something. You're my best friend."

I feel a whole swirl of emotions, like a pile of leaves caught up in a sudden gust of wind. I'm a little upset that Fina didn't ask me before telling Ms. Singh, but also grateful that she was trying so hard to protect me. And embarrassed that a teacher had to come to my defense.

Mostly, though, I still just feel sad.

"You're my best friend, too," I say. "Thanks for trying."

"I'll stick my gum in Edie's hair when she's not looking," she offers. "Ruby's, too. I'll call their parents and pretend to be the principal and say they're failing all their classes."

"You're going to pretend to be Mr. Keeler?" I say.

"Sure I am," she says in her deepest baritone. "I'll do anything you want."

When I don't laugh, she loses the fake voice. "What

do you want to do, Emma? Right now, I mean. Stay here? Go to lunch?"

"You go. I have makeup work I have to do."

Her face falls in confusion. "Really? You want to be alone?"

"Yeah," I say, not exactly sure why I'm saying it or if it's even true. "For now."

"Okay," she says uncertainly. "If that's what you really want."

She picks up her bag and walks slowly to the door, glancing back at me one last time as if she's hoping I'll have changed my mind.

Somehow, I get through the rest of the day. And Fina was wrong, by the way. Ms. Singh's speech does not make things go back to normal. It's true that fewer people seem to step out of my way as I walk down the hall, so maybe they did listen to the part about me not being contagious.

But wherever I go, whispers follow behind me like bits of toilet paper stuck to my shoe.

And even though everyone is talking *about* me, nobody but Fina says a word *to* me.

When I get home, I play it all over in my mind. Every sideways glance, every single whisper.

I wonder if this is what my life is going to be like from now on. Because if so, I think I would rather be homeschooled.

30

The next morning, I stare into the mirror for a long time. And the longer I look, the worse I feel. The patches above my eyebrows are spreading down past my temples. My bangs can't cover them anymore. The ones at the corners of my mouth are lengthening into a pale ropy circle around my lips.

It's funny. Before I got vitiligo, I never understood how Mom and Lily spent so long looking at themselves in the mirror. I guess it was easy not to care what I looked like until I looked . . . *different.*

I reach for my concealer, then hesitate. The counter is dotted with little plastic tubes and glass bottles of my makeup. But what's the point of wearing any of it anymore? Everyone thinks I look like a zombie underneath it anyway.

What does it matter if I show them what's really there?

So I drop the concealer into the drawer beside the sink. Then I sweep the rest of the makeup in, too.

When I come down for breakfast, Boomer is the only one who doesn't stare at me.

They're used to seeing my patches by now. But not in the morning before school.

Dad looks only for a second. Then he says, "Morning, Butterfly," and slides over a plate of toast.

Lily stares up from her laptop, her mouth slightly open. I can't quite read her expression. But when Mom looks up, I know instantly that the mom who rubbed my back and watched Netflix with me earlier in the week is gone.

"Honey?" Mom says softly. "Did you run out of makeup?"

"I didn't run out."

"Is that how you're going to school?" she asks, taking a tiny sip of orange juice.

"Yes."

There's a tense silence.

Then, "Are you sure you—?" Mom starts.

Anger bubbles up inside me. I should have known Mom would react like this. I push back my chair so suddenly that Boomer startles and skulks away upstairs. "It's *my* face, Mom," I say. "Not yours. And I can do what I want with it."

"Emma, I just—"

"Mom," Lily mutters.

"Emma's right," Dad says, then turns to me. "You look great, hon."

Tears prick my eyes as I take a piece of toast, swing Gram's bag over my shoulder, and go out to wait for the school bus, squinting against the sunlit frost that sparkles across every yard.

When the bus arrives, I clench my hands into fists. As I walk down the aisle to my normal seat, I keep my chin held high, but I'm careful not to look at anyone. I want them to see me, but I don't want to see their reactions.

Ruby gets on a few minutes later. I think I feel her hesitate as she walks back to sit with the Graces, but I don't look up at her.

I do when Edie gets on, though. We lock eyes for a second, and as she takes in my face—both shades of it—her mouth rounds. Then she looks away.

At school, it's the same. People stare as I walk by. They fall silent first, then start whispering again. I try to imagine that I am back in the Spinney, that their whispers are just the wind rustling in the trees.

But I can't.

Fina isn't at school yet when my bus arrives, so I go straight to homeroom and don't see her until English class.

"You didn't wait for me this morning," she says as she sits down next to me, sounding hurt.

"Sorry," I reply. "It was cold out."

She looks at me and does a double take. But instead of gawping like everyone else, she smiles. "No makeup," she chirps, pushing her glasses farther up the bridge of her nose. "Cool."

I look down at my warm-up.

After class, Ms. Singh crouches by my desk.

"Feeling better?" she murmurs.

"A little."

"I'm glad," she replies. "You know I'm always here if you need anything. Or if anyone gives you any trouble."

At lunch, Fina and I sit at our usual table. I glance at the empty seat where Ruby used to sit, then across the cafeteria to where she's sitting beside Edie. I wonder if she's happier there than she was here with us. I wonder if she thinks telling Edie about me was worth it.

Fina tries to keep me distracted. She talks about how her dad has finished *Pretty Little Liars* and started watching *The Vampire Diaries*.

"If you don't mind sharing a roof with the most embarrassing dad of all times, maybe you could come over this weekend," she says. "Sleepover?"

"Maybe," I say. But I don't mean it.

I know Fina is trying as hard as she can to act like everything is normal, but somehow it feels like things are different between us now. Like in *The World at the End of the Tunnel* when Jack is taken to the hobgoblin king's castle and thrown in the highest tower.

A damp, mossy wall surrounded him. Jack put his hand to the stone. On one side of the wall was him, Jack, and on the other were birds and horses and trees and clouds and everything he had ever known and loved.

That's exactly how I feel. Like I'm on one side of this wall and Fina's on the other. Her side is bright and cheery, and my side of the wall is dark and lonely.

I know what you're thinking. Letting myself feel so defeated is like letting Edie win. But it's not just Edie's text.

I could probably get over that—over all the whispers and the stares, too, if I knew they were going to go away eventually. Like the time I threw up during the third-grade spelling bee, and for a while, I was totally humiliated, but after a week or so, nobody even remembered.

The stares aren't going to go away this time, though.

Nobody can forget about my vitiligo when my face is a constant reminder.

Even if I wanted to keep wearing makeup, what about the patches on my toes, which are now threatening to cover my feet entirely? And the ones on my elbows and neck? Am I supposed to wear jeans and turtlenecks for the rest of my life?

I glance around the cafeteria at all the kids talking and laughing. Not wondering what they're going to look like when they wake up tomorrow. It's just a normal day for them.

I'm not sure if I even have a normal anymore.

That night at dinner, Mom asks me how my day was (I lie and tell her it was fine), but nobody says anything else about my vitiligo or my lack of makeup. We talk about Lily's next round of college applications, and Mom tells everyone that Arnold O'Shea has officially hired her.

Which is my cue to push the rest of my stir-fry away and go upstairs. But I can't sleep. So I lie in bed, listening to Boomer snore and imagining Mom hanging out at Edie's house.

If they ever meet, I bet Edie will put on the sweet innocent face she does around teachers. She'll be all polite, and Mom will come home wondering why I told her Edie wasn't a nice girl when clearly she is. Mom will wonder why I can't be more like her.

Finally, I throw my covers off and go downstairs.

The kitchen is dark and empty. No Gram waiting with warm pie. No Gram to comfort me or tell me what to do. Even the smell of her is gone, like she was never really here. I pour myself a glass of milk and sit down at the table.

"It's not fair for you to just leave me like this, you know," I whisper to the empty chair that used to be hers. "Right when I need you the most. You shouldn't have done it. You shouldn't have died."

I stare at the chair for a long time, silent tears rolling down my face, a ball of anger hardening in my stomach.

When I go back up, I hear something coming from Mom and Dad's room. Mom should be over the moon. She's just gotten the biggest account of her career.

But through the crack under the door, I can hear her crying, too.

31

When I go back to school on Monday, something has changed.

People aren't whispering about me anymore. They aren't staring.

Instead, they look right past me in the hall. Like I'm invisible.

And somehow, this almost feels worse than the staring and the whispering. Because at least then I felt like I existed.

I tell myself I should be relieved. It's better this way, right? Better to be invisible than to be a freak. Even Edie just stares forward in English class, pretending like I'm not sitting right beside her. Which is probably not that hard, because I don't raise my hand or say anything all class. All day, actually.

Fina stays by my side as much as she can, like a body-guard. At first, she still tries to pretend like everything is normal. She smiles and laughs and talks.

But everything is not normal, and when I don't smile or laugh or talk back, she stops trying to make conversation. Her smile dims. We walk silently through the halls together.

At lunch, Fina makes another attempt. "See that girl?" she asks, taking out her sandwich and nodding to a tall girl across the room. "She's in my social studies class. She's really funny, actually. Maybe we could invite her to sit with us sometime."

"Or you could just sit with her at lunch from now on if you wanted," I say.

I don't say it to be mean. I really, really don't. I was just thinking that it would be good if Fina had some other friends. Friends who will laugh at her jokes and make her laugh, too. It's bad enough that I heard Mom crying again last night. I don't want to be responsible for making Fina sad, too. I don't want her to be stuck on the dark side of the wall just because I am.

But when Fina looks at me, there are tears welling in her eyes. She picks up her tray, throws her trash away, and walks out of the cafeteria without a backward glance.

And as she disappears, I can't help thinking that I

might have just lost my only friend. The only person at school who actually still sees me.

That night, I go to the bathroom to take a shower, but instead, I walk over to the mirror and study the spots on my elbow that are now sprinkled down my forearm like breadcrumbs from Hansel and Gretel.

Except that Hansel and Gretel used the breadcrumbs like a map to find their way back home.

Whenever I have a problem, I like to retrace my steps, Gram said. *Go back until I figure out where things started to go wrong.*

My skin is kind of like a map, too. You know, the two-tone ones where continents are patches of green in the ocean of blue?

Except my map is a map of my differences. Every chalky island on my skin is another reason that I don't fit in.

As I return to my bedroom, an owl hoots outside like it's agreeing with me. I look over to where *The World at the End of the Tunnel* lies on the table next to the bed, untouched. I haven't picked it up since last week.

Here is something I'm not proud of. That ball of anger that I felt in my stomach the other night? It hasn't gone away.

I still miss Gram, but whenever I think about her

now, the anger is there, too. I keep wondering why she bothered with all these fairy tales—"Hansel and Gretel" and the rest.

All stories have truth in them, darling Emma, I hear her remind me. *Especially fairy tales.*

But how can fairy tales be true when they all end the same way? Happily ever after.

That's not how Gram's story ended.

And why was it so important to her to make me believe in the charmed folk? In magic? If magic was real, then she could have used it to get better. But she didn't. She died.

Gram lied to me.

Magic and fairy tales and happily-ever-afters— they're all just make-believe.

I'm not like Hansel and Gretel. I can't follow my spots back to a happy ending. I can't retrace my steps to who I used to be. Because it's not just the outside of me that's changing. With every new spot I get, I feel further away from Emma, and more and more like someone I don't know.

So what's going to happen if my patches keep spreading and spreading?

I look down at my moonlit skin. I imagine someone taking an eraser to me and rubbing and rubbing until there is nothing left of Emma at all.

32

The village girl had been right. Ivy's shadow had gone. No matter how many ways she turned beneath the winter sun, she could not get it to return.

Next to disappear were her feet. Two days later, she bent to pick up a dropped spoon, only to find that her toes had begun to flicker like the dying flames in the hearth.

Day by day the flickering spread. It crept from her toes to her knees, from her fingertips to her elbows.

"It's the witch's curse," Ivy said to Shilling. "She told me I would disappear, and now I am."

She read through every page of every book her gran had owned, but none of them contained advice on how to reverse a witch's curse.

The days passed, and Ivy's heart welled with sorrow until not a crumb of hope was to be found in Poppy Cottage.

Then one night, there came a pounding at her door. Afraid it was the witch, Ivy peered out her window to see half the village standing in front of the cottage. The pounding came again. She opened her door, for if she did not, the villagers would surely break it down.

"Yes?" she said, keeping far back from the light of their torches. She prayed to the shadows to keep her secret.

A man with the chest of three men stepped forward. Ivy recognized him as the baker. "Are you the remedy woman's girl?" he growled.

"I'm her granddaughter," said Ivy.

"We've heard strange stirrings coming from this cottage," he said. "Moaning and howling."

"And now," said a boy stepping forward, "my sister says that the remedy woman is dead."

After all these years, Ivy recognized his laughing blue eyes. A mean light danced in them now. His sister—the one who had brought the pie—stood next to him, eyes downcast.

"That's not all she tells, neither," said the baker. "She says you've got no shadow. Is it true? Step out into the light where we can see you, girl."

Shilling growled, but Ivy could see that the villagers had weapons that flashed in the glow of the torches. "Be still, Shilling," she said.

She took a step out of the house, and as she did, she felt her whole body flicker. A gasp rose up among the villagers.

"She's unnatural!" cried one.

"She's freakish!" shouted another.

"She's wicked!" yelled a third.

"No," said the baker, his lip curling. "She's cursed. And as long as she stays here, her curse will keep spreading. Rotting our crops, sickening our children, poisoning our wells."

Ivy said nothing. The man was right. She was cursed. And perhaps it would spread. What did she know of curses? Her gran had not bothered to teach her about such matters.

"Go," the man said. He pointed toward the forest. "Go now, and do not return here. You will not be welcome."

Ivy did not move. Inside the cottage were Gran's things. Her books. Her remedy jars. All that Ivy had left of her.

But then the boy picked up a rock and threw it at her. Ivy let out a shout of pain, and the boy laughed. A girl picked up a second stone and threw it, and then it seemed they were all bending down and searching the ground for stones.

Ivy reached for the wooden crutch her gran had left her and held it out like a weapon.

"Come, Shilling," Ivy said. "Run!"

Ivy swung the crutch, and the crowd parted. She and Shilling ran, rocks nipping at their heels, through the villagers and into the trees. They ran deep into the forest, stopping only when they came to the clearing where they had buried Gran. There, Ivy collapsed upon a bed of white snow.

Shilling whimpered and nudged his warm nose against her body.

"No, Shilling," she said, stroking his head and planting a soft kiss on his nose with her flickering lips. "You've done all you can do for me. You should go now."

The wolf dog gave one last cry before he turned away and loped off into the darkness.

Then Ivy closed her eyes and waited to disappear completely.

When I finish writing the chapter, I lie back on a bed of fallen leaves. I close my eyes, the journal lying open against my chest. Tears streak down my cheeks.

I've only been there a few minutes when I hear it.

SNAP.

Boomer growls. My heart seems to yank the rest of me up from the ground. I look around, wide-eyed. And then I see her.

Standing between two trees, one hand on her hip, is Fina.

"Hi, Emma," she says.

"What are you doing here?" I ask, wiping the tears away.

She knots her arms in front of her chest and takes a couple steps forward, looking serious. "I went to your house. Your mom said you come back here a lot. It took me a while to find you, but . . ." She takes a step closer. "We need to talk."

I bite my lip. Has Edie sent another message to the whole school? Or is Fina here to tell me she doesn't want to be friends anymore? "About what?"

She looks at her feet and kicks a little pile of leaves. "I miss you," she says. "I wanted to make sure you're okay."

More tears well in my eyes. They start out as tears of relief, but then a lump rises in my throat and I sink back to the ground, my face buried in my hands. And Fina is there, lifting me up and hugging me while I cry for what feels like a really long time. Boomer sits loyally on my other side, occasionally nudging me with a concerned nose.

When finally my sobs slow down, I drop my hands from my face. "I don't—I don't want to disappear, Fina," I say. "I don't want to stop being me—being *Emma*."

I kind of expect her to ask me what I'm talking about, but she doesn't. Instead, she looks me straight in the eye and says, "I see you, Emma. You can't disappear as long as I see you, right? But you gotta stop pushing me away."

"I'm sorry," I say. "I just feel . . . separate from everybody. Like no one else can understand what's happening to me."

A gust of wind blows through the trees, making Fina pull her jacket tighter. "I'm trying to understand," Fina says. "But it's kind of hard when you aren't talking to me."

She's right. I know she is. I need to talk to her. I owe her that much, after she came out here looking for me even though I know I hurt her feelings. But it still takes me a few seconds to summon up the words, to figure out where to start.

"Well," I say finally, "I keep asking myself why this happened to *me*. And right after Gram died. It just feels like, one minute, everything was fine, and the next minute, nothing was the way it was supposed to be anymore. Like I was cursed."

"I don't know about cursed," Fina says, "but my mom says bad things always come in threes."

"I only said two."

"You forgot about Edie."

I fish out a smile. It's small, but it's real.

"Keep going," she says.

"When I first got diagnosed," I say, taking a deep breath, "I was really worried that it would get worse and people would stare at me all the time. And then it *did* get worse, and Edie sent that text, and my fear came true. But now it's like people don't even see me anymore. Like I don't exist. And that feels even worse."

Fina reaches over and plucks a yellow leaf from my hair. "Yeah. I get that. But don't you ever think that maybe you're kind of . . . making yourself invisible?" she asks, twirling its stem between her fingers. "I mean, I know everything has been super hard since Edie's text. But people probably *aren't* going to look at you if you don't talk to anyone or look at anyone or raise your hand in class, you know? It doesn't help. Neither does telling me to sit somewhere else at lunch."

I have a sudden vision of the Apple Lady, walking around the village like a ghost, never talking or looking anyone in the eye. I think about how people ignore her or cross the street when they see her coming. And for the first time, it occurs to me to wonder what made her that way. Maybe something happened to her, too. But maybe she didn't have a Fina to come looking for her.

"It's not that I didn't want you to sit with me," I say.

"I just don't want you to have to be Fina, the girl who's best friends with that girl with vitiligo. I can't escape my skin, but *you* can."

Fina pulls a face. "Emma," she scolds, "I am your friend because you're awesome, and I'm awesome, and awesome people stick together. And by the way, it's not just you who needs me. I need *you*, too. Moving really sucks, and you're the only thing that's made it kind of okay. I don't know what to do without you."

I feel my stomach twist with guilt. I've been so caught up in thinking about what I'm going through that it didn't even occur to me that Fina might need a friend right now, too. That I may be missing Gram, but she's missing her whole family back in California.

"I'm so sorry," I say. "You're my best friend."

"I know," Fina says simply. "And I don't care what you look like or what people say, but for the record, I think you look great, and people are stupid."

"I wish everyone thought that," I murmur, feeling the lump rising in my throat again. "Or at least that my mom did. She cries a lot at night. I think—I think she's ashamed of me."

"I bet that's not true," Fina says. "I bet she's just worried about you."

"You don't see the way she looks at me sometimes. Or how Lily stares at me like I really am a ghost."

"Well, you can always come live with me and I'll be your sister, and me and my mom will think you look amazing," replies Fina, grinning.

I let out a little sob-giggle. "Even after I hurt your feelings?"

"I'm sure you'll make it up to me."

"How?"

"By not giving me the silent treatment anymore," she says, leaning over to pet Boomer, who is nudging her thigh with his wet nose. "And also by telling me what this place is."

"It's—" I start. But I don't know what to say. How much can I tell Fina? How much do I want to?

"It's really cool," she decides before I can say anything, standing and climbing onto Throne Rock. "Look! This rock is like a big chair!"

"A throne," I correct her.

"Oooh, like the one in Fernlace," she says. "And look at that huge tree! It's like the Council Tree where all the Goldengrove elders meet. The stream could be the Ivory River."

Funny, I've never thought of it that way before, but she's right.

"Yeah," I say. "Except without all the deadly rapids. My gram's been bringing me here ever since I was little."

It's actually really weird seeing another person here

who isn't Gram. But it's nice to hear something besides silence in the glade again.

"I can see why," she says, gazing around. "There's something really special about it."

So I tell her everything. About the first time Gram brought me here and what she said about the charmed folk who came over on the ships from Europe. About the stories Gram and I wrote together about them. About how, after Gram died, I started one last story, and how I opened the journal one day to find someone else had written in it, too.

Behind her glasses, Fina's eyes grow wider and wider the longer I speak. When I've spilled out everything I know, she gazes around for a minute, thinking. The forest is silent once more.

"You really saw them?" she asks finally. "The charmed folk?" There's something in her voice that sounds a lot like hope.

"I used to," I say. "Not anymore, though."

Her face falls a little. Then a wrinkle appears between her eyebrows. "But wait. So, you don't know who's writing to you?"

"No clue."

"And that doesn't, like . . . freak you out?"

"I don't think so," I say. "Whoever it is must have known Gram. Gram obviously trusted them enough to tell them about the hollow and how we wrote stories together."

"But, Emma! We *have* to figure out who it is," she says. "Aren't you dying to know?"

"Um, I guess so."

Actually, I'm not sure I *have* been dying to know. Because having my mysterious pen pal felt like having a little bit of Gram back. Because maybe even after everything that's happened, I still wanted to believe in that last shred of magic.

"Emma?" Fina murmurs. "I know you said you don't see them anymore. The charmed folk. But do you think—could we maybe just pretend? Could we pretend that this is the Goldengrove, and we're Jack and Sarah? Or are we too old for that?"

"No," I say. "We're not."

She beams. "In that case," she says, "I'll be Sarah. You be Jack. Boomer, you get to be the hobgoblin king."

And we spend the rest of the morning running around the Spinney, pretending it really is the Goldengrove, climbing the Council Tree and waving sword sticks at Boomer, who seems to be having the time of his life playing the hobgoblin king.

When we finally leave the glade, we're both out of breath. We have dirt on our cheeks and twigs tangled in our hair. And neither of us minds a bit.

33

I'm not ready for Fina to leave when Mr. Ramirez shows up to take her home that afternoon. I don't want the spell to break. When she was here, it was like the wall between me and the rest of the world wasn't a wall anymore. It felt more like a curtain that could be lifted away.

But as the weekend draws to an end, I feel a familiar weight of dread in my stomach that grows heavier and heavier. And when I wake up on Monday morning, I feel almost too heavy to get out of bed.

When I finally do, I catch my reflection in the bathroom mirror. Sometimes, like today, it's still a shock to see myself, the splashes of pale across my face. They remind me of the paintings Gram left in her studio, the bits of blank canvas peeking out between all the colors.

All the things she left unfinished.

Saying all that stuff about not letting myself be invisible was easy enough in the Spinney, where there was no Edie to sneer at me, nobody to gawk at me or pretend I'm not there. What if I get to school and the curtain falls again, leaving me alone once more?

There's no point in worrying about things you can't change, Gram's voice chides, *and you can't change what people think of you.*

But this time, Gram's words sound hollow to me. Maybe you can't change what people think of you, but sometimes what people think changes *you*, whether you want it to or not.

Just as I'm finishing my cereal, there's a knock on the front door. Mom and Dad exchange a puzzled look, then Mom goes to answer it.

"Well, hi, Fina!" I hear her say. I feel my heart rise like a kite, and I get up and run to the door. Sure enough, there's Fina, waiting on the doorstep.

"Good morning, Mrs. Talbot," she says. "I thought I might ride the bus with Emma today."

"How nice," Mom replies, then waves to Ms. Ramirez. "I'll just go say hi to your mom."

"You didn't have to come," I say to Fina, but I'm not sure I've ever been happier to see her.

"Yeah, well, I thought you could use some company,"

she replies. "And also, I have an idea. About your pen pal. A *plan*."

We walk to my stop. It's really cold this morning, so we both kind of hop back and forth from one foot to the other to keep warm. Fortunately, the bus pulls up pretty much right away.

Fina scooches in next to me on the squeaky blue seat, and we huddle close so she can whisper her plan.

"I'll bet you this person comes to the Spinney at night," she says. "Because whoever they are, they don't want to run into you. They want to keep their identity a secret. But why? That's what I want to know. Anyway, we should have a sleepover on Friday, and we can sneak out of your house just like we did on Halloween. Then we go to the Spinney and wait."

"So, basically you want to have a stakeout?"

She grins. "Basically."

"But what if the person doesn't come that night?" I ask. "What if they come before then?"

"Go to the Spinney as soon as school's over," she says, "and take the journal out of the hollow. Don't put it back until Friday. They'll probably come and check, and when it's not there, they'll come back again until it is."

"Maybe," I say. "Maybe not. Sometimes it takes a while for them to write back."

Fina shrugs. "Then we do it again the next Friday. What's the worst that can happen? Either way, it's an adventure!"

"Yeah," I grumble. "And if my mom catches us, it'll be our last."

The bus stops for Ruby to get on. She bites her lip when she sees Fina sitting next to me and glaring at her. Under Fina's gaze, Ruby seems to wilt like a thirsty rose. And weirdly, I find myself feeling kind of sorry for her.

"Traitor," Fina mutters.

"Yeah, but look," I say, nodding my head toward the back. Ruby is sitting by herself across the aisle from the Graces, staring silently out the window. "She doesn't seem very happy."

"She shouldn't be. Who would choose to hang out with those girls?"

Fina rolls her eyes, but I shoot another glance back at Ruby, thinking. Remembering.

"You know what she said about the kids at her old school making fun of her?" I ask.

"Yeah."

"I bet she told Edie about me because she thought if she could just hang out with the popular girls, nobody would make fun of her anymore."

Fina pushes her glasses up the bridge of her nose. "My guidance counselor back in California always said that kids who are bullies are usually kids who have been bullied themselves," she says. "But it still doesn't make it okay."

"No," I say. "But at least I get why she did it. I don't think it was to be mean."

"So, are you saying we aren't going to concoct an elaborate revenge plot to get back at her?" Fina asks, giving a dramatic sigh of disappointment.

"You've done enough plotting for one day," I say, giving her a light shove. She curls her fingers together and does an evil-mastermind laugh, which dies away when we pull up to Edie's stop.

As Edie walks by us, Fina hisses like a teakettle just before it boils. "I don't care what my guidance counselor used to say," she mutters. "Some kids are just plain mean."

34

Even with Fina beside me, I still feel anxious as I walk into school that morning. I try to focus on our conversation instead of whether people are looking at me or not. I laugh when she makes a joke about Mr. Owens. I feel okay until we have to go our separate ways for first period.

Then during social studies, I turn around to pass back a worksheet to see a quiet girl who transferred into my class last week—I think her name is Skyler—totally staring at me. Her eyes are all round. If she's new to the school, she might not know about my vitiligo. I face forward and make sure not to look in her direction again.

When I tell Fina about Skyler at lunch, she thinks for a while, then says, "You know that part of *The World at the End of the Tunnel* when Jack and Sarah are surrounded by the clover elves? And the elves are just staring and pointing arrows at them?"

"Yeah," I reply.

"And Jack and Sarah are like, 'Uh-oh. Did we do something wrong? Are they going to shoot us?' But then the clover elves all start to talk in Chitterish, and the one who can speak English explains that they're just amazed by Sarah's freckles and Jack's buttons?"

"And then they realize that the elves have never seen human children before," I finish. "They're just curious."

"Exactly. So maybe when people stare at you, it's not because they're thinking there's something wrong with you. Maybe they're just curious. Or maybe they look at you like people stare at sunsets or interesting paintings. Because you're unique, you know?"

I take a long sip of juice. "Unique," I echo.

"You know what I'd stare at?" she asks.

I raise my eyebrows.

"Ninjas," she says, and giggles, "doing the Electric Slide."

Here is something I love about Fina. You never, ever know what she's going to say next.

"Um . . . and panda bears doing forward-tuck rolls?" I ask.

Fina claps her hands. "Oh, oh, yes, and kittens chasing disco ball lights!"

I'm giggling now, too.

"Mr. Yardley doing karaoke," I say.

"Edie trimming her nose hairs!" says Fina, gasping for air.

We both throw our arms down on the table and dissolve into hysterical laughter. When we can finally sit up straight again, I catch sight of someone else staring at me from across the cafeteria. Edie.

There's no way she could have heard us talking about her. But she's still looking at us like we're the cause of a really bad smell. I don't mind, though, because for once, I think, it has nothing to do with my vitiligo.

The bell rings then, and Fina and I have to go our separate ways. The echo of our lunchtime laughter sits in my belly for the whole afternoon.

I'm not exactly sure I believe what Fina said about why people stare at me, but for the rest of the day, I think about it. And I wonder.

The next day, I get called on in social studies to answer a question. And in English, I raise my hand when Ms. Singh asks someone to explain the difference between mood and tone.

Both times, I get the answer right. Both times, nobody acts like there's anything weird about it. A couple kids turn to look at me while I talk, but most just keep looking bored. Nobody gasps or laughs or whispers. I'm just a kid getting called on in class.

For the first time since Edie's text, things feel kind of normal.

That is, until I go to the bathroom during fifth period.

As soon as I open the door, I hear someone crying in one of the stalls. I have déjà vu, and I know exactly why. The crying girl is barricaded in the same stall *I* hid in after Fina showed me that text.

The girl stops crying when she hears me come in. A few seconds later, she blows her nose and flushes the toilet. Then she opens the door.

If you had asked me this morning who would end up crying in the bathroom later today, I would have definitely said me.

I would *not* have put my money on Edie O'Shea.

She stops dead when she sees me, staring at me with red, puffy eyes. For a few seconds, neither of us says anything. Edie walks to the sink and washes her hands, then splashes water on her face.

"I know it's stupid to ask you," she says quietly, looking at her own reflection instead of me, "but could you just, like, not tell anyone about this?"

"Um, okay," I murmur, too stunned to think of anything else to say.

Edie shoots me a weird look, either a grimace or a

kind of failed attempt at a smile, and leaves without another word.

As I walk back to class, I can't stop thinking about how seeing her crying in the bathroom is kind of like seeing a fish flopping on dry land.

Unnatural.

By the end of fifth period, I'm still so busy thinking about it that I don't even notice Austin barreling through the doorway into the computer lab right as I'm trying to get out.

We knock into each other, and he spirals away from me, lifting his hands to his chest and making a face. Like if he touches me, I'll burn him.

But it's *my* cheeks that are burning. And there are at least ten people in the hall watching.

"God, you're such a klutz, Austin," says an annoyed voice. I turn to see who spoke.

Ladies and gentlemen, once again, Edie O'Shea.

"Uh, sorry," he mumbles to Edie, who's standing behind him looking deeply unimpressed. "I mean, sorry," he says, this time to me, before streaking off into the lab. A couple people laugh, and then everyone turns back to their lockers and their conversations.

Edie marches off down the hall, leaving me alone to wonder what exactly just happened.

35

For the rest of the week, *I'm* the one stealing glances at Edie, trying to detect any hint of the girl I saw crying in the bathroom. But she seems pretty much normal. Well, normal for Edie O'Shea. The only two things out of the ordinary are the faint shadows under her eyes, and the unusual quiet that has descended over her lunch table.

She hasn't said another word to me about what happened in the bathroom or about Austin. Did she snap at him because she was worried I would tell someone what I saw? And what's she crying over that she's so embarrassed about?

She didn't need to worry, though. I told Fina about what happened with Edie and Austin. ("She probably has a guilty conscience," Fina replied. "Who knew

Edie had a conscience to begin with?") But I don't tell her about Edie crying. Because I know if things were reversed and it was Edie who saw me crying in the bathroom, she would tell everyone.

And I don't want to be like Edie.

The rest of the week is surprisingly okay. Maybe the scene outside the computer lab has something to do with it, but nobody else does anything mean the rest of the week. Or maybe people are just getting used to the new me.

I still get the occasional stare, but I try to remember what Fina said on Monday. When I catch a group of eighth graders looking at me before homeroom on Friday, I force myself to smile instead of look away.

And they actually smile back.

Still, it's a relief when school lets out on Friday afternoon. Especially because Friday is stakeout night.

Mom comes and picks me and Fina up from school. We both sit in the back, even though I know Mom hates that because it makes her feel like a chauffeur.

"It's so nice to see you again, Fina!" she says.

"You, too, Mrs. Talbot."

"How's school going? Are you liking it so far?"

"Yeah," says Fina. "It's smaller than my old school, and the kids aren't *so* bad." She shoots me a look and nudges me in the ribs.

"Does your family have big Thanksgiving plans?"

Even though I know that Thanksgiving is next week, the word still sends a jolt through me. Thanksgiving was Gram's favorite holiday. With Mom's family so far away, we always spent it with Gram. It will be my first big holiday without her.

I feel a sharp arrow of sadness, followed by an awful hardness at the thought. I guess even though things are kind of getting back to normal, I can't stop feeling like Gram failed me somehow. Like she taught me the wrong things. Like she didn't prepare me enough for what it would be like when she was gone.

You should know that I don't want to feel this way about her. I just do.

"My mom has already started cooking," Fina is saying. "Even though there's only the three of us this year. She likes to have everything planned out, I guess."

"Sounds like my kind of mom," says Mom. Which is funny, since Ms. Ramirez is definitely *not* Mom's kind of mom. I wonder what she thought of Ms. Ramirez's purple hair.

That night, Fina and I eat dinner with Mom, Dad, and Lily. Somehow, having Fina there changes everything. The mood is so much lighter, and I don't feel Mom's eyes tracing the outlines of my patches, trying to tell if they've gotten bigger or not. She's too busy talking Fina's ear off about the one trip she took to LA in college and how she went Rollerblading at the beach and rode a Ferris wheel and saw some guy named Sean Connery in Hollywood.

Fina and I lock eyes when Mom talks about his "dreamy accent" and nearly burst out laughing. Even Lily seems giggly.

"Well, he *was* the best Bond," Dad says—whatever that means—with a resigned sigh.

Fortunately, everyone goes to sleep early that night, so Fina and I don't have to wait forever to sneak out of the house. Just like on Halloween, I give Boomer a bone to distract him, and then I creep out to make sure all the lights are off.

Fina has my backpack strapped to her shoulders, chock-full of stakeout supplies: binoculars, a flashlight, and lots and lots of snacks. I bring the journal from the sycamore tree, which I've kept in my room all this week, hidden in the corner of the closet.

We bundle up, sneak out the back, and slink into the little brick lane behind Morning Glory Cottage. It's only eleven o'clock, but the average bedtime in Lanternwood is probably closer to eight thirty, which might explain why we don't run into anyone.

Hopefully, not *everyone* is asleep, though. Hopefully,

my mysterious pen pal is still awake.

In all the times I've visited the Spinney, I've never gone there at night before. The air is cold and sharp as we cross the meadows, and the dark trees loom up before us.

"It's like the Dimwood," Fina whispers.

"It totally is," I say, imagining screeching banshees circling overhead and grinning ogres waiting in the shadows to snatch us up.

At the exact same time, we reach for each other's hand.

"Are you sure you want to do this?" I ask. "We can go back if you want."

Fina hesitates for just a second, glancing toward the forest. Then she shakes her head. "If Jack and Sarah did it, so can we."

So we duck under the barbed wire.

Even though I know this forest by heart, we go slow and walk soft, so we don't give ourselves away. We don't dare use Fina's flashlight or even our phones, because if my pen pal *does* come, they'd be able to spot the light from a mile off.

An owl hoots in a tree overhead and Fina startles. She grips my hand tighter.

"It's okay," I say. "It's not really the Dimwood. There's no evil hobgoblin king here."

"Right," Fina says. "Right."

When we get to the glade, I return the book to the sycamore hollow. Then we have to figure out where to hide. There's a mostly full moon tonight, but it's cloudy, too. Every time a cloud crosses over the moon, we can barely see anything other than the outline of the trees. But when the sky is clear, we can make out the branches and rocks and leaves, all sketched in silver.

We decide to sit behind Throne Rock. It's close enough to the hollow that, even if it's cloudy, we can still make out some detail. And it's big enough to hide the two of us.

Fina takes out her binoculars, some Twizzlers, and a big bag of Donitas—these crunchy ring-shaped Mexican snacks her mom lets her have in her lunchbox on Fridays. We each take one, crunch into it, shush each other, then giggle, then shush each other again. Then we reach for more.

Fina loops the binoculars around her neck. "Let's talk suspects," she says. "You said it must be someone who knew your gram really well. Who could that be?"

"Mom, Dad, Lily," I say. "Some of the villagers. There's Old Joe and Older Joe and Gloria and Ruth. Oh, and then there's—"

The instant it comes to me, I can't believe I haven't thought of it before.

"The flowers," I murmur.

"Flowers?" Fina asks. "Is that the name of another villager?"

"No," I say. "No, they were in the graveyard. The morning after Halloween, someone left my gram flowers. And I'm pretty sure I know who it was."

"Why didn't you tell me this?" Fina asks.

"Because that Monday was the day everything, you know, happened. And then I just kind of forgot about it."

Fina nods. "Fair. So who is it? Who left the flowers?"

"His name is Professor Swann."

"Were they friends?"

I shake my head. "I don't know," I say. "They must have been closer than I thought, because why else would he leave her flowers?"

"Do you think—?" Fina starts. "I mean, could he have, like, loved her?"

I remember how he cried after Gram's funeral. I think about what Ruth said when I asked her about him. *I seem to recall he had a flame for someone else.* Is it possible that the flame was for Gram? Could Professor Swann have—

"Oh, my god," I whisper. "Fina, give me the backpack."

She hands it over, and I dig to the bottom for the familiar shape of the book that's always there. I pull it out, turning to the first page, and shine the light of my phone down to read.

The World at the End of the Tunnel

By R. M. Wildsmith

For my muse and best friend.

"I knew it," I say breathlessly, staring at the worn writing. "I knew the handwriting in the journal looked familiar, but I couldn't figure out where I'd seen it before."

"I don't get it," Fina murmurs.

"This book was Gram's. I always thought my grandpa wrote this inscription because of what it says, but you can't really read the signature, can you? It matches, Fina. The handwriting matches the journal's."

"So you're saying that whoever wrote this inscription—"

"—is my pen pal," I finish.

We stare at each other. I haven't even begun to wrap my head around what this all means when we hear a rustling noise, followed by another. The noises get closer and closer. Footsteps.

My spine goes very, very stiff at the same time that my heart goes bonkers in my chest. Fina points frantically at my glowing phone screen. I click it off.

Silently, Fina shifts her weight to peek out from the side of the rock again. Then she gives a tiny gasp.

I lean to the other side until I can make out the shape of someone moving through the trees, heading straight for the sycamore. It's too cloudy now to make out anything other than a silhouette.

When the figure gets to the tree hollow, it stops, pulls out the journal, and flips through the pages. Looking to see if there's a new chapter, probably. Then the figure closes the journal again. Fina reaches down to her chest for her binoculars and takes the tiniest of steps forward.

I see where her foot is going to land right before it happens.

She steps right onto the bag of Donitas, and a huge *CRRRUUUUNCH* sound fills the night.

The figure whips its head in our direction, just as the moon finally peers out from behind the clouds, and for a second before the figure turns and runs, I see a face.

I gasp in recognition.

It is not Professor Swann.

It's the Apple Lady.

36

"*So tell me* again," Fina says, sitting up in my bed with two pillows propped behind her. "Who is this lady? What do we know about her?"

Even though we didn't get a lot of sleep last night, Fina and I both woke up bright and early today.

"The Apple Lady," I reply. "I've only ever seen her when she's going to church or walking in the morning. She comes out to pick fruit. Blackberries or apples or whatever's in season. She always wears headphones and she doesn't ever speak."

"What's her real name?"

"I don't know."

"Where does she live?"

I shake my head.

"Did your gram know her?"

"She must have," I say. Well enough for the Apple Lady to write that Gram was her "best friend" in her inscription. Except that I remember this one time Gram and I had passed her picking blackberries on our way to the Spinney. She'd looked up only for a second before turning back to the bramble. I could hear the tinny sound of music coming from her headphones.

"Why doesn't she ever talk to anyone?" I had asked Gram.

"Some people just keep themselves to themselves," was all she'd said. "And we have to respect that."

I had asked Gram a question about the Apple Lady. So why didn't Gram tell me that she knew her? That they had apparently once been best friends?

Because she was hiding something, says a voice in my head.

I suddenly remember the look Gram used to get sometimes when she was telling me her fairy tales. Like she was somewhere far away from me. Someplace I wasn't allowed to see.

And I remember the day she told us that she had breast cancer, and explained that she'd known for a while but didn't want to tell anyone until she knew she was dying.

I always thought that Gram was my best friend in the world. But suddenly she feels like an illusion. Like a character from one of her own stories made of ink and paper instead of flesh and blood.

"That's not a lot to go on," Fina says, tapping her mouth. "It feels like instead of solving a mystery, we've just opened a whole new one."

A little trickle of cold air floats in from a gap between the window and the sill. I pull the covers up over my shoulders.

Fina's right. I want to know what Gram was hiding and why. And fortunately, I think I know where we can get some answers.

A few minutes later, we're all bundled up in our scarves and gloves. We're just about to walk out the door when I hear Lily's voice.

"Where are you guys headed?"

I turn around to see her curled up on the couch, her laptop, a mug of tea, and a bunch of papers spread over her lap.

"Um," I say, "out?"

"Emma's giving me a tour of the village," Fina says.

Lily smiles. "That's cool. Have fun."

"Thanks?" I say, although it comes out as a question. I think this is the most Lily has said to me since my makeup tutorial. Since when does she care where I go on Saturday mornings? Or whether I have fun?

"So where *are* we going?" Fina asks as soon as we get outside.

"To find someone," I reply.

We walk by Ruth's house first, but she's not in her yard today, so we start in the other direction, heading for Gloria's place. Halfway there, we hit the jackpot.

Ruth and Gloria are outside the village hall. Old Joe is leaning against his tractor, which he's pulled over to the side of the road so he can watch Gloria teetering on a ladder, strands of Christmas lights in her hands.

"Tighter, Gloria, tighter!" Ruth demands, banging her cane.

"Did I ask for your help?" Gloria snaps.

"Hi, Ruth," I call. "Hi, Gloria. Hi, Joe."

Three heads turn to see who's calling them, and they all lift their hands to wave.

"This is Fina," I say, pausing as we reach the lawn of the village hall. "This is Gloria and Ruth and Ol— I mean, Joe."

Fina waves at them. "Here, let me help," she says, striding over to the ladder and holding it steady. I follow her, take the knotted pile of lights on the ground, and start untangling them.

I can feel Old Joe studying my face as I walk by. I haven't been out in the village much since I stopped wearing makeup, so I'm sure he's wondering about my patches. He doesn't say anything, though. Good. We have more important things to talk about.

"Well, thank you, dears," Gloria says. "Now *that* is what I call helpful. You know, I've used these same lights for fifty-two years."

"Isn't it a little early for Christmas lights?" Fina asks.

"Certainly not," Gloria replies. "Thanksgiving is right around the corner, and people expect these lights to be lit as soon as they're done with their turkeys. They come from miles around to see them."

It's one of Lanternwood's traditions. Every year, once we're done with Gram's apple pie, we come and see the lighting ceremony. Every year, someone from the village gets chosen to plug in the lights on the village hall, and then, one by one, everyone else in the village switches their Christmas lights on. There are always a couple of Hanukkah houses, too, all done up with blue and white.

"Aren't they beautiful, Emma?" Gram had whispered last year, putting her arm around me and tilting her head against mine. "This is why I love this time of year. It's when the world finds out how resilient it is. It may be dark and cold, but we band together and we hang lights and sing songs. And before you know it, spring is right around the corner!"

Her breath hung in the air like an echo.

I didn't know yet that she was sick. That it was our last Thanksgiving together.

"Some things just don't change," Ruth is saying now, tipping forward to make sure we turn our attention to her. "But most everything does. You girls will learn that soon enough. Oh, your bones are fine now, sure. But one day they'll get to aching like mine, and then you'll think of old Ruth and say, 'She knew what she was talking about'!"

"Don't listen to her," Gloria says with a sigh. "So nice of you girls to come and help us."

"Just out for a walk on this fine fall morning?" Old Joe asks.

"Actually, no," I say. "I was wondering if you could tell us something."

"Any old thing?" Old Joe asks. "Because I've got a nugget or two of wisdom still rattling around in this old clunker." He taps the side of his head, and Gloria clucks her teeth.

"Maybe another time," I say, shooting him a smile. "I wanted to know about somebody who lives in the village. Or at least, I see her here sometimes. But I don't know her name or anything about her."

"Well, go on, then."

"I've always called her the Apple Lady," I say. "Because I've only ever seen her out in the mornings picking fruit."

Old Joe nods. "Ah. You mean Madeline. Madeline Mitchell."

"Madeline Mitchell," I repeat. At last, my pen pal has a name. One I've never heard before.

"She's an odd one, and there's no denying it," says Ruth.

"Been in this village as long as any of us," Old Joe adds, adjusting his cap.

"So, she lives in Lanternwood?" Fina asks.

"Well, technically she lives just outside it," Old Joe replies. "She lives in the house on Briar Hollow Lane. The *only* house on Briar Hollow Lane, all the way down at the end."

I squint up at him, shading my eyes from the sun. "Briar Hollow Lane? I thought there was nothing down there but a water treatment shed. That's what Gram told me."

I look from Old Joe to Gloria in time to see a little frown cross over her face. Another lie, then.

"Well, it was a white lie," Old Joe says, as if reading my thoughts. "Kids can be cruel to folks like Madeline. Not you, of course. But maybe you tell someone, and they tell someone, and the next thing you know, kids are daring each other to ring her bell in the middle of the night."

"But did Gram know her?" I ask.

Old Joe nods. "Sure. They were friends a long way

back. I think Madeline used to visit your gram when she was still ill."

Gloria sucks in a sharp breath. Ruth looks suddenly interested. I feel my forehead wrinkle. "You mean when she had cancer?"

Old Joe shakes his head, slow as a cornstalk swaying in the breeze. "Naw, I mean when she was a child."

"Now, Joe," Gloria chides, her voice sharp. "I'm sure Emma's not interested in ancient—"

"What do you mean?" I interrupt.

Nobody says anything for a minute. They don't move, either. They just stand there, frozen, like three very wrinkly statues.

Then Old Joe's jaw starts to work side to side. "Well, now," he says sheepishly, "I'm not really the person to be asking about that kind of thing. In fact, I'd, uh, better be getting back to the fields. You tell your folks I say hello. Nice to meet you, Fina."

He tips his hat at her, climbs up into his tractor, and rattles off.

Gloria looks furious. Ruth wears an amused smile. I have never been more confused in my life.

"What was he talking about?" I ask. "Gram never told me anything about being sick."

"Emma, some things are between family to discuss," Gloria says, turning back to her lights.

"Aw, psh," Ruth says, waving her free hand. "Don't you think that can of worms is open now, Gloria? Yes, your gram was a sickly child, Emma."

"Joe, that old busybody," Gloria grumbles. "Always had a mouth the size of Texas."

"But sick with what?" I ask, ignoring her.

Ruth and Gloria exchange a look. "Now, that we can't tell you and not because we don't want to," Gloria says. "One spring, she just stopped coming to school as much, and in the fall, she didn't come back. We were told she was too sick to do much besides stay in Morning Glory Cottage."

"They took her to the beach for the sea air, sometimes," Ruth corrects her.

"It was the mountains for the mountain air," Gloria argues.

"There were all sorts of rumors flying," Ruth says, tapping her cane against the sidewalk. "Polio. Tuberculosis. A schoolteacher died from meningitis that year, remember, Gloria? She was so young. Pretty thing, too."

"Isabella Fortune," I say, thinking of the stone in the graveyard. "Gram told me about her."

Gloria nods. "Poor woman. Anyway, I'm not sure anyone outside the family really knew what was wrong with your gram," says Gloria.

"How long did she stay in the house?" I ask.

257

"A long time," Gloria says.

"A year," Ruth adds, "or two."

"Two *years*?" I ask, my mouth dropping open.

My head is buzzing, and my heart is beating fast, for some reason.

"Oh, they came to church service most weeks," Gloria is saying. "'Course, her daddy was the mayor back then and thinking about running for governor, so it would have looked bad not to have the whole family there. But they came in late and left before it was over, as I remember. She was too fragile to be caught in a crowd. I visited her once or twice, but it was a bit—well— frightening. Your great-grandmother kept her room so dark. The light gave your gram headaches."

"Then one day, she was back," Ruth barks, snapping her fingers for dramatic effect. "Still a sickly thing to look at, but recovered, apparently."

"And you didn't ask her what was wrong?" Fina asks.

"It was a different time," Gloria replies. "In those days, illnesses weren't talked about in the open. They were whispered about behind closed doors. Anyway, it was obvious your gram wanted to put it behind her. It was the kind thing to do not to ask imprudent questions. We were all just thankful she was back again."

My hands tremble a little as I untangle the ancient lights from one another. At the same time that I'm hurt that Gram kept all this from me, I feel a deep pain in my heart for her. What could keep a child that sick? Was it cancer? Could you get cancer as a child and then again when you were old?

"But what about Madeline?" I ask. "Joe said she visited Gram. Maybe she knows more."

Gloria gives her narrow shoulders a brittle shrug. "Maybe. All I know is your gram and Madeline were thick as thieves after your gram came back to school."

"But they grew apart in the end," Ruth adds.

"What happened?" Fina asks. "Did they have a fight or something?"

"Nothing as dramatic as that," Gloria said. "But as Ruth says, Madeline has some strange ways about her. From the time she was a child, she was timid as a church mouse."

"Afraid of the world," Ruth croaks, before coughing loudly into her mittened hand.

"Your gram was timid, too, when she first recovered," Gloria says. "But she had a love for, well, just about everything. The river. The meadows. People, most of all. She had a gift with people. But Madeline, she wasn't like that."

"She was afraid of people more than anything," says Ruth.

"I suppose nowadays, she'd have been diagnosed with something," Gloria says, shaking her head. "Sent to a doctor, gone to therapy. Perhaps she could have been helped. But in those days— Well, after school, we saw her less and less until she just sort of—"

"Disappeared," Ruth finishes.

The word sends a chill through me. I think of how I ended the last chapter of the story, with Ivy lying alone in the snow, waiting to disappear.

Is that what happened to Madeline?

And if I didn't have Fina, could I have ended up the same way?

Then I realize: Madeline *did* have a Fina. Gram.

But if they were really such good friends, how could Gram have let Madeline fade away? Why hadn't she fought for Madeline like Fina fought for me?

I feel like my grip on Gram is slipping away faster than ever.

"Now, *my* old bones need a break," says Gloria, clutching the small of her back. "I have a pot of tea in the hall. Would you like to come in?"

"No," I reply. "We have to get going. But you guys have been really helpful. Thanks a lot."

"Nice to meet you," Fina says.

"Emma, dear?" Ruth says before we can turn away. She juts her wobbly chin forward and squints at me. "What's all that white stuff on your face?"

I hesitate a moment, glancing at Fina. "Skin," I say. "It's just my skin."

37

If I had my way, we would run to Briar Hollow Lane right now to pound on Madeline's door. But when we get back to Morning Glory Cottage, Ms. Ramirez's car is already parked outside.

She's inside having coffee with Mom, who, embarrassingly, is in her Pilates clothes for her class later today. Except Ms. Ramirez doesn't seem to notice how embarrassing she is. She's laughing at something Mom said. Like they're friends or something.

I'm just about to ask if Fina can stay longer—another night, even—when Ms. Ramirez drains her cup and stands to go.

"We're volunteering with some of my students to help clean up the highway adopted by the college," she says. She checks the time on her cell phone. "And we are officially late."

"I'll go get my stuff," Fina says.

Once we're upstairs, she grabs my hand. "Don't go see Madeline without me, okay?"

I hesitate.

"Seriously, Emma," Fina says. "I know she's your pen pal or whatever, but it sounds like she's kind of strange. You shouldn't go by yourself."

"And also, you're curious to meet her."

Fina grins. "*And* I'm *dying* to meet her. I'll tell my mom we have to work on a project after school next week. We'll go then, okay?"

"Fine," I grumble. "But if you weren't my best friend . . ."

"Oh, but I am, Emma," Fina says, grin widening. "Oh, but I am."

After Fina leaves, I find Dad in the backyard trying to get the lawn mower to start.

"Hey, Dad," I say, sitting down on a mossy bench between two rosebushes.

"Hey, Butterfly," he says, looking up in surprise.

"I was wondering, do you know much about Gram's childhood?"

He wipes his hands together and tilts his head in

thought. "Not much, actually. Obviously she grew up here. But she didn't like to talk about growing up a lot, I think because she had a tough relationship with her parents—your great-grandparents."

"Tough like how?" I ask.

He rubs a hand over his stubbly jaw. "I'm not sure. I just always got the sense they didn't get along. They died when I was little, but I think they were very stern people. Not a barrel of laughs like your mom and me." He winks, and I roll my eyes. "Anyway, I guess her father had to have been a serious person, to be the mayor and all. He even tried to run for governor at one point. I think he might have been more interested in being a good politician than a good father, actually."

"Do you know if Gram was ever sick as a child?" I study my own father's face closely for any sign that he might be hiding something. But he just thinks for another moment, then sits down beside me on the bench and shakes his head.

"Not that I know of. Are you wondering about her cancer? Because I don't think anyone could have seen that coming. That's just the way life is sometimes, you know?"

"Yeah, I know," I say. At least, I'm learning.

He sighs and pulls me closer so he can kiss me on the head. "This happens when people die," he says. "You start thinking of all this stuff you wish you had asked them. You kick yourself for not taking the time to do it when you had the chance."

I hadn't thought of it that way. Would Gram have told me the truth if only I had asked?

"There's so much I didn't know," I say quietly.

"You knew Gram's heart, Emma," Dad says.

A few weeks ago, I would have agreed with him. But now I'm not so sure.

After Mom leaves for Pilates, I decide to take Boomer for a long walk. I need some space to think about everything I heard today.

Lily is still on the couch, which is weird, since she and Mom usually go to Pilates together.

"Study break," she says. "Want to join? I was thinking *Mean Girls*."

One of the only movies Mom, Lily, and I all like. Why is Lily being so nice to me this morning? I don't get it, but that's one mystery that's just going to have to wait.

"No thanks," I say. "Boomer needs to go out."

She looks the slightest bit disappointed as we leave. I think back to what she said when she was doing my makeup, about it being hard to make friends at her new school. Is that why she's suddenly being nice again? Is she so desperate for company that she wants to hang out with me?

Once Boomer and I start walking, though, my thoughts quickly turn back to Gram, my mind running over what Fina and I found out this morning.

Gram was sick as a child. Maybe for years. And when she recovered, Madeline Mitchell was her best friend. Until something happened between them. Except, if they weren't friends anymore, how did Madeline know about the journal in the sycamore hollow?

The journal! Madeline took it last night when she ran. Could she have returned it by now? Maybe she's written another chapter of the story. Or maybe she saw who was spying on her in the woods last night. Maybe she'll have written me a note explaining everything.

Boomer and I fly down through the meadows and into the Spinney. I tell myself not to get my hopes up. That Madeline probably hasn't had time to write back yet. Or that she might be too angry about our stakeout to write again at all.

But when I come to a stop, breathless beside the sycamore tree, I see that the journal has indeed been returned to the hollow. And when I flip eagerly through the pages, I see a new chapter waits for me inside.

After Ivy had been alone for some time, she felt the sudden presence of someone nearby in the forest. Someone watching her.

Then she felt Shilling's warm tongue against her frozen cheek. She opened her eyes to see the great wolf dog standing over her, feebly wagging his tail.

"Shilling," she said, her voice hoarse with frost, "I told you to leave me here."

But over his silver shoulder, she noticed something strange. Two trees that had not been there before. And the longer she looked, the surer she was that they were not trees at all but girls, just like she was—only with bark instead of skin, long spindly branches for arms, and hair made of willow branches. One of them held in her wooden hands a stone cup.

"Drink," she said. "It will do you good."

Ivy took the cup and drank the liquid inside. It tasted of mulled blueberries and wild honey and afternoon sun. As she drank it, warmth spilled down her throat and spread throughout her insides until they were filled with summer.

She looked around the clearing then and found that she was surrounded by all manner of forest creatures—owls and foxes, dormice and squirrels, bees and deer and rabbits.

Except the longer Ivy stared back, the more certain

she was that they were not animals at all. They had begun to shimmer. Suddenly, the foxes were elves with red cheeks and ginger hair. The dormice were timid gnomes that looked up at her with wide eyes. The bees were a colony of fairies, fluttering busily around their queen. The deer were fauns who bowed to her over their hooves.

"I don't understand," she said, drawing nearer to Shilling, who was, thankfully, still a wolf dog. "What's going on?"

"Magic, of course," said one of the tree girls, who Ivy thought might be a pixie.

"But Gran told me that all magic creatures were driven into extinction," said Ivy.

"Almost," said the other pixie. "Now we live only in the oldest of forests, and we take great precautions to keep ourselves hidden."

"Only your gran could see us for what we truly are," said one of the fauns.

"Why?" Ivy asked.

"Your grandmother was the Keeper of the Forest," said the fairy queen, who wore a crown of clover and sat upon a throne of holly leaves. "A protector of its magic. As long as she was here, no harm could come to us."

"But now she's gone," said the first pixie. "And the

forest is in grave danger."

"And you," piped the second pixie, "are the only one who can save it."

"Me?" gasped Ivy. "Why me?"

"Because, child," the fairy queen explained, "you are of the forest. Your gran found you here as a babe, just as the last Keeper found her. You may look like a normal human girl, but you've more magic in your veins than any who stand before you. If you could look inside yourself, you would find a heart made of balsam bark, bones made of river rocks, and vines instead of veins, with the morning dew running through them."

Ivy clutched herself, shaking her head. "No," she said. "If this was true, my gran would have told me."

"She could not," said the faun in an airy voice. "The Keeper is forbidden to share the secrets of the forest."

"But now you are Keeper," said the first pixie.

"And you must banish the witch," said the second pixie. "Or we are lost."

"Even if I am what you say," Ivy protested, "I am cursed. Can't you see how I flicker? I'll soon disappear altogether."

Even now, she could see only the barest outline of the girl she had been before.

"Magic," said the fairy queen placidly, "is all about how you see things."

"The villagers saw it, too," said Ivy.

"Because you believed it to be true," said the fairy queen, "and so it was."

"But you must fight to see the real truth," said one of the elves, who until now had not spoken.

"The truth!" chanted the nearby gnomes. "The truth!"

"Change the way you see, girl," said the fairy queen, "and you will change who you are."

"You mustn't disappear," said the first pixie, "because if you disappear, we will, too."

Ivy closed her eyes. She summoned the last seed of strength she carried within her, which she had not known she possessed. She could not let disappear all the creatures Gran had cared for.

She felt the dew of the forest surge through her vines, felt her balsam bark heart begin to pump with hope.

And when she opened her eyes again, she saw herself for what she truly was. Strong and sturdy as the tallest tree in the forest. Fast and pure as the clear river running through it.

Ready to face the witch.

38

On Sunday morning, I am woken up by a rumble of thunder and Boomer—who hates thunderstorms—inching closer to me in bed. All night long, I dreamed of trees coming to life and witches flying over them.

I open the curtain, letting the stormy light in. When it hits my skin, it turns my vitiligo patches almost to silver. They actually look kind of beautiful.

I look down at my arms, lightly tracing the outline of my patches and thinking about Ivy's story.

The Keeper is forbidden to share the secrets of the forest.

Is Madeline trying to tell me something? That there's a reason Gram kept so much from me?

Ready to face the witch.

Is this an invitation to come and see Madeline? She *is* the one who wrote the woman in the white cloak into the story, after all. Maybe that's how she sees herself. But why? The witch in the story kills Ivy's gran. But Madeline didn't kill my gram. Cancer did.

There's something about the way Madeline writes that's so familiar. Like how the magical creatures shimmer into sight just like the charmed folk used to do for me.

I think there's something else, too, though—something staring me right in the face that I'm just not seeing.

Change the way you see, girl . . . and you will change who you are.

Another crack of thunder, and Boomer leaps out of bed and cowers by the door.

"Come on, boy," I say, throwing off the covers, "let's get you some breakfast."

He follows me downstairs, where Lily is just sitting down at the table to eat her omelet. Mom and Dad are nowhere to be seen.

"Morning," I say.

"Morning, Emma."

I fix Boomer's breakfast—nothing distracts him like food—and am sitting down to pour myself a bowl of cereal when I realize Lily is staring at me.

She thinks she's really good about doing it only when I can't see, but I can feel her gaze. She might as well be tapping my shoulder.

I look up, ready to tell her to mind her own business, but there's something funny about the way she's staring at me. Like she might be about to cry.

"What's wrong?" I ask. "Oh, no . . . did you . . . ? Is it Yale?"

"No, that's not it," she says, and I swear her eyes are welling with tears. First Mom, then Edie, now Lily. It's like an epidemic.

"What? Why are you looking at me like that?"

She sighs. "It probably sounds stupid, but I'm just, well, really proud of you."

My mouth drops open a little.

"And maybe a little bit jealous, too."

It drops more. Lily? Jealous of *me*? "Why?" I ask.

"You're my little sister, Emma," she says, swiping a tear. "But you're like a hundred times braver than I've ever been. If it was me who had vitiligo, I would probably think it was the end of the world."

"Um, is this supposed to be making me feel good?" I ask. "Because if it is—"

Lily rolls her eyes, more at herself than me, I think. "Sorry. What I'm trying to say is that I love how you aren't afraid to be who you are."

I blink a few times. Since when is this how Lily sees me?

"I thought you were ashamed of me."

She shakes her head, silky hair shining under the kitchen lights. There's another rumble of thunder outside. "Of course not, Emma! Why would I be ashamed?"

"Because you and Mom always want everything to be perfect, like you are. I thought that's why you taught me to do my makeup. Because you both wanted me to hide my patches."

A crease shoots down between Lily's eyebrows like a lightning bolt. Her chin trembles. Suddenly she doesn't look so perfect. She just looks like my sister.

"Have you ever thought that maybe we just act perfect because we're afraid?" she asks, her voice thick. "Afraid that if we don't get into perfect schools or have perfect Instagram posts, people will see the truth? That we have flaws, too? And then—and then—"

In case you're wondering, the answer is no. I have never, ever until this moment thought of Lily or Mom as being afraid. Of anything, besides maybe grass stains. "Nobody's perfect, Lily," I say quietly.

She takes a big bite out of her omelet and talks as she chews, something I'm pretty sure she's never done in her entire life. "Sometimes I think— I've spent so long trying to be perfect that it's all I have. Without perfect,

I don't really know who I am."

"You're my sister," I say. "That's who."

"A sister who is so *not* ashamed of you," she replies, grabbing my hand from across the table. "I showed you how to do your makeup because, if it were me, I would wear it. Because I'd be afraid. But it's not me. It's you. And I think if you want to wear makeup, it's cool. And if you don't, that's *really* cool."

"Why didn't you tell me any of this before?"

"You stopped talking to me!" she says, a hint of frustration rising in her voice. "I was trying to be supportive, and you were giving me the cold shoulder. I thought you were the one who didn't want anything to do with *me*."

I squeeze her hand. Besides the night Lily did my makeup, this is the only other time I can ever remember actually feeling like I had a real sister instead of a stranger living in the next bedroom.

It feels extremely wonderful.

But I can't help but feel bad, too. I knew Lily was going through kind of a hard time, and I haven't been there for her at all.

"I'm sorry I gave you the cold shoulder," I say. "And I'm really not that brave."

It's funny. Lily thinks I'm brave because I'm not afraid to show the world who I am, but I don't even know who that is anymore.

"You're braver than you think."

"Well, maybe you are, too," I say. "When are you going to tell Mom? About wanting to take a year off?"

"Maybe tomorrow. Maybe never. I think I'll wait and see if I get into Yale first. If I do and they let me defer a year, she probably won't be as upset."

"I'll be there when you tell her. You know, for moral support. If you want, I mean."

Lily smiles. "Thanks, Emma. *You* should talk to Mom, too. Tell her what you told me."

"Maybe," I mumble.

She takes a thoughtful sip of her coffee.

"Sometimes I wonder," she says slowly, "if I'd spent more time with Gram, like you did, if I would be a little braver, too. Gram was so . . . original, wasn't she? The long dresses and the parasols and stuff. I always thought it was weird, but now I think she was pretty cool. She wasn't afraid of what anyone thought."

"So, why didn't you?" I ask. "Spend more time with her?"

She shrugs. "You two had your little club. And I always got the feeling that maybe Gram looked down on me sometimes. Both of you. Because I'd rather fit in than stand out."

"Maybe I did sometimes," I say slowly, "but not Gram. I don't think Gram looked down on anybody."

"You remind me of her, you know. You have her spirit."

"Really?" I ask. I look down at my hands for some reason, like I'll be able to see the shape of her palms in mine.

"Really," says Lily.

Suddenly, I fling myself out of my chair and wrap my arms around her. Because even with all my questions about Gram, it still means everything that Lily would say something like that to me. "Thanks, Lily," I whisper.

My sister hugs me tight in answer.

39

It rains all morning. After breakfast, Lily leaves to go to a study group, and I start back up to my room. I keep thinking about what Lily said. *You have her spirit.*

Dad told me I knew Gram's heart.

I want to believe them so badly. But how do I know if it's true? How do I find the real Gram?

Whenever I have a problem, her voice echoes in my head, *I like to retrace my steps.*

Maybe if I retrace *her* steps, I can find something to explain what she was hiding. My heart lifts as I think that maybe she even left me something to explain it. I just haven't found it yet.

I take the last few stairs two at a time. I decide to start with the studio because that's the one room in Gram's house that no one's been in much since she died. She could have left something there for me in plain sight and I wouldn't know it.

It hits me as soon as I walk in—that smell of paint and canvas so strong that, for a second, I'm sure I'll look up to see Gram sitting at her easel.

I think part of the reason no one's really come in here is because none of us knows what to do with the paintings that she never finished.

They're all landscapes—of the river and meadows mostly, one of Old Joe's farm at sunset, and one of a garden with a lily pond. I've never seen that one before—the painting or the garden. Gram was painting it in the same broad, swooping strokes and bright, contrasting colors that she always used. They made everything come to life.

Tearing my gaze from the unfinished paintings, I search the room top to bottom. The rain beats on the old windowpanes, making them rattle as I look in her desk drawers, then in her filing cabinets. I even walk around, bouncing lightly on each floorboard in hopes that one might be loose.

But there's nothing.

Disappointed, I pad down the hall to my room. I look under the bed, run my eyes over the family pictures atop the bedside table, then search the bureau drawers.

My heart gives a hopeful leap when I find a stack of pictures in the bottom bureau drawer, but they are all of Gram, Grandpa, and Dad right after he was born. Turns out, he really *was* a fat baby.

The last place I search is the closet.

And that's where I find it, tucked up in the very darkest corner, behind one of Gram's floor-length dresses.

A small green shoebox with faded golden writing.

It takes me a while to realize that I've seen it before.

It was the winter afternoon years ago when I'd come in to find Gram looking out the window at the snow, and she'd been angry at me for not knocking. She had been so strange that day, telling me I didn't ever have to come to Morning Glory Cottage if I didn't want to. *I want this house to be a happy place for you*, she'd said.

There had been two things on her lap: *The World at the End of the Tunnel* by R. M. Wildsmith. And this shoebox, which she'd shoved under the bed. But then we'd started reading *The World at the End of the Tunnel* for the first time, and I had barely given the box another thought.

But now, all these years later, here it is.

I pry it open carefully because the box is really old, the cardboard soft under my fingers.

Inside, there are three things. The first is a book of poems by somebody called Gerard Manley Hopkins. I flip through it to see that someone—Gram, probably—has underlined certain phrases and words and starred some of the poems.

I put the book aside in favor of the next thing I see in the box: a picture.

It's a framed family portrait of a man, a woman, and a girl. The man stands over them both, with a hand on each of their shoulders. The photo is in color, but deeply faded. And there's something very odd about it. Nobody is smiling.

The man kind of resembles Dad, except he wears a smugly satisfied expression that I can't imagine on Dad's face. The woman has an upturned nose and a prim smirk that I can't quite call a smile because there's no joy in it.

They certainly look stern.

And the girl—the girl is a teenaged Gram. Actually, she looks a lot like Lily. Her hair is curled into cheerful ringlets, and she wears a bright, pretty dress, but if you look past those things, you can tell that she's unhappy. In fact, she's wearing the very same look she wore that day I came in to find her holding this shoebox. Like some secret sadness had followed her all the way from this picture to that moment.

I gingerly place the photo on top of the poetry book and pick up the last thing in the box. It's a little notebook, the pages brittle as fallen leaves. Inside, the lined sheets are covered with drawings instead of writing. Little sketches of fairy couples dancing in the moonlight, gnomes peeking out from hollowed trees, a stone palace with turrets spiraling up from each corner. Every page is filled.

I run my fingers over the tiny valleys made by the pen that pressed against these pages so long ago, and I remember the only thing Gram ever told me about her childhood. She used to play in the Spinney as a little girl, too.

Did she do these sketches in the Spinney? Sketches of things she saw, or imagined she saw? And how old was Gram when she did these? Was it before or after that picture was taken? And was the picture before or after her illness?

The truth is, Gram didn't leave me answers in any of these objects. And the more I stare at the sad girl in the picture, the more I feel like I never really knew her at all.

40

When I go down for breakfast on Monday, Lily is sitting on one side of the table. Mom has some blueprints laid out on the other. In one of the bottom corners, it says, O'SHEA HOUSE.

I literally glance at them just long enough to see the name before Mom appears behind me and starts rolling them up. "Don't look at those, please."

"Geez, Mom, it's not like they're state secrets," Lily says. "Anyway, *you* left them out."

I reward Lily with a smile. I could get used to this whole getting-along thing.

But when I turn around, Mom is staring at me with her eyebrows knitted together in the expression she has when she watches the six o'clock news.

"What?"

"You—you've got a new one," she says, brushing her thumb against the skin beside my nose.

I run upstairs to look in the mirror. Mom is right. There's a new spot on the right side of my face, just between my cheek and my nostril.

It's a tiny little spot. It shouldn't be such a shock, especially because, in lots of the pictures I've seen of people with vitiligo, it forms a pale mask around their eyes, mouth, *and* nose. I already have it around my eyes and my mouth, so what should it matter if I have it around my nose, too?

On the bus, I try to convince myself that I'm fine. I remind myself that things are already going back to normal at school.

But then in math class, when I finish rummaging in my backpack for my homework, I look down at my desk to see a folded piece of paper.

On it are two words.

Hey FREAK!

I look around, but everyone is staring at their notebooks or up at what Mr. Owens is writing on the board. One of the Graces sits behind me, right beside Sean. Was it one of them? Or was it Skyler, the girl who I caught staring at me last week?

I crumple up the note, my eyes burning with tears.

How could I have actually thought that just because I had one okay week that things were going to be normal again?

In the library at lunchtime, when Fina asks me what's wrong, I show her the note. She looks at it and scowls. "Who wrote this?"

"I don't know. The Grace with braces, maybe. Or Sean, or someone else. Someone left it on my desk. And there's more. I have a new spot."

I point to my nose.

"I can barely see it," Fina says, squinting hard behind her glasses.

"It'll probably get bigger," I say. "I thought—I thought I was kind of okay about it now. But maybe I was just okay because last week I didn't see any more spots. And nobody called me a freak."

Fina squeezes my hand. "I'm sorry someone wrote this note," she says. "And maybe there will always be a few stupid people who are mean about your vitiligo. I can't pretend that that doesn't suck. But there's also me. And I don't think you're a freak, no matter how many spots you have. Do *you* think you're a freak?"

I actually think about this for a while.

A few weeks ago, I might have said yes. It's true that

I have pale patches on my face and neck and elbows and toes. That *is* still weird, even to me. But when I look in the mirror now, I don't see a disappearing girl anymore. I see more than just my patches. I'm starting to see Emma again. Plain old normal Emma.

"No," I say finally. "I think I look different from most people. But I'm not a freak."

"So, whose opinion do you trust more? Yours and mine? Or Grace and Sean's?"

"Yours and mine, I guess."

"Thank god," Fina replies. "I was really worried for a second there. Besides, there are tons of people in the world like you, remember? Didn't you say it was like one in a hundred?"

"Yeah," I say. "I did."

She grins, and for some reason, I suddenly think again about Gram and me, standing in front of the village hall lights last Thanksgiving. How she said she loved this time of year because it was when the world finds out how *resilient* it is.

I didn't actually know what resilient means. I had to ask Gram.

It means not giving up, even when things are really tough. Like how plants can live through winter in the frozen ground and still bloom again in spring.

And I guess maybe looking different from most

285

people means I'm just going to have to be resilient now, too. To hold on tight to the Emma that I almost let slip away before. Because Fina's right. I'm not always going to be able to control whether people call me names or write mean notes.

But I also can't let those things control me.

"Emma?" Fina says. "Did I say something wrong?"

"No," I reply. "No, I was just thinking. Everything you said was right. Totally, one hundred percent right."

Then we spend the rest of the lunch period talking about what Dad told me about Gram's childhood and what I found in her closet.

"Madeline Mitchell is the only one who can answer my questions about Gram," I say after I'm done. "We have to go talk to her. Tomorrow."

"Tomorrow," Fina says with a nod. "After school."

41

The rest of the day is surprisingly okay. I feel like I just got back a test that I thought I had flunked, but I actually did really well.

I got a new spot *and* got called a freak. And I survived.

I'm okay. And the fact that I'm okay somehow makes me feel much better than okay.

There really is something to this whole resiliency thing.

When the last bell rings, I find myself hovering outside Ms. Singh's doorway. I wait until the last few kids trickle out, then I step in.

"Hi, Ms. Singh."

She looks up from the papers she's shuffling on her desk and smiles. "Hi, Emma," she says. "How's your day been?"

"Pretty good. What about yours?"

"Long but good," she replies.

"Ms. Singh? I, um, heard someone say that you know someone else with vitiligo."

Technically, I heard it myself, but I still don't want Ms. Singh to know I was standing outside her door when she lectured everyone about being nice to me.

All afternoon, I've been thinking about what Fina said. There *are* other people like me. Lots of them.

Her eyebrows lift before she shakes the surprise from her face. "That's right," she replies. "Two people, actually. One friend from high school and one from college."

"What do they do?" I ask.

"Hmmm, well, one's a lawyer," she says. "The other does something with music production, I think. He lives in Hollywood, anyway."

"Oh, wow," I say. "And are they—I mean—what does their vitiligo look like?"

"Well, the lawyer has some on her face, and the music producer has it mostly on his hands and feet, I think. I don't keep in touch with him much. But the lawyer is one of my good friends. If you ever—well, if you want to talk with someone about it, I'm sure she would be happy to talk to you."

The whole time I felt so alone because of my vitiligo, I never even thought about talking to someone else who had it. Never thought, until today, that it might help me feel less lonely. But actually, it would be really nice to talk to somebody who's gone through what's happening to me. Someone who doesn't have to try to understand. Who just . . . *understands*. "Thanks, Ms. Singh," I reply. "That would be great."

"Sure thing. I'll give her a call after the Thanksgiving break. And Emma? Are things, you know, going okay for you? Here at school, I mean?"

"They're—" I start, thinking about the crumpled note now lying in the library trash can. "I think they're going to be, Ms. Singh. I think they're going to be more than okay."

"Glad to hear it, Emma," she says, beaming.

A few minutes later, while I'm waiting for Mom to pick me up, I google "famous people with vitiligo" and scroll through the list. Turns out, not only is there a supermodel with vitiligo, there are actors and singers and politicians— even a ballerina. The pale spots sprinkled across her dark chest twinkle in the stage lights like stardust.

And the best part is, the comments section of the article isn't filled with trolls calling the people in the article awful names.

It's filled with people saying how beautiful they are, how unique and brave.

My chest feels warm inside by the time I'm done

reading. The feeling floats with me out into the parking lot when Mom's car pulls up.

"How was your day, sweetie?" she asks.

"It was pretty good."

"Well, that's great!" she replies brightly. "We need to stop at the grocery store before we go home. There're still some things I need to get for Thanksgiving. Actually, can you pull my list out of my bag? I want you to write down a couple more things before I forget them."

I grab her briefcase in the back seat and start rummaging through the papers inside.

"No, not my briefcase," she says. "My purse."

But I'm already pulling out a list from the briefcase.

Not a grocery list. Another list.

"Emma, put that back, please."

But I've already started to read it. And the more I read, the more the warm feeling slips away.

Questions for Dr. Howard:

Any sign of repigmentation from the light box/creams?
Supplements/natural remedies to try?
Special diets—do these work?
Scientific trials—any promising?
What about acupuncture?
Depigmentation cream—more details?

I stare at the questions. My chest is cold and clammy now. Mom is saying something about wanting to be prepared for our next appointment, but I'm not really listening. All these questions are about treatments. Ways to get rid of my vitiligo.

I don't say anything for a long time. The tears I was fighting this morning are back.

Because as long as I have a friend like Fina, I can be resilient at school. I can make myself not care what the Graces and the Seans of the world think of me.

But I can't do that with Mom. I can't not care what she thinks of me. She's the person who's supposed to love me no matter what.

"Depigmentation cream, Mom?" I ask. "Seriously?"

I remember reading about that. It's for people with vitiligo covering a lot of their bodies who decide that getting rid of the rest of their pigment is better than being split into two colors or waiting for the rest of their color to fade away.

But my patches are still really small compared to those people's. Can my own mother really want to strip all the color left in my skin? The color I've always been proud of—the one *she* gave me?

"Well, not for now, of course," she says. "It's just to get a sense of what our options are for the future. In case, you know, the treatments we're trying now don't work. I've seen pictures of people who have no pigment in their skin, and they look very normal. Just fair-skinned."

"Would you just STOP thinking about how to make me normal, Mom?"

The words burst out of me like racehorses galloping from their gates.

"I know it must be really hard for you to have a polka-dotted daughter and everything, but maybe you could just try to *get used to it*."

I hear Mom give a little gasp. She pulls over to the side of the road and puts the car in park. I stare straight ahead, not bothering to wipe the tears running down both cheeks.

"What do you mean, Emma?" she asks, her voice shaking slightly.

"From the second I got diagnosed," I say over the sound of my blood, which seems to hum with anger, "all you've cared about is getting rid of my patches. All the creams and the light treatments and sending Lily to do my makeup. But now that I'm not wearing makeup anymore, you want me to be some guinea pig for scientific trials or take away the rest of my color so I can fit in again."

"Emma, I—"

But I can't stop the words now. "Every time you look

at me, I see you staring at my spots, trying to see if I have new ones. It's like I'm not even your daughter anymore. I'm just this big problem you can't wait to fix so you can go back to having a perfect life. Well, news flash. I'm not perfect. And neither is Lily, by the way. I'm sorry you didn't get a daughter like Edie O'Shea, but you know what, Mom? Edie isn't a very nice girl. And I would rather have spots and be nice than be popular and mean."

Now I'm done. I wrap my arms around myself, hunching my shoulders, and start to sob. Mom slowly reaches over and pets the back of my head. I scoot against the window, away from her hand. There's a long moment of silence.

Then, "Emma," Mom says again, her voice soft. "Maybe I haven't been— I haven't done the best job supporting you. I see that now. But believe it or not, up until this moment, I really thought I was doing the right thing."

"How is making a list like this supporting me?"

"I thought *you* wanted to get rid of your spots," Mom says. "You seemed so scared when you were diagnosed. So I've been researching anything that might help. Or at least give you some hope. Of course I don't want you to do the depigmenting cream. And I'm not going to put you in some trial. I just thought it would be nice for you to know if there's anything promising for the future. But was I wrong about you wanting to treat your vitiligo?"

"No," I say, sniffling. "Maybe. I don't know. I just want to know that whatever I want, it's okay with you."

She reaches over again to stroke my head, and this time I don't pull away. "Emma, of course it's okay. I thought you— Well, it doesn't matter. I should have said that right away. Maybe I didn't listen well enough. Maybe I just thought you were scared because I was."

"Scared of what?"

She sighs. "If you ever have kids, you'll know that your first priority becomes their happiness. You want to do everything you can to keep them safe and happy. You want the world to be kind to them, and that's not always something you can control." She gives a little cough, but it's not enough to disguise the waver in her voice. "When we found out you had vitiligo, I was so worried that your world might become a crueler place. I know how awful kids can be about stuff like this."

I glance at Mom. Her eyes are glistening as she stares at me. "You do?"

"Of course I do," she says. "When I was your age, I got bullied a lot at school."

"You *did*?" I'm not sure I've ever really thought about Mom being my age, but if I had, I would definitely have

294

imagined her as the most popular girl in school.

"I did. I wore hand-me-downs from my sisters because your grandma said there was no point in buying new clothes when we had perfectly good ones. She cut my hair herself, and she wasn't very good at it. She didn't know how to style it like the other girls did. And the worst part was, I had terrible acne, but I wasn't allowed to wear makeup."

Mom laughs a little and shakes her head. "As soon as I got to college, I found a part-time job and saved up all my money for new clothes. I bought magazines to teach myself to do my makeup."

I cock my head, trying to imagine Mom as a dorky kid with a bowl haircut and pimples. But I can't. It is literally impossible to see her as anything other than beautiful.

"Why didn't you ever tell me this?"

"It's not something that makes me happy to talk about," Mom says. "And when I became a mother, I didn't want you and Lily to go through what I did. I wanted to give you every advantage I could. I've always tried to protect you however I can. That's what I thought I was doing these past few months."

"So, you aren't ashamed of me?" I ask. "Not even a tiny bit?"

"Not even a microscopic bit ashamed," Mom says.

"Just very, very worried. Especially since Ms. Singh called us that week you were 'sick' to say that you were going through a hard time at school."

My heart skips a beat. "She *did*?"

Mom nods.

"What did she tell you?" I ask. "Why didn't you say anything?"

"She said that there were some rumors going around school about vitiligo and that she would address them with the students. And your dad said that if you didn't tell me, it was probably because you didn't want me to know. I wanted to say something, but I decided he was right."

I can't believe Mom's known all this time. Can't believe she knew and, instead of trying to get me to tell her all the details and find a way to fix it, just watched Netflix with me and rubbed my back. Is *that* why she's been crying at night? Not because she's ashamed, but because she's been worried about me getting bullied?

"Emma," she says, "I want you to tell me the truth now. Are kids still giving you a hard time? Is it Edie O'Shea?"

I hesitate a second before answering. "Some kids are always going to be stupid," I reply. "But I have Fina. I'm resilient. So you don't need to worry about me so much, okay?"

Mom nods. "Okay. But maybe just a little bit?"

She brushes the back of her hand against my cheek. "Yeah," I say. "Just a little bit would be nice."

"And about Edie," Mom says, then stops, biting her lip.

"What?"

"Well, I shouldn't really say anything. I'm only telling you this because I trust you not to tell anyone and because it might help you understand why Edie has been mean."

I lean in closer, waiting.

"You know the house I'm designing for her dad?"

"Yeah."

"Well, it's just for her dad. Not for Edie or her mom."

My mouth drops open. Is *that* why Mom rolled up the blueprints so quickly this morning? "You mean her dad is leaving them?"

"He already has," Mom says. "He's living in an apartment until the house is done. Something about the demands of his career being too much to balance with a family."

"That's awful," I murmur, picturing Edie red-eyed in the bathroom last week. Now I understand why she was crying. I would be, too. I can't imagine how terrible it would make me feel if Mom or Dad decided that I was "too much to balance."

"Yes, it is," says Mom. "If Edie has been bullying you,

this doesn't excuse it, but it might help explain it. It might help you see that it's got nothing to do with you."

"It's because she's so unhappy," I say.

"And misery loves company," Mom replies. "You're pretty smart for a kid your age, you know that? Smart *and* resilient. I'm so proud of you, Emma. If you ever doubt that again, all you have to do is ask, and I'll be here to remind you."

"Thanks, Mom," I murmur.

She puts the car in drive.

"Hey, Mom? One more thing. Can Fina come over after school tomorrow? We have, um, a project we're supposed to work on."

"Sure," says Mom. And as we pull away, I can't help but feel guilty. Guilty for lying to Mom about tomorrow after she told me the truth about Edie.

But not quite guilty enough to take the lie back.

42

The sun is already starting to go down by the time Fina, Mom, and I pull into the driveway of Morning Glory Cottage the next afternoon. My foot has been tapping against the floor the whole way. All day, all I've been able to think about is finally meeting Madeline Mitchell.

As soon as we get in the door, I tell Mom that Fina and I are going to walk Boomer.

"I thought you had a project to work on?" Mom asks.

"Fresh air is good for the mind, Mrs. Talbot," Fina says innocently.

"Well, don't stay out too long," Mom says, tucking a strand of hair behind my ear. "Dinner is in an hour or so."

Fina and I walk along High Street, where golden

light spills out from the windows of the houses and into the purple afternoon.

When we come to the bend in the road where the church is, we break into a run, sprinting past the orchard and the farm fields until we come to Briar Hollow Lane.

"Looks creepy," Fina murmurs, staring down the narrow, gravel road with piles of dead leaves strewn across it. "I wish we'd come when it was lighter."

"Do you want to go back?" I ask, even though I really hope she says no.

"Are you kidding? No way. And Boomer will keep us safe, won't you, boy?"

Boomer looks up, wagging his tail. Fina and I link arms and start walking. The only sounds are the leaves crunching underneath our feet and Boomer panting happily. The farther we walk, the harder he pulls.

We don't talk much. I wonder if Fina's heart is thumping in her chest like mine. If she is also thinking about Jack and Sarah stealing through the hobgoblin king's castle, looking for a way to the dungeons to free the fairy princess.

Though each corner in the corridor, each flight of steps, brought with it the possibility of new dangers, the children carried on. They had come with a mission, and they would leave with a princess.

After what feels like miles, we round a curve in the road and gasp.

A huge house looms in front of us. There's just enough light left in the sky to tell that it's white. It's three stories, or four if you count the turret that points into the sky. There's a dim glow on in one of the first-story rooms, but that's it.

This was a house that was built for a big family. For Christmases and birthday parties and summers packed with distant relatives. And now it's practically empty. You can tell by its wobbly silhouette that it's in bad shape, too.

It's like a beautiful cake baked for a wedding that never happened. And now it's been left to slowly crumble away.

"I can't believe I didn't know this was here," I whisper.

"I can't believe one little old lady lives there by herself," Fina replies.

As we get closer, we see the house is surrounded by a foreboding iron fence. But the gates leading from the drive are open.

"Almost like she's expecting company," Fina says, staring at me with moon-wide eyes. "Just like you said."

"I guess we should go knock," I say. With every tip-toed step we take, my legs feel more unsteady. My palms are sweating inside my gloves. But I make myself keep going. I have to know why Madeline's been writing to me. To know what she does about Gram.

Holding hands and breathing nervous puffs of frost into the night, we make our way onto the porch. Boomer's tail starts going nuts when we step up to the door.

"Together," Fina whispers, and each of us raises a hand and knocks gently.

My heart is beating so hard it actually hurts. I hold my breath, waiting for the door to creak open.

But it doesn't.

"Madeline?" I call after a moment. "It's Emma Talbot. I just want to talk about my gram."

Nothing.

I knock again, more firmly this time. "Madeline?"

When there's still no answer, I stand on my toes and look through the frosted windowpane in the door—the only window in the whole house that doesn't have blinds over it.

And what I see sends a bolt of fear through me.

"Fina," I say, "look. On the floor."

She stands on tiptoe next to me, drawing in a sharp gasp as she takes in the trail of red leading up to the door. "Oh, my god," she whispers. "That looks like . . . blood."

I try the handle, but it's locked. "Come on," I say, taking Fina's hand and leading her off the porch. "There's got to be another way in."

43

We stumble around the side of the house. But when we reach the back, we find that the yard is enclosed within a brick wall. I assume it's brick, anyway. It's hard to see with all the ivy growing over it.

"Look!" Fina says. "There's a door!"

I squint through the dim light to see she's right. You can just see a little iron ring that must be a handle. We both grab it at the same time and pull, then push. The door stays firmly shut.

Fina turns in a circle and points at an oak tree behind us. "I bet you I can climb that," she says. "And see that branch? It goes right over the wall. I can probably get across it and jump down."

"Are you sure?" I ask. "Maybe we should call the police."

But Fina is already climbing into the low branches of the tree. I start after her, but she looks down at me and shakes her head. "You stay here, and I'll open the door," she says. "I don't know if the branch can hold both of us."

So I stand there, biting my lip as she clambers onto the branch and sits down, then begins to scooch across it until she's reached the other side of the wall. "What do you see?" I ask.

"A garden," she says. "Hold on."

Then she takes hold of the branch with both hands and slides off it.

CRACK!

"Fina!" I yelp at the same time I hear her cry out in fear or maybe in pain. The broken branch snaps back up without her.

"Fina, are you okay?" I call. From the other side of the wall, she lets out a sob in answer. "Hold on! I'm coming!"

I push with all my weight against the door, but it won't budge.

Then Boomer and I are sprinting around, looking for another way in. It's so dark now and there's so much ivy that I don't know if I would be able to see another door even if there was one.

You have to find a way in! a voice in my head screams. *Fina is hurt! Madeline might be, too!*

But I run the whole way around the wall without seeing another way in. I turn back, planning to look again, to start tearing at the ivy if I have to, but Boomer doesn't budge. "Not now, Boomer!" I cry, pulling at his leash. "Come on!"

Instead, though, he lifts a paw to scratch at the wall. I pull back the curtain of ivy where he's scratching and see moonlight shining off another door handle.

"Good job, boy!" I say, taking hold of the handle.

I pull. It doesn't budge.

Then I push, and the door swings open.

Even though it's dark and nothing is blooming, I know the garden I'm standing in is extraordinarily beautiful.

In the corner closest to the door I came in, there is an ancient double swing-set covered in rose vines. Two oaks stand like twin guardians by the back wall, and between them is a greenhouse. At the center of the garden is a sunken lily pond with little mossy stairs that curve all the way around it.

I realize I've seen the lily pond before. This garden is the one I didn't recognize—from Gram's unfinished painting. So she's been here, and I bet Boomer has, too. That's how he knew about the door.

Fina is nowhere to be seen.

"Fina!" I call quietly. "Fina, where are you?"

I turn to see the back door of the house hanging open, and my thoughts suddenly go wild. I think of Hansel and Gretel being lured to the witch's house to be eaten.

What if this is a trick, too? What if Madeline Mitchell has done something with Fina?

I guess I'm about to find out.

I head for the door, my fingers tightening into nervous fists. Boomer trots in behind me.

The first thing that hits me when I step inside is the smell. Cooked apples.

I take another step. The furniture is old, but it looks well taken care of. The curved wooden arms of the delicate sofas shine with polish. The walls are covered in old paintings and photographs. There's no sign of Fina here, or anyone else, for that matter.

I force myself to keep going, to walk through to the next room—a dining room with a table big enough for me to lie flat on and spread my arms wide and still not touch any of the corners—and then find myself in the kitchen, where the counters are completely covered with jars and jars of homemade jam. There's a steaming pot on the stove, and I bet anything there are apples in it.

I move on to the front hall, and see what was spilled across the floor.

Not blood. More jam, and shards of glittering glass strewn across the tile.

"Fina?" I whisper again.

I'm just about to try the next room when something on the little table by the front door catches my eye. I do a double take.

The name itself isn't a shock. I've known it for years, after all. But I have no idea what it would be doing here, in this house, atop that table, typed on a crisp white envelope.

I pick the envelope up and study it.

Getty Publishing Group
195 Broadway
New York, NY 10007

R. M. Wildsmith
PO Box 47
Lanternwood, NC 27660

Before I can stop myself, I pull a letter from the envelope, which has already been opened.

Dear Mr. Wildsmith,
I hope this letter finds you well. I am writing one last time on behalf of all of us here at Getty to express

our hope that you will allow us to move forward with the fiftieth-anniversary edition of THE WORLD AT THE END OF THE TUNNEL. *As you know, sales for the book have been modest the last ten years, and we believe this edition will bring your story to a whole new generation of readers who will treasure it as so many have done before them.*

I know you are a very private individual, but perhaps we could speak on the phone at your earliest convenience? I am available to you at the number below, night or day.

Warmly (and a bit desperately),

Alexandra Homer
Head of Editorial, Getty Publishing Group
195 Broadway
New York, NY 10007
ahomer@getty.com
212-555-9191

44

I feel a long breath leave my body as I quickly thumb through the rest of the envelopes on the table. They are all the same—all addressed to R. M. Wildsmith, all from the Getty Publishing Group.

But what are they doing *here*?

"Emma," croaks a voice.

I whirl around.

Madeline Mitchell is standing behind me. Boomer's tail goes crazy again, and he wags his way over to her. She gives him a stiff pat on the head. Of course if he's been here, he must have met her before.

I'm still holding the letter in my hand. "Ms. Mitchell," I say. I mean to let it go, but my grip around the sheet of paper only tightens. "I didn't—I don't— Where's Fina?"

Her gaze lands on the letter. I've seen her before, of course, but I've never really *seen* her until now. The sunken cheeks and blue-gray eyes, the wispy eyebrows and silver hair, the shoulders knotted around her ears.

"You'd better come with me," she says finally, without even looking at me. Her voice comes as a shock. Like hearing a painting speak. "Watch your step. I'm afraid I—I was startled to see you and your friend walking up the drive."

She gestures to the broken glass, then turns around and disappears through a dark doorway.

After a second's hesitation, I follow her through another kind of living room and into a study. A bright fireplace sends light dancing over the shelves and shelves of books stacked every possible way. The room is filled with the smell of their pages.

A big chair is in front of the fireplace, and nestled up in it is Fina. Her left foot is propped on a stool with a bag of frozen peas over her ankle.

"Emma!" she says, sitting up when she sees me.

"You're okay," I say breathlessly, rushing over to her. "I heard you yell, and by the time I found a way in—"

"Madeline brought me in," Fina says. "She was just going to find you. She thinks I sprained my ankle."

"That's all?" I ask. "I thought you were really hurt or something."

Fina makes a face. "It *does* hurt."

"Would you like a s-seat?" Madeline asks quietly, gesturing toward a chair on the other side of the hearth. She still doesn't quite look at me when she speaks. Her voice rattles like a cold wind blowing the last of the autumn leaves from the treetops.

"Okay," I say uncertainly.

I can't tell if she's angry or not. She seems more nervous than anything. Her hands chase each other in circles on her lap as she takes a wooden rocking chair in the darkest corner of the study. Boomer circles around the room once, then lies down next to her.

Isn't she going to say anything about the fact that she just caught me reading mail that wasn't mine? Or that Fina and I broke into her garden?

I pass the letter to Fina before I sit, giving her a meaningful look. She glances down, and her eyes widen as she starts to read. And then, for a long, extremely uncomfortable minute, no one says a thing. The fire crackles.

"Um," Fina says finally, holding up the letter, "what is this?"

"Why do you have R. M. Wildsmith's mail?" I ask.

Madeline leans forward just far enough so her face is lit in the orange glow of the fire.

"I think you can put it together," she rasps.

And she's right.

Madeline Mitchell suddenly transforms. She is not the Apple Lady anymore. She never has been. All along, she has been the fairy queen in beggar's clothes.

"*You're* R. M. Wildsmith?" Fina asks. "*You* wrote *The World at the End of the Tunnel?*"

Madeline flinches, like a spark from the fire has just landed on her skin. She begins to rock, back and forth, back and forth. "The answer to your first question is yes, technically speaking, I am R. M. Wildsmith. Or as close as anyone alive could be. The answer to the second is more complicated."

"But I thought R. M. Wildsmith was a man," Fina says.

"People are good at assuming things," Madeline says quietly.

"But you didn't correct them," I reply. "You never told anyone who you were?"

"No."

A thought strikes me like lightning. "Gram," I murmur, thinking of the hours and hours we spent together reading *The World at the End of the Tunnel.* "Did she know the truth?"

Madeline Mitchell does the weird, flinchy thing again. Then she gives a bark of humorless laughter. "*Know* the truth?" she says. "She *is* the truth."

Fina and I glance at each other. "Is that some kind of riddle?" she asks. "I mean, we know you two were friends."

Madeline's lips pucker. For the first time, she looks at me. Just for a second. "Friends," she repeats, as if testing out whether her tongue can form the word. "Yes, I suppose we were. I am—I'm sorry for your loss, Emma. Your grandmother was a good woman. The best I ever knew."

"She's been reading me your book ever since I can remember," I say. "But she never said anything about you."

"She was protecting me."

"From what? Why didn't you want me to know? Why do you hide away from everyone?"

Madeline pulls a quilt from the back of the chair and wraps it around her frail frame. She doesn't say anything for another long minute. Instead, she gazes at the patterns of light on the ceiling until her eyes seem to mist over. I'm just starting to wonder if she's, you know, *all there* when she looks down at me again. The fire sparkles in her eyes.

"Your face," she says. "You have vitiligo?"

I feel my body give a little jerk. What does my vitiligo have to do with anything?

"Um, yes?"

"Why does that matter?" Fina asks, scowling.

"I wondered. Your story. Ivy slowly disappearing into the snow. It seemed too much of a coincidence. I assume it started to spread after your gram died?"

I nod slowly. Goose bumps creep up my arms. How does she know that?

"I think—I think I'll tell you a story of my own now," Madeline says. "Yes, I think it's what she would want."

"You mean Gram?"

Madeline ignores me. She keeps rocking backward and forward in her chair. Backward and forward. "I know what people say about me, you know. They call me odd. Strange. Crazy. When I was a girl, the names weren't any nicer. I've never liked people, you see. Never understood them.

"I went to school, but only because my parents forced me. Every day there was torturous. The rest of the time, I stayed here, safe with my books and my garden. Until night fell. Then I would go for walks in the forest on my own. I liked the quiet. The company of the trees and the moon. How I wished *I* could be the moon, watching everything from the safety of the distant sky. How peaceful it would be."

Her voice trails off in a kind of whisper, and she looks lost in her wish.

"I liked knowing I wouldn't run into anyone," she

says after a moment. "Until one night I did."

Backward and forward she rocks, all the time staring into the fire.

"She told me she was a fairy princess escaped from the house where she was being kept by an evil pair of goblins. They had locked her away from the world, and only at night, when they were deep asleep, could she be free from their tyranny. Every night, when the moon rose, she rose with it, and through the woods she ran, laughing into the wind.

"We became friends, the two of us, the fairy princess and the outcast child. Neither of us belonged to the day, so we lived our lives at night, and what wondrous lives they were. How the world transformed when the fairy princess looked at it. Streams became vast rivers; rocks became castles. The forest became a kingdom trapped under a curse of darkness."

"You mean Gram," I interrupt as the pieces click into place in my mind. "She's the girl you met in the woods? The fairy princess who had been locked away?"

Madeline nods.

"But we thought she was sick," Fina says. "That's why she couldn't go out."

"*No*," Madeline snaps, slapping her hand down on the arm of her chair. She stops rocking. "Her parents were the ones who were sick."

"What are you talking about?" I nearly shout. Why can't she just say what she means?

She glances at me again. "You haven't yet guessed?" she asks. "You do know that your condition can be hereditary?"

For a second, I don't know what she's saying. Then I remember the pamphlet Dr. Howard gave me. The one that said vitiligo can sometimes run in families. "But Gram didn't have vitiligo," I say slowly.

"Some secrets hide themselves away in the shadows like me," Madeline rasps. "Others hide from us in plain sight."

I picture Gram sitting next to me in the Spinney. Her long flowing dresses, fifty years out of style. Her fingers twirling the handle of her parasol. I always thought it was to protect her dove-white skin.

What had I thought when I first got diagnosed? *I almost wish I'd inherited Gram's skin color instead. Then you would barely be able to see a difference between my spots and the rest of me.*

I think about the pictures I've seen online, of people with vitiligo who have lost all their color, who turn the most delicate shades of pale. Pale like Gram.

The pieces all fit so snugly, I can't believe I never saw it before. But then, Gram hadn't told me, had she? And until a few months ago, I had never even *heard* of vitiligo.

"She didn't always look the way she did when you knew her," Madeline says. "The paleness crept up on her slowly. It took many months for it to cover her completely. At least, the parts other people could see."

"I don't understand. If all that was wrong with her was vitiligo, why did she have to stay inside during the day?"

"I've told you, haven't I, that her parents were the sick ones? They were the kind of people who did everything for show. All that mattered to them was their reputation. And things were different back then. Conditions like vitiligo were not well understood. They frightened people. People would have talked behind cupped hands. Your gram might have become an outcast, like me. Her parents couldn't let that happen. So she spent her days with only her tutor and her books for company. They told her they were protecting her. That it was for the best."

I feel like someone has punched me in the stomach. I think about everything I went through at school after Edie's text. I can only imagine how much worse it would have been sixty years ago, before you could google vitiligo and find out what it really was.

But that's no reason to keep a child locked away from the world. I feel heat rising in my cheeks as I imagine Gram trapped in Morning Glory Cottage, forced to live behind her curtains. All because of something she couldn't control. The same something that's happening to me.

The pages of my mind flip back once more to the snowy afternoon when I'd run into her room to find her staring out the window.

I don't want you to ever feel like you have to come, do you understand? she said. *I want this house to be a happy place for you.*

Because it hadn't been a happy one for Gram. Morning Glory Cottage had been more like a prison. And Gram had been just like Rapunzel, locked up in her tower.

"Madeline?" Fina asks softly. "You said that it was Emma's gram who came up with the story about the fairy princess captured by goblins and a world that's been cursed with darkness. But that's—that's the story from *The World at the End of the Tunnel*."

An electric jolt goes through my heart. *The World at the End of the Tunnel* had sat there that snowy day, right on Gram's lap. Along with the shoebox containing the picture of her parents, the book of poems, and the sketchbook.

A sketchbook full of fairies and gnomes and palaces. I had thought they were drawings Gram had done of the charmed folk in the Spinney.

But what if they were creatures from the Golden-grove? Characters from *The World at the End of the Tunnel*?

Barely able to breathe, I look over at Madeline. Glistening tears are gathering on her cheeks. The wrinkles on her face catch them like silver fish in a net.

"When your gram lost the last of the color in her skin, her parents rejoiced. She was *normal* again." Madeline spits the word out. "They told everyone she'd miraculously recovered from her illness. It had been so long since anyone had seen her properly, no one even noticed that her skin was a different color. Besides, it *would* be pale, wouldn't it, after months and months stuck inside? The curse was broken. She no longer had to live her life by night.

"She went back to school and made other friends. She was so very good at it. Oh, she and I were still friends, too, of course, but it wasn't the same. It was never the same. Then she grew up and went away to college and met her husband. I was the only one who still remembered the fairy princess and the world cursed to darkness. I was the only one who still lived in the Dimwood, yearning for the day it would transform into the Goldengrove."

"But—" Fina says, "I mean, why did *you* write the story?"

"She left the story!" Madeline cries. "She pulled me into it and made me believe. She finally gave me a world where I could belong. And then she left! So one day, I sat down, and I began to write. I invented a boy and a girl to go into the Goldengrove, and I used the tales your gram had spun to create their adventures. And then I—I sent it to a publisher."

"You stole her story?" I whisper.

"I had nothing else," murmurs Madeline, rocking again. "I didn't know—I had no idea—what it would become. I didn't think she would ever see it."

"But she did," Fina says. "Everyone saw."

"Her copy of the book," I say suddenly, another puzzle piece lodging in place. "There's an inscription in it. *'For my muse and best friend.'*"

It had never even occurred to me that the inscription was from the *author*. That it meant that Gram was the muse for the book itself.

"She asked me to sign it," Madeline says miserably. "I didn't want to. It was the only copy I ever signed. You see why I signed no more. You see why no one can ever know the truth about R. M. Wildsmith."

Madeline's hand floats to her mouth as a sob escapes her lips.

"B-b-because there is no R. M. Wildsmith," she says, hiccuping. "There was only a girl who was bitter in her

320

loneliness and a better girl who found it in her heart to forgive the other. She was never even angry with me. After her parents died and she returned to Lanternwood, she came to see me. She told me she understood. She said she was happy for my success, as if it were ever really mine. I thought she had forgotten me, you see, but I was wrong. She was the only one who didn't. Until the very end, she came. She visited. She kept my terrible secret. And now I am alone again."

Tears are rolling down my cheeks, too. Because all at once, I understand why Gram kept so much from me. Not because she didn't trust me, but because she didn't want to betray Madeline's secret. And my heart is nearly bursting with pride. Gram, *my* Gram, was the one who dreamed the Goldengrove and the Dimwood into life.

At the same time, though, I feel heavy with the weight of knowing everything she had to go through. Everything that Madeline is *still* going through. I'm not the only one who misses Gram terribly. She was Madeline's best friend, too.

"Did you leave the flowers on her grave?" Fina asks. "Was it you we saw in the graveyard on Halloween?"

Madeline is blank for a moment, then gives a nod. "From my greenhouse," she says. "I didn't mean to frighten you. I don't like talking to people. It's very—difficult for me."

"That's why you wear your headphones when you walk," I say. "So no one will try to talk to you."

"Music," she mumbles, her voice childlike now. "It calms me. I go to church to hear it. And it gives me the courage to go out walking. I don't like them to go to waste, you know. The berries and the apples. Flowers and the trees—I understand *them*. Being with them makes me feel less alone. It's people that make me feel lonely."

I cross the room and kneel down in front of Madeline. "You're not alone," I say.

I take one of her hands. Her skin is thin and soft as silk. I squeeze her hand—gently—because I know it's what Gram would do if it were me sitting in that chair crying. Because when I was alone and afraid after Gram died, it was Madeline who wrote back to me in the journal.

"Such a kind child," she says. "Just like your grandmother. Who else would be so kind to an old fraud?"

"But you aren't a fraud," I say. "Not really. People don't just read that book for the story. It's the way it's written, too. Besides, if you hadn't turned Gram's stories into a book, nobody ever would have gotten to read *The World at the End of the Tunnel*. Gram loved it, you know. She must have read it to me a dozen times."

Madeline gives a little sniff, and for the first time since we've come, her face seems to relax a bit. "Your

322

gram told me everything about you when she came for her visits," she says. She reaches her free hand out like she's going to stroke my cheek, but then she folds it back in her lap. "She told me when she took you to the Golden— Ah, but she called it something else with you. The Spinney, wasn't it? She told me when she took you there the first time."

"And the journal?" I ask. "Did you always know about it?"

"She told me how you took turns writing in it. I still walk in the woods at night, and sometimes I would go there and read the stories in the journal. I read the chapter you wrote after she died. I don't know what possessed me, but I thought—I thought you would be missing her, like I was. I thought perhaps you would be less lonely if someone wrote back."

"You were right," I reply. "I did miss her, and it did help. A lot."

Madeline says nothing to this. Like the idea she could actually help someone sounds impossible to her. Like she really does think of herself as a fairy-tale witch.

"We can keep visiting you," I say. "Just like Gram did."

Fina nods. "Definitely."

"No," Madeline says. "No, I couldn't ask that of you."

"It's what Gram would want," I reply. "And—" I hesitate for a moment. But I know what I'm about to say is true. And I think Gram would want me to say it. "She would want you to let your publishers do that new edition of *The World at the End of the Tunnel*."

"Yeah," Fina says eagerly. "It's like the letter says. Think of all the kids who would read it!"

"No," says Madeline again. "I am done taking credit for someone else's ideas."

"You wouldn't have to. You could tell the truth. You could write it in the new edition. Maybe—maybe it would make you feel better?"

Then I think about all the people who would come in droves to see the Spinney—the real Goldengrove—if they knew the *whole* truth.

"You could stay anonymous," I add quickly. "No one would know your real name or even Gram's."

She gets that faraway look again as she stares into the fire. "I—I hadn't thought . . . ," she starts, but then her voice trails off.

Suddenly my phone begins to ring. Madeline jumps in her chair like a bird startled from its branch. "Sorry," I say. I pull the phone out of my pocket. It's Lily.

I silence the call and look at the time. Seven o'clock. We've been gone almost an hour and a half. I glance over at Fina. "We have to go," I say.

Madeline clears her throat. "Your parents will be worried," she replies, standing up.

She's right. They will be worried. And I've never been so grateful in my life to have someone to worry about me like that. Someone who cares about me enough to worry.

I help Fina to stand. "I'll tell them to come get us at the top of the driveway," I say. I don't want them pulling up in front of Madeline's house and knocking on her door. Something tells me she's had enough company for one night. "Can you make it that far?"

"Yeah," Fina says, putting her foot down and wincing. "I think so."

I text Mom where to get us. Then we follow Madeline back to the door, where Fina hands her the letter from the publisher. "So, will you think about the new edition?" she asks. "And what Emma said?"

"I will," Madeline says slowly. "I will . . . think about it."

I smile at her as she opens the door and cold air rushes in. Fina hobbles out onto the porch.

"Madeline," I say, "thank you for telling us the truth. It means a lot. But can I ask you one more thing?"

We need to go—Mom is probably going to be really mad at me—but I just have to know. There's one thing Gram kept from me that I still don't understand.

Madeline looks at me, waiting.

"Why do you think Gram didn't tell me about her vitiligo? Is it because she was ashamed, like her parents were?"

She blinks, slowly, then shakes her head. "Your grandmother was never ashamed of who she was. But I think she wanted people to see the color she put into the world. Not the color that had been taken from her skin."

"Yeah," I reply, imagining Gram sitting by the river, a paintbrush in her hand. "That sounds like her."

"Interesting that your vitiligo should come on after she died," Madeline murmurs just as I turn away.

"Why?"

"My understanding is these things are often brought on by—what's the word?—*traumas*."

I'm pretty sure Dr. Howard's pamphlet said something about vitiligo getting triggered by certain things—except it used the word "stress." I never thought about it being triggered by Gram's death, though, because "stress" is a word you use to describe how you feel before a big test. Not how you feel when your grandmother—who also happens to be your best friend—dies.

"I thought I was cursed," I mumble. "First Gram and then my skin."

Madeline reaches out once more, her hand trembling slightly, and this time she does brush it against my cheek. "You are not cursed," she says. "Every spot you get is just more proof."

"Proof of what?"

"Of how much you loved your gram, of course. Of how much you'll always love her. And there is nothing in this world more beautiful than love, Emma Talbot."

As I turn to go, my heart feels like it's splitting open and being mended back together at the very same time.

45

Mom and Dad aren't just worried when Fina, Boomer, and I appear at the top of Briar Hollow Lane. They're furious. Then they see that Fina is limping, and they go back to worrying.

"What happened?" Mom says breathlessly. "Why didn't you call us? What are you doing out here?"

Instead of answering, I throw my arms around her, then Dad.

"Let them get in the car, hon," Dad says over my shoulder. I release him, and he opens the back seat door and helps Fina in, Boomer jumping in after her.

He and Mom ask Fina about a dozen times if she thinks her ankle could be broken, and by the time she's finally convinced them that it doesn't hurt that much, we're home. So it's not until we're back sitting around the table in the kitchen of Morning Glory Cottage— me, Fina, Mom, Dad, and Lily—that I get to explain where we've been.

I tell them everything.

Well, almost everything. I don't tell them about sneaking out of the house on Halloween or about our stakeout. I do tell them about the journal, though, and how someone was writing to me and how we figured out that it was Madeline Mitchell.

I tell them what we heard from Old Joe, Gloria, and Ruth, and Dad's face goes pale. Mom brings her fingers to her lips.

"Sick?" Dad asks. "What was she sick with?"

Fina and I take turns explaining everything Madeline told us. About *The World at the End of the Tunnel* and Gram's vitiligo.

Then a few seconds tick by in silence.

Dad rubs his face with his palms, shaking his head. "I can't believe she never told us."

"Which part?" Mom asks.

"Any of it," Lily says. "All of it. How could Gram's parents be so cruel?" She bites her lip. Her eyes shine.

Mom, who is sitting between me and Lily, puts an

arm around each of us, but she looks at me. "I know. The world was a different place back then, but I can't imagine doing something like that to a child, then or ever. I really can't."

"Her long dresses and that parasol," says Lily. "I thought she just liked dressing weird."

"She was always so careful about her skin," Dad muses. "Always. She used to say she burned very easily. I just thought she was being overly cautious."

"But she had no pigment in her skin," finishes Mom. "So she *had* to protect it from the sun. Or she could have done a lot of damage."

"Now I know why she didn't like talking about her childhood," Dad says quietly. "But it's easy to see where her imagination came from, isn't it? It's how she got through it."

"I found her sketchbook upstairs," I tell them. "It's full of drawings of fairies and things that she did, probably when she was stuck inside. All her ideas."

"Let me get this straight," Lily says, running a hand through her hair. "You're saying that our grandmother was a famous author? Or she would have been, except this Madeline woman plagiarized her story?"

"The ideas were all Gram's," I say. "But she was never angry at Madeline for using them. She's been visiting her all these years. And I bet she was glad that Madeline got the book published. Otherwise, nobody would have ever gotten to read it."

"I wondered why she liked that book so much," Dad says. "She was always trying to get me to pick it up as a kid."

There's a knock at the door, and Boomer starts barking his head off.

Mom gets up. "That must be Fina's parents."

"What are you going to tell them?" Fina asks.

"Everything," Mom replies. "But only when I call your mom tomorrow morning. Hopefully by then, you'll have told them everything first."

Fina nods. "Fair enough, Mrs. Talbot."

Mom and I walk her to the doorway, and when we get there, Fina wraps her arms around me in a big hug.

"Being friends with you," she says, "has turned out to be a pretty cool adventure."

46

At long last, Jack and Sarah laid down their swords. The hobgoblin king had fled into the night with his queen, leaving his wrought iron crown to clatter to the ground. Sarah picked it up and flung it out the window after him. And then a most strange and wonderful thing happened. The sky, which had been black as an empty hearth since the children arrived, burst into a garden of color. Slowly at first, then all at once, it blossomed purple, then pink, now orange and gold.

Somewhere, the escaped fairy princess was laughing to make the sun rise, and Jack and Sarah began to laugh, too. From all over the

kingdom came sounds of merriment and rejoic-
ing. The curse was lifted, the darkness banished.
Dawn had broken over the Goldengrove at last.

I feel goose bumps prickling up and down my arms. It's late, but I can't sleep, so I've been reading the last chapters of *The World at the End of the Tunnel*. It feels so different now, knowing that Gram is at the center of it all. I find myself looking for her behind every line. And for the first time since she died, I feel like I've found her again.

When I've read until the very end, and Jack and Sarah are tucked once more into their own beds, I creep out of mine. I go downstairs and look in the freezer. There's mint chocolate-chip ice cream. Not exactly a warm slice of Gram's apple pie, but it'll have to do.

I take the carton, sit down in my usual seat, and look across the table at the one where Gram always sat.

And for a moment, if I close my eyes and open them again in the just right way—if I look *through* my eyes instead of with them, like Gram taught me—I can almost see her there. I can imagine her, at least. Her skin the color of clouds just before the sun starts to set, her long silver braid hanging down her back, a crooked-tooth smile dancing on her face.

"Can't sleep, darlin'?" she says.

"No. My head is too loud."

"Ah, yes. Thoughts can be pesky that way. Care to share one?"

I take a bite of ice cream, feeling the coldness of it seep into my tongue.

"I'm sorry, Gram," I say. "I've been angry at you. For telling me all those fairy tales. For making me write them, too, and most of all, for making me believe in them. You always said there was truth in every story, but after you died, all I could see were lies."

"Oh? What kind of lies?"

"Like how those stories always have happy endings."

"And you don't believe in those anymore?"

"I don't *not* believe them," I say, thinking. "But I don't think they're the truest part of the fairy tales. I think they're just the part people remember."

Gram's smile deepens. "Go on."

"The true part is that there's always a battle. Jack and Sarah had to fight the troll army and the hobgoblin king. Hansel and Gretel had to beat the witch and find their way out of the forest. I don't think you can know how your story ends, but the ending is always better if you're willing to fight for it. That's why you told me all those stories, and made me write my own. That's what you wanted to teach me. To fight for myself."

"Very good," Gram says. "But there's another reason, too. Can you guess?"

I think about this for a minute, digging my spoon around the ice cream carton to find the biggest chocolate chips. "Your sketchbook. Dad says your imagination is what helped you get through the time you were trapped inside."

"Imagination is one of the greatest gifts we have. If we build it up strong enough, it can be anything we need it to be. A home. A friend. A whole entire world."

She's still smiling. Drinking me in with her eyes.

"A world like the Goldengrove," I say.

Gram winks. "My secret is discovered at last, hmm? Was it wrong that I hoped one day you might uncover it?"

"No," I say. "And I understand why you didn't tell me about Madeline and the book. But I wish you'd told me about your vitiligo, Gram. It would have made it so much easier for me to know that you had it, too."

"I knew you would have a battle to face one day," Gram says. "But I didn't know it would be this one. If I had, of course I would have told you. But I didn't want to worry your father or you about something I didn't think would happen. And I didn't want anyone to worry about *me* or treat me any differently."

I nod. "Yeah. I get that. But, Gram? I'm really sorry for what your parents did. I thought I had it rough with Mom, but I was wrong."

I've been wrong about a lot, come to think of it. I was so set in my own way of seeing things that I forgot that there is always another way to look at them.

Gram flicks her wrist. "It's just like you said, Emma. We all have our battles. I fought mine, and I won. Now you're fighting yours. And I'm so proud of you."

"Madeline says that each one of my spots is more proof of my love for you."

Gram's eyes sparkle. "And proof of your courage and strength."

"I never needed a lot of those things until you died."

"Well, the battles we fight always change us. When we're fighting them, all we can see is how they wound us. But they can change us for the better, too."

I wonder how different Gram would be if she'd never gotten vitiligo. If she ever would have imagined the Goldengrove or grown up to paint the world full of color.

I wonder if she would have been so kind to an outcast like Madeline if she had never known what unkindness felt like.

Maybe without her vitiligo, she wouldn't be the Gram I know. Maybe she would have turned out to be someone else completely.

"It's getting late," she says softly.

"I don't want to leave you, Gram," I reply. Tears fill my eyes.

"It's all right. You know where to find me now, Emma. And for what it's worth, I *did* get my happy ending. I got you."

I blink back my tears, and when I open my eyes again, she's gone. I'm the only one sitting here at the table.

But somehow, I don't feel alone.

47

There really should be a rule against having to go to school on days when there is absolutely no way you can concentrate. When Fina and I meet in our usual spot the next morning, she just keeps shaking her head and saying, "I can't believe it. I *can't believe* it."

We huddle together by the corner of the building, trying to stamp away the cold. "All that time, Emma, you've been playing in the Goldengrove. *The* Golden-grove! *And I've been there, too!*"

"I know," I say, smiling. "And you recognized it. Remember? You said the sycamore tree reminded you of the Council Tree. I bet it *was*. And the stream was the Ivory River, and Throne Rock was Fernlace. It's funny, I never thought about any of that until you pointed it out. But you saw it right away."

"I guess sometimes you can't see things that are right in front of you," she replies. "I mean, your own grandmother—she invented the Goldengrove. Aren't you freaking out?"

I laugh. "It's weird. I probably should be, but I guess . . . it doesn't feel like that much has actually changed. I always knew Gram was amazing at coming up with stories."

"Yeah, but I mean, don't you wish she'd told you? That she came up with *that* story?"

"I don't think so," I say. "Because she couldn't have told me without telling me about Madeline, could she? She didn't want to betray her friend. Besides, if I'd only ever thought of the Spinney as the Goldengrove, I never would have come up with my own stories, you know?"

"Okay, good point," Fina says.

I feel someone looking at me, and sure enough, when I glance around, there's a girl standing by the flagpole, staring. It's Skyler, the same girl I caught staring at me in math class last week. I try to ignore her.

"Were your parents mad?" I ask.

"A little," Fina says. "But then my mom found out

that my dad still hasn't gotten a turkey for tomorrow, and she kind of forgot to be mad at me anymore."

"Um," squeaks a voice.

We both look up. Skyler has moved closer. She's standing almost right next to me, clutching her books tightly to her chest. "You're Emma, right?" she says. "I think we have math together."

"Yeah," I reply, glancing at Fina.

"I'm Skyler," she says. "I, um, I like your boots."

"Oh, thanks." I look down. I'm wearing the same boots I wore yesterday, and they're still splattered with mud from walking up and down Briar Hollow Lane. I have a feeling that Skyler did *not* come over here to talk about my boots.

"You guys are new here this year, right?" she says, her ears turning scarlet as she speaks. "I just started this month. This girl in my gym class, Ruby, she said— well—it's stupid—but she said I should come talk to you."

By now, Skyler's voice is little more than a nervous whisper. She watches as Fina and I exchange a bewildered glance. *Ruby* sent Skyler to talk to us? But why?

Fina waves to Skyler. "I'm Fina."

Skyler tries to wave back and ends up dropping some of her books. Fina and I both lean down to help her with them.

"Hey!" Fina says, picking up a book called *The One and Only Ivan*. "I love this one!"

"Oh! Me, too," says Skyler, breaking into a toothy smile. "It's my third time reading it."

I hand her back her social studies book and a math worksheet. "Mr. Owens assigns a lot of homework, huh?"

"Yeah," she says. "There's way more homework here than at my last school. Or maybe that's just seventh grade."

"Maybe," I say. "Hey, why did Ruby tell you to come talk to us?"

Skyler looks sheepish. "I told her I was, um, having a hard time making friends. And she just said you guys were really cool."

So that's why Skyler walked over here. Why she's been staring at me. Not because of my patches or my boots. Because she wants to be friends.

Fina and I share another look.

"Well, even Ruby is right about something once in a while," Fina says, grinning. "Where are you from?"

"Florida," says Skyler.

The bell rings, and the three of us walk in together, swapping stories about our old schools. Fina is still hobbling a little. Her mom and dad took her to an urgent care place last night, and it turns out Madeline was right. She sprained her ankle but not very bad.

"What happened to your leg?" Skyler asks.

"It's a long story," Fina says.

"There'll be lots of time to tell you later on," I add.

It turns out Fina and I aren't the only ones too distracted to pay attention in school today. In all my classes, everyone is talking about Thanksgiving break. At least some of the teachers are smart and decide to let us watch movies instead of actually trying to teach us stuff.

The one person who doesn't seem excited about the long weekend is Edie. I steal glances at her table during lunch that day while Fina is telling Skyler about her plans to initiate her into the New Kids Brigade, which include an elaborate secret ceremony, apparently.

My eyes keep going back and forth between Edie—dragging her fork through her food, her eyes glued to the table—and Ruby, who is talking to one of the Graces.

Halfway through my tacos, Ruby catches me looking at her. For just a second, she holds my gaze. Then she gives me the tiniest nod and looks away. And I think that maybe her saying those things to Skyler was her way of apologizing to me. Of trying to tell me that she wishes she hadn't done what she did.

Edie doesn't look up at all. I wonder if her dad is going to have dinner with them tomorrow, and if not, if Edie's thinking about what it's going to be like having Thanksgiving without him. I wonder if she's told any of her friends, but my guess is she hasn't, since she asked me not to tell anyone about seeing her crying.

I feel a pang of sympathy for her. Because I've just realized that, no matter how popular Edie seems to be, in this moment she is just as lonely as Madeline Mitchell.

48

I take the school bus home that afternoon, and when I walk into Morning Glory Cottage, Mom is on the phone in the kitchen.

"Sounds good," she chirps, waving at me when I appear.

Lily is sitting at the table reading something. As I draw nearer, I see it's *The World at the End of the Tunnel*. Not my copy. This one looks like she just bought it from the bookstore.

"Thought we were too old for books like that?" I ask.

Her lips twitch into a smile. "Okay, okay. You were right about this one. It's pretty good so far, actually. Even for a highly sophisticated college applicant like me."

"Great," Mom says. "We'll see you tomorrow! Two o'clock."

"Who are we seeing tomorrow?" I ask once Mom hangs up.

"Well," she says, smiling mischievously, "I called Ms. Ramirez this morning to check in about last night. Turns out Mr. Ramirez forgot to buy a turkey. We got to chatting, and we thought we could do a joint Thanksgiving."

"*Really?*" I squeal. I haven't said anything to anyone about it, but I've been kind of dreading tomorrow. The empty spot where Gram should have sat. Having Fina there will make it so much better.

"Both our families are missing people this year," Mom says. "So it seemed like the right thing to do."

She plants a kiss on my head, then goes upstairs to find a recipe from some old book.

I feel like a weight has been lifted off my shoulders. But annoyingly, I find my thoughts drifting back to Edie and the empty spot that will probably be at her table tomorrow. Even though I know she's the last person I should be feeling sorry for, I do. It's hard enough to miss someone you've lost. I can't imagine how hard it is to know that that someone doesn't miss you back. At least, not enough to come home.

"Hey, Lily?" I say suddenly.

"Yeah?"

"I need a favor."

She looks up from the book, raising an eyebrow.

"I need you to drive me somewhere. Tonight. And I need to borrow your book."

I think my luck may be finally starting to change, because just before ten, Mom realizes that she got buttermilk instead of heavy cream and says in an irritated voice that she'll have to go to the store.

"We'll do it," Lily and I say together. This is much better than sneaking out yet again.

Mom stares at us suspiciously. "It's too late," she says.

"There's no school tomorrow, Mom," I argue. "It doesn't matter if we go out."

"We just want to help," Lily adds convincingly. "You're already doing so much."

Here are two things you should know about Lily.

    1. She is a great liar.

    2. She is an even better sister (see #1).

"Since when do you girls do things together?" Mom asks, putting a hand on her hip.

"Honey," Dad says, looking up from the movie we'd been watching with him on the couch, "don't look a gift horse in the mouth."

"Oh, all right," Mom says. "But drive slow."

"We will," Lily replies, chancing a smile at me. "Very, very slow."

Five minutes later, we're in the car.

"I still don't understand why we're doing this," Lily says.

"I know," I reply.

But Gram would understand. She would say that what I'm doing is right. That sometimes the best thing you can do is forget about your own battle for a while and help someone else. Especially someone who is fighting a losing one.

Soon, we pull up in front of a big house with a yawning front lawn of grass that, even in the dark, you can tell is neatly clipped. All the lights are off, but somewhere on the first floor, blue television light splashes out from the windows.

"Just wait here," I say. "It'll only take a sec."

Then I climb out of the car, into the freezing-cold night, clutching the book tightly to my chest. Silently, I walk up to the porch, and I'm just about to set the book down there when the door swings open.

Edie O'Shea stares out at me from her dark house.

"Emma?"

I freeze. This was not part of the plan.

"What are you doing here?"

I look down at Lily's copy of *The World at the End of*

the Tunnel. At the story I've cherished for so long. The one that helped Gram get through her darkest years.

And suddenly I feel very, very stupid.

What am I doing here with this book? Edie is going to think I'm crazy. She's going to tell everyone at school that I'm stalking her or something.

But then I think again of Gram, and I take a deep breath.

"I just—I was going to leave this for you," I say, cheeks warm despite the cold.

Edie reaches out a hand for the book. "I've heard of this one," she says, "but I've never read it."

Her voice is different away from school. Less certain. She looks up at me and narrows her eyes. "Why did you bring this to me? After I've been so—you know—"

"Mean?" I say, before I can stop myself. Edie stiffens.

"Look, I just thought tomorrow might be kind of hard for you. And this book has gotten me through some, um, hard stuff. I just wanted you to know someone was thinking about you. That someone cared."

She crosses her arms over her chest. "You know about my dad, don't you?"

"Yeah," I admit. "My mom is working for him. Designing his new, um, house."

Edie sniffles. "I know," she says sharply. "Your mom is the reason I found out my dad was leaving, actually.

I found her business card in my dad's briefcase. That's when he told me. And I kind of hated you after that."

I feel my eyes widen with surprise. All along, I thought this was about that stupid poem. But it was so much bigger than that. "I didn't know until a couple of days ago," I reply. "And I won't tell anyone."

I'm about to turn to go when Edie speaks again. "You probably don't believe me, but I'm sorry," she says quietly. "For the picture and the text and all that. The first time I saw you on the school bus without makeup, I knew I shouldn't have done it. Because it wasn't ever really about, you know, your skin. But I didn't—I couldn't tell you that."

"Well, you kind of made my life miserable for a while," I say. "And nobody deserves to feel like I felt. But I know it sucks, what's happening with your dad. I know what it's like to lose someone. Just . . . don't do it to anyone else, okay?"

Edie nods. There's another uncomfortable moment of silence.

"Well, I should—" I say just as Edie says, "Thank you for the—"

We both laugh nervously.

"I still don't get why you're being so nice to me," Edie says. "It's kind of weird, but it— Well, thanks. I actually really like reading, you know."

"Good," I reply. "I hope you like it. Happy Thanksgiving."

"Happy Thanksgiving, Emma."

Then I turn away. And I have the strongest feeling that somewhere, Gram is really, really proud of me.

49

When I come downstairs the next morning, the kitchen is already filled with wonderful aromas. I have a mug of hot cocoa and toast for breakfast while Mom and Dad bustle around.

"Going to be a cold one today," Dad says as he chops the rosemary.

"I heard they're calling for snow," Mom replies from the sink.

"A white Thanksgiving?" I ask, smearing a little extra butter on my crust and giving it to Boomer, who has been sniffing around the turkey waiting to be stuffed on the counter.

"Stranger things have happened." Dad winks at me.

"Hey, Mom?" I ask.

"Uh-oh," Mom says. "I know that voice. That's the voice of a girl whose about to ask for something. Something big."

"Not really," I say. "It's just, I was thinking—do we have room for one more at dinner?"

Mom turns the faucet off, flicking the water from her hands before she turns to look at me. "Are you thinking about Madeline Mitchell?"

I nod.

She glances at Dad. "We'll have plenty of food," he says. "It sounds like the Ramirezes are bringing enough to feed the whole village."

"Well, it's fine by me," says Mom. "The more the merrier."

For a while, I sit next to Lily on the couch. She's watching the Macy's Thanksgiving Day Parade while I thumb through a new book. Well, a new old book. *The Collected Works of Gerard Manley Hopkins.*

It's hard for me to really understand most of the poems inside, but Gram has made little notes in the margins. Questions and comments and things. She obviously read this book many, many times. I even found a poem where she must have borrowed the name "Goldengrove" from. It's about a girl looking at an autumn forest.

Which reminds me. There's something I have to do. A story I have to finish.

So I set the poems aside, bundle up, and take Boomer out to our own autumn forest. We trace our usual path along High Street, past the church, and down to the meadows. Boomer breaks into a sprint when we cross under the barbed wire.

The woods are bright with sunlight but quiet as midnight. I run my hands along the trunks of the trees as I walk, listening to the golden crunch of the leaves under my feet.

The cold is sharp against my cheeks, but I don't mind it. It's the kind of cold that reminds you that you're alive, that you have a whole day stretching out ahead of you and you just never know what it will hold.

When I get to the grove, I pull the journal out from the sycamore hollow. As I do, I notice something I never have before. The gray bark on the sycamore tree. Bits of it have begun to peel away, exposing pale patches of new bark underneath. I smile, running my hand over the sycamore's trunk before turning away.

Ivy's story isn't finished yet. It needs one more chapter. I sit down on Throne Rock and write furiously, until my hand starts to cramp. Until I've said everything I need to say.

I'm just getting up to return the journal to the sycamore hollow, where Madeline can read it, when I stop.

Gram always made me read our stories out loud when we finished them.

Because stories are like spells. They don't work properly unless you tell them out loud.

So I flip back in the journal to the beginning of the story. "Okay, Gram," I say. "For you."

I clear my throat.

"'Once upon a time,'" I start, "'there was a humble cottage that sat halfway between a village and a great wood, as if it could not decide to which it belonged.'"

I tell my story to the Spinney, just like I've told so many before. The way I look may be different now, but my voice is the same as always.

And as I speak, I feel something strange happen. A breeze ripples through the treetops, and all around me, I can sense movement. I feel the familiar sensation of eyes—many eyes—upon me. Except this time, I don't mind. This time, I smile.

Because if I were to look up, I am sure I would see a gnome popping her head up from the patch of moss closest to me. Others would appear next to her as they work their way out from their burrow, all of them resting their pointed chins in their little palms.

I would see the fauns arriving soundlessly, settling themselves in a graceful ring around the sycamore's trunk.

And a rock in the middle of the stream, unrolling itself into a forest troll, its heavy eyes blinking ever so slowly.

The fairies drifting to the ground in the falling yellow leaves, twinkling inside them like dewdrops.

And Gram, sitting by the stream in her long cotton dress, her face lifted toward the sky, listening.

All of them gathering for one last story.

All of them waiting to hear the end.

Ivy's new friends insisted that she eat and drink before setting out to meet the witch. The fauns took her to a comfortable den, the pixies lit a fire to warm her, and as she ate, the others told her stories of Gran and of how she had found Ivy as a baby by a stream and how Ivy had filled every corner of her wild heart.

Then they left Ivy once more, so she could think of a plan to banish the witch.

"How can we defeat her, Shilling?" Ivy wondered, curled under a knotty blanket given to her by the gnomes. "What do we have that she doesn't?"

She glanced to the corner of the den, where the crutch Gran had been carving when she died rested against the twiggy wall. Except when Ivy looked at it now, she saw that it was not a crutch at all, but a half-finished sword.

Ivy knew then what she must do. She knew Gran had left her the sword so she could fight this battle. She borrowed a knife from the elves and set to work at once, whittling the wood into a sword, finishing what her gran had started.

And when she was done, she crept out from the den in the middle of the moonless night, when all the forest creatures were fast asleep. For she was the Keeper of the forest, the protector of its magic, and this was her battle and hers alone to fight. Only Shilling went with her, prowling on silent paws.

Holding the wooden sword by her side, Ivy strode through the forest until she came to its dark heart, to the grove of thorny trees.

And there, in the center of the trees, was a cottage, just as Ivy remembered it.

"Come out, witch!" Ivy called, raising her sword high. "Come out and do battle with me, the Keeper of this forest."

Presently the witch appeared in her white fur cloak, holding her long wooden staff. She cackled when she saw Ivy standing in the snow. "You think you can defeat me, girl?" she shrieked. "We'll see about that, won't we?"

Ivy swallowed down her fear as the witch swept closer, holding her staff as if it were a club. Ivy raised her sword.

"I will give you one last chance, silly girl," snarled the witch as she approached, her face bathed in shadows. "Run now. Leave this forest forever, and I shall spare your life."

But Ivy had come to face the witch. And face the witch she would. She lifted her sword behind her just as the witch's staff began to whirl in the air. Ivy let out a great cry and swung her blade.

When Ivy's sword hit the witch's staff, a very strange thing happened. For a moment, all was still. Then suddenly the forest was filled with bright light, and in its glow, Ivy caught sight of the witch's face beneath her hood. And she gasped, for the old woman's face had changed once more, and Ivy could not understand what she saw.

In the next instant, the witch was ripped from sight, the light faded away and Ivy and Shilling were left alone in the grove. But not quite alone, for moving through the trees was a pulsing, bluish light. As it drew nearer, Ivy saw that it was the woman in white, and she raised her sword again, fearing the witch's tricks.

"Peace, my child," said the woman, "for I am no witch. She has been vanquished, thanks to you."

"If you are not the witch, then who are you?" Ivy asked.

The woman stopped in front of Ivy and drew off her hood. The face beneath seemed carved from pearl. "I am the same figure you saw in the forest all those years ago," the woman said. "I am the moon that hangs in the sky, that watches over this forest and all forests, and that sometimes likes to walk among them on moonless nights."

"But I saw you," Ivy said, "leaving Poppy Cottage just before my gran died. You killed her!"

"I did not," said the woman calmly. "I came only to tell her that it was her time to go, just as I tell the tides each day and night. Just as I must tell all things eventually. I came to tell her that all would be well, that I would watch over you in her absence."

"Then who was the witch who put a curse on me?" Ivy asked, still uncertain.

"I think perhaps you can answer that for yourself," said the woman in white.

"It was me," Ivy said quietly, remembering the face she had seen in the flash of light, just before the witch disappeared. It had been the mirror image of her own. "I am the witch."

"In a manner of speaking," said the woman kindly. "Your fear created the witch. Fear that without your grandmother to love you, you would not be worthy of love any longer. That without her to see you, you would simply disappear."

"Was the witch ever real, then?" Ivy asked. "Or have I only imagined her?"

"Certainly your fear made her real. But because of that, all you needed to do to vanquish her was to be brave. You have proved yourself a worthy guardian for this forest tonight. You came on your own and risked your life to save the forest and all its magic. You are its true Keeper."

The woman in white bowed her head to Ivy, who bowed her own head in return. Then the woman turned to go.

"Wait," Ivy said. "Please—can you take a message to my gran for me?"

The woman smiled, and Ivy could feel its warmth upon her face. "Tell her yourself," she said. "For she is all around you."

Then the air shimmered, and the woman in white was gone.

By the time Ivy and Shilling made their way back to the fauns' den, daylight had broken and the forest creatures had all awakened. When she told them that the witch had been vanquished, they gave a great cheer that echoed all through the forest. They began to sing and dance, and preparations were made for a great party to celebrate the defeat of the witch and the coming of the new Keeper.

And while Ivy slept that morning, the creatures built her a cottage of her own. They crept to Poppy Cottage and brought back Ivy's bed, Gran's books, the pots and pans and remedy jars. And when Ivy woke up, she found she had a new home in the middle of the forest, where the creatures could visit her often. She would never again be alone.

As the cold of winter left and the color of spring returned, the forest creatures quite forgot about the witch.

Ivy did not forget.

Ivy knew that, as sure as summer would follow the spring, trouble would find the forest again one day. And when that time came, she would stand and fight.

But for now, there were sunshine and tulips and foxgloves that bloomed at her heels.

For now, her balsam bark heart beat steady in her chest.

50

When I look up, Boomer and I are alone once more in the Spinney. As I knew we would be. And I think that's okay.

Before she ever brought me here, Gram told me that if there was one thing she believed, it's that there is magic in the world for those who want to see it.

I always thought when Gram talked about magic, she meant fairies and fauns and forest trolls.

I'm not sure if I'll ever see the charmed folk again, at least not the way I once did. But I know now that there are other kinds of magic in the world.

Like how some people are shape-shifters. You think they're one thing, and then suddenly they turn into something else completely. Wicked mothers and sisters

361

can become your biggest cheerleaders. Old witches become enchantresses, and kindly grandmothers hide forests of secrets behind their twinkling eyes.

Or like how sometimes, the right person walks into your life and you walk into theirs just when you need each other most. Like you're each other's lucky charms.

Or the way that people can live on inside you for a long time, even when they're supposed to be dead and gone.

And maybe there are such things as curses, too. But there's also magic in the ways people find to overcome their curses, and maybe even find a way to make something beautiful out of them.

I know now that people *can* disappear. But they can also come back.

I guess what I'm trying to say is that I always used to think of magic as this kind of treasure waiting to be found, like a robin's egg or a five-dollar bill dropped on the street. Or a forgotten railroad tunnel that can lead you into another world entirely.

But now, I think magic is more like something you have inside of you. Like love or kindness or stories.

I close the journal and put it back into the hollow for Madeline to find. Ivy's story is finished now. My story, on the other hand, is just beginning, and I have no idea how it's going to end.

Some mornings, I still wake up and examine my skin for signs that my treatments are working. Thinking that I could find a breadcrumb trail to follow back in time, to when I had only one color of skin.

But today, I looked at my reflection and saw a different girl than the one I was before that first spot appeared on my toe. Not just plain old Emma, but a girl who is totally one of a kind. I saw a girl who is braver than she used to be, and kinder, too. A girl with beautiful sycamore skin.

I saw a girl who takes after her gram.

And I know that no matter what my skin looks like tomorrow or next month or next year, I'm going to keep fighting for that girl.

I will never let her disappear again.

51

Nobody answers when I knock on Madeline's door a few minutes later. Not even when Boomer whines and scratches at the door.

"Madeline?" I call.

I don't hear her. There's no curtain twitching. But for some reason, I am sure that she can hear me.

"I just came to tell you that if you wanted to come to my house for Thanksgiving, I would really love that," I say through the door. "My parents, too. Fina will be there and her parents. I know it's a lot of people, and I understand if you don't want to come. But even if you don't, I'll be back to visit again. It's what she would want, so no arguing, okay?"

There's no answer.

"I'm going to go now. Dinner's at three o'clock. Oh, and by the way, I finished our story."

I wait a second longer, just in case the door cracks open, but it doesn't.

"Happy Thanksgiving, Madeline," I say.

As Boomer and I pass by the church on our way home, I glance over at the graveyard. Then I do a double take. Professor Swann is there, standing at Gram's grave.

I kind of forgot about him, and my theory that he might have been in love with Gram, after Fina and I found out who was really writing to me in my journal. Who had really left the flowers on the grave, and written the inscription in Gram's copy of *The World at the End of the Tunnel*.

But there he is, standing over her grave on Thanksgiving. And I need to know why. I tug Boomer through the church gates and into the grassy graveyard.

"Hi, Professor Swann," I call.

It's not until he turns around and we're a little closer that I realize he's not standing in front of Gram's grave at all. He's standing in front of Isabella Fortune's. The teacher Gram liked who died so young.

"Hello, Emma," he says. His hat, for once, is pressed against his chest instead of on his head. He beckons me over. "Come to visit your gram?"

"Kind of," I say. "I saw you in here, and I wondered— well, was she a friend of yours?" I nod toward Isabella's grave, remembering how untidy and overgrown it had been the day of Gram's funeral. Now a rosebush has been planted over the neat grass.

Professor Swann's eyes swim. "She was my first true love," he replies, turning to stare at the name like he might see her face there if he looks hard enough. "My *only* true love, to tell you the truth, Emma. She was a schoolteacher here in town. She probably taught your gram, actually."

"She did," I say. "Gram told me about her. She said she was a great teacher."

"Yes, she was," agrees Professor Swann. "I didn't visit her here for many, many years. It was too hard. But then, at your grandmother's funeral, I saw her grave so overgrown, and I knew I couldn't stay away any longer. She doesn't deserve to be forgotten."

For a moment, he looks lost in thought. Or memory, more likely. Then he shakes his head and pins a smile on his face. "Anyhow, happy Thanksgiving, Emma."

"You, too," I say. I remember what Ruth said about Professor Swann not having any family. "Professor? Do you have—I mean, do you have plans for dinner today? You could come to our house if you wanted. We'd love to have you."

Madeline isn't the only lonely person in Lantern-wood. The only one who could use a little company. And like Dad said, we have plenty of food.

He hesitates, leaning his head to one side. "Well, if you're sure."

"I am."

Professor Swann smiles. "In that case, I'd be very grateful." Then he settles his hat back on his head, takes one last look at Isabella's tombstone, and follows me out of the graveyard.

Mom and Dad are clearly surprised when Professor Swann walks in behind me and Boomer, but they usher him in. The Ramirezes have already arrived, and Ms. Ramirez immediately starts up a conversation with Professor Swann about what Hampstead College was like when he taught there.

I find Fina talking to Lily in the kitchen. I've never seen it so full of food. Mr. Ramirez made chili corn bread, and Ms. Ramirez made pumpkin empanadas and Brussels sprouts with chorizo. The dishes sit alongside Mom's mashed potatoes and cranberry sauce, and Dad's green beans with almonds. From the oven comes the mouthwatering smell of turkey.

For the first time since Gram died, the house feels really full.

I pull Fina aside, and I tell her about going to Madeline's house.

"Do you think she'll come?" she asks.

"I'm not sure," I say, just as her phone rings. It's her grandmother calling to wish her a happy Thanksgiving. She puts the phone on FaceTime and introduces me to all her family, who are together in San Diego. Her grandmother says it's eighty degrees there, and Fina pulls her sweater tighter around her, even though the oven is keeping the whole house toasty.

"Do you miss them a lot today?" I ask once we hang up.

"Yeah," Fina says. "Abuelita especially. But I'll get to see her at Christmas. And anyway, I've got you!"

"Yeah," I say, wrapping my arms around her and squeezing. "You do."

Lily pulls out a board game she's been too cool to play since she was like ten, and the three of us play while the grown-ups finish cooking. Every few minutes, I look over at the door, but nobody rings the bell.

So I'm actually a little sad when Mom says it's time for dinner. But when we sit down, Lily and Professor Swann start talking about study abroad programs, and Mr. Ramirez and Dad get into a dad joke-off. Their jokes get worse and worse, but everyone just laughs harder and harder. We eat firsts and seconds and thirds until I literally can't have another bite. And that's *before* dessert.

By the time the knock comes at the door, I've almost forgotten I was hoping for Madeline to come.

Everything goes quiet as we all look at one another.

"Is someone going to answer that?" Ms. Ramirez says.

I shoot up from my seat and walk to the door. I open it and have to hide my disappointment. Old Joe is standing on the doorstep.

"Happy Thanksgiving, Emma!" he says.

"Happy Thanksgiving, Joe."

"Gloria sent me. The lights are about to go on. And she wants you to plug them in this year."

"*Me?*" I ask. "Why me?"

"I learned a long time ago not to question Gloria," he says, shaking his head.

I laugh. "Okay. Hold on. I'll get everybody together."

"Great," Old Joe says. "And here—this was sitting on the stoop when I walked up."

He hands me a hot dish covered in tinfoil.

I shut the door and bring the dish into the dining room. There's a note stuck on it.

"What is it?" Fina asks. "What does the note say?"

I unfold it and read aloud the words—written in familiar handwriting. "'Dear Emma, Thank you for your invitation. I'm sorry I couldn't make it.'"

"That's all?" Fina asks, her face falling.

"No," I say. "There's a P.S."

Keep knocking.

I hand Fina the note so she can see for herself, then pull back the foil from the dish. Inside is a warm apple pie.

After we all have our hats and gloves firmly on and scarves wrapped tightly, we walk the short distance to the village hall, where people are gathered around, talking and wishing one another happy Thanksgivings. Professor Swann has to stand on tiptoe to see over the crowd. Old Joe goes to stand by Older Joe, who is wearing a truly terrible purple wool hat and has cranberry sauce caught in his white beard.

There are also a few kids from school here with their families, and lots of people I don't recognize. People who drove here to see the lights go on. The crowd takes up the whole street in front of the hall.

Gloria waves me up when she sees me. I grip Fina's gloved hand and drag her with me, weaving through the crowd of strange and familiar faces.

"Aha," says Gloria. "Finally! We've been waiting."

As if we had an appointment.

"But why me?" I ask. Usually the person who gets chosen to plug in the lights is someone who's done something really special for the village that year.

"Because, dear," Gloria says simply, "it's what your gram would have wanted."

She claps her hands and calls for everyone's attention. Before I have time to think about what she said, I suddenly become aware of hundreds of eyes turning in my direction.

I can't remember ever being in front of this many people. My dinner seems to flip in my stomach. Even in the dusky light, I'm sure they can make out my patches.

"Is everybody ready?" Gloria calls.

"Just do it, Gloria!" Ruth cries. "Some of us have bad backs!"

A few people laugh. I wonder if anyone is staring at me, whispering to the person next to them. *Do you see her face? What's wrong with it?*

And you know what?

Maybe they are and maybe they aren't. I decide I don't care. A smile creeps up my face. It's Thanksgiving. My best friend is standing beside me. Nobody is going to ruin this moment.

"Countdown!" Gloria demands, handing me the end of the string of lights.

"Five!" someone yells.

A snowflake appears in the sky. It lands on Ms. Ramirez's coat. Her eyes light up when she sees it. Fina and I look at each other and grin. "Four!" we yell.

Mom has one arm wrapped around Dad's waist and the other looped over Lily's shoulders. Lily squints up at the sky. Nearby, a kid calls out, "*Snow!*"

"Three!"

That's when I see a dark figure in the back of the crowd. I squint, but all I can make out is a shape, standing slightly away from everyone else in the shadows.

"Two!"

A snowflake lands on my nose. I bend down toward the outlet, gripping the end of the light strand firmly in my hand.

"ONE!" everyone shouts.

I plug in the lights.

When I stand up again, I look for the figure I saw. But there's nobody. Whoever it was has just slipped out of sight.

Everyone starts to clap and cheer. One by one, up and down High Street, the houses turn their lights on. The crowd gasps as rooftops and doorways and yards begin to twinkle and glitter. Color spills from everywhere. The village is bathed in its brightness.

The lights illuminate the snowflakes that have begun to fall faster and faster. People are looking up and pointing. Fina tries to catch a snowflake on her tongue, and suddenly everybody—even Ruth—is laughing and clapping their hands like little kids.

Snowflakes land on the ground. On noses and ears and eyelashes and cheeks.

The entire world is suddenly dappled with white.

And it is magical.

Acknowledgments

This book starts and ends with Aki Laakso. Thank you for inspiring this story, and for encouraging me to write it when I wasn't sure I could. Your strength, determination, optimism, and—above all—your kind heart have made you a wonderful husband, and I know they will make you the best father a kid could ask for.

Thanks to Sarah Davies and Polly Nolan for their enthusiasm for this book, their never-ending well of patience and support. I am prouder than ever to be part of the Greenhouse family.

To Alyson Day for giving this story a home and for her confidence in me to tell it. Thank you for all the passion you poured into this book! That goes for the whole team at HarperCollins: Megan Ilnitzki, Manny Blasco, Jon Howard, Laura Mock, Joel Tippie, Emma Meyer, and Aubrey Churchward. Thank you for all your dedicated work to make this story into a real live book.

To Yaoyao Ma Van As for creating a spellbindingly beautiful cover that captures the essence of Emma's soul and her story.

Special thanks to those who lent their time, experience, and expertise to show me how to write this story in the best way I could. To Dr. Edith Bowers for taking the time outside the office to read and offer me her feedback, and for taking such good care of her patients inside it. To Dr. John Harris for reading, for patiently answering all my many questions, and for being an incredible resource and advocate for those in the vitiligo community. To Julia Lodewick, Aki Laakso, and Jesica Perez for lending me their wisdom and sharing their life experiences to help me craft the characters in this book. And to my beta readers, each of whom made critiques and suggestions that were instrumental in transforming this manuscript into a novel, and each of whom has become an inspiration to me in her own right: Kristin Gray, Supriya Kelkar, Tae Keller, Jen Petro-Roy, and last but never least, Nancy Ruth Patterson.

To the Cramp for being a combination of writing critique/support group, and wonderful people to boot: Paige Nguyen, Keith Dupuis, Christie-Sue Cheeley, Scott Reintgen, Emmalea Couch, and Kwame Mbalia.

Finally to Mom, who continues to read every piece I write and offer thoughtful feedback on them all. And to Dad, who always gets around to it eventually, and always lets me know he's proud when he does. You guys are pretty great.